Ger'Marcco Trayham

To contact the author you can email him at: polodadon.gt@gmail.com or Tra_now@yahoo.com on any social networks

In Loving Memory of

Margaret L. Trayham &

Candice P. Jones

Based on a true

Story...

Every Which Way

It was 5:15 a.m. as Trey leaned over and picked up his cellphone that had seemed to have been vibrating for the twentieth time. It was annoying him, as it lay against the glass nightstand next to his side of the bed that he shared with Scarlett. Squinting with one eye open, he managed to press a button on the brightly lit phone to cut off its alarm. Having noticed it was Monday morning and he had an hour and forty-five minutes to shower, get dressed, cook breakfast, and be out of the house by 6:30 a.m. in order to make it on time for his 7 a.m. shift. Trey dreaded these moments, when he was forced to get out of bed leaving Scarlett's side. He lightly placed his cell phone back on the nightstand, as to make as little noise as possible. Placing the sheets over his head, Trey turned and pressed his nude body against Scarlett's back and butt, placing his left arm underneath the pillow they shared to lay their heads on, while wrapping his right arm around her waist to pull her closer. He planted a light kiss on the back of her neck, while whispering her name.

"Scarlett?"

"Yes babe," she whispered back, letting him know that she was awake and just as comfortable as he was. She inched her butt closer to his dick to let him know that she wasn't ready for him to get up, and leave her side to start his work day. "Don't get up yet baby, lay with me for ten more minutes!" As he laid there smiling and still holding on to Scarlett, Trey knew this was going to be an interesting day on the job, if he still had a job that is. After being out sick with the flu for a whole two weeks, he knew he was on work probation for using all of his sick days, and calling out sick when he knew he was actually fine. A stunt like this could land Trey in the unemployment line, and he knew that he couldn't call out again. Trey had gotten sick on the job, and had a doctor's permission slip for being sick for two weeks, he thought to himself; that maybe they would give him another chance, Scarlett thought otherwise.

Scarlett

With being his live-in girlfriend for three years, she knew from watching him take his job for granted, that it was only a matter of time before he would be fired. "I hate this freaking job", what he would sometimes say to her during conversation's they would have on his lunch break.

Scarlett would encourage him to do something different, but it would seem to go in one ear and out the other, and eventually the subject would be dismissed as if it never began.

"But babe, if you hate your job why don't you apply somewhere else or another department at least?" "I am babe, but anyway... how about if I come to your job on your lunch break and eat you for desert?!"

"Mmmmmmmmmm, come and get me daddy! Mommy will be waiting with open legs", she would jokingly say and right before she hung up, she would remind him to apply for another department.

"I know, I know, I am baby...See you at 4:00 p.m. with those legs open!"

Growing up in the streets, while being raised in a broken home, with only his mother to help raise and teach him how to be a man, only male role models Trey had were the neighborhood drug Dealers and Pimps, whom everyone including him respected and looked up to because of their big cars, nice jewelry and money. Trey knew that his role models never worked a regular paying 9-5 job, he knew from watching and paying attention, on days he didn't go to school he knew these same people never left the neighborhood, and if they did they would return as quickly as they left, wearing the latest fashions or with a different ride. One sunny afternoon while Trey was taking out the trash, a white Mercedes Benz with tinted windows pulled up beside him. Caught off guard by the fancy car quiet and sudden approach, Trey's first instinct was to run, but being mesmerized by the beautiful sight of the car, with its chrome wheels and matching tints, had him stop and stare in awe of what set before his eyes. As the driver's window rolled down slowly, Trey smiled at the familiar face.

"Trey boy what's up young cat daddy," said Ronnie in his usual greeting.

Trey knew Ronnie all too well with their constant run ins around his house either exiting Trey's mother Italy's room in the morning when Trey was on his way to school or entering Italy's room in the wee hours of the night when Trey would walk to the refrigerator still half asleep from being awakened from the loud music that did little justice to muffle the constant female moans and groans that came from her room. Trey knew of his Mom's entertaining, and being involved with different men of different races, from over hearing them late at night when he would sneak downstairs and put his ear to her door, only to tip toe and sneak back upstairs and climb back in bed just in time before Italy would come upstairs to look in his room and check up on him. With keeping up with his constant snooping and sneaking up to her door late at night, he later found out that Ronnie was Italy's lover and pimp, and that she made money from massaging and performing sexual acts for different men from all walks of life, and not only was she doing it at night, but she would see most of her "clients" throughout the day while Trey was in school. With knowing this, it never seemed to bother him, he loved his mom so much that even if it did bother him he didn't let it show, and he would never mention what he knew to her or anyone else. He would go about his day as if it never happened, because to him his mom was the greatest ever, and in his eyes she can do no wrong.

"Hey Ronnie, what's up?"

"What's up with you young cat daddy, what are you doing out here?"

"Just taking out the trash for Italy!" Trey said smiling.

"Okay, young cat daddy, tell your mom I said hello, and I will see her later..." Ronnie said, before rolling up the window and pulling off, leaving Trey staring at the vehicle as the sun glinted and danced on the rims, before it vanished down the street. That same day, Trey told Italy about his run in with Ronnie, while she sat him down and had a conversation with him about her lifestyle and why she did the things she did; that changed his life forever. Holding nothing back she gave him all the details, from when she first began after the abrupt divorce from his father when he was two years old, to how different men made her feel wanted and desired as a woman. Italy described the loneliness and abandonment she felt, from not only her husband, but her family as well. While the money afforded her a lifestyle she never had, and gave her the ability to see that Trey; her one and only son, was provided with everything that she could never afford as a child.

One of the conversations that stood out the most in his adolescent life and still to this day is when she told him, {"If you ever lose your job and can't make ends meet, use what you got to get what you want Trey...Nice looks, a nice physique, good hygiene with a personality that will have a woman hand you the panties that she's wearing will get you ahead in life. But remember, use it while you have it, because you won't have it forever!"}

As he laid there holding Scarlett, and reflecting on the conversation's, and the times he and Italy shared, he decided to call his supervisor to inform him that he was returning today, that way if he was in trouble he wouldn't have to ride all the way there, only to return right back home. Removing his head from beneath the sheets while still pondering the thought to call, he decided what the heck, they were either going to tell him to come in, or fire him. Placing another light kiss on the back of Scarlett's neck, he climbed out the bed and picked up his cell phone from the nightstand and headed to the living room, as to not disturb Scarlett and to give himself a little privacy. Dialing his job, while pacing the living room floor, still in the nude, he waited patiently for an answer, until his supervisor finally picked up, "Maintenance!"

"Mr. Jowell, this is Trey, how are you?"

"I'm fine Trey, how can I help you?"

Ready to end the conversation, Trey got straight to the point on why he called,

"Well, I was calling because I was supposed to return back to work today and I wanted to know if I am to come in, and do I still have a job?"

"Unfortunately Trey, you don't have to come in, because as of Friday you were terminated, and a letter was sent out to your home. I know you still get direct deposit so your final paystub will be mailed to you this upcoming Friday. I wish things were different, but there's nothing any of us can do about this. Is there anything else I can do for you?" Mr. Jowell asked his former employer ready to terminate the call.

"No thanks, Mr. Jowell, you were a big help", he said feeling a little disappointed, but most of all relieved.

As he hung the phone up, he continued to pace the floor, asking himself what he was going to do next. The bills still had to be paid, and food still had to be put on the table. He knew he would have to come up with something soon, because there was no way Scarlett would be able to handle everything on her own. Had he listened to her, and found employment

8

somewhere else, he knew that he probably wouldn't be in this position. "Shit!" he yelled out loud feeling disturbed about the thought of being unemployed with no other source of income.

Trying to devise a plan, he decided to take a shower. After about twenty minutes Scarlett entered the bathroom quietly, startling him when she pulled the shower curtain back and stepped inside. "So, I'm officially unemployed." He said to her, never once turning around or removing his head from underneath the water. Moving her body in front of his, to position her body under the shower so that the water can hit both of their bodies, she hugged him tightly and whispered, "Don't worry baby, I know something will come through for you. How do you feel?"

"I'm good babe, he stated flatly while adding, I'm just going to figure out some kind of hustle to bring money in, get unemployment and use those checks to pay our bills with."

"Ok baby, we'll get through this, in the meantime let me taste this juicy dick, and then I want you to hit this kitten really good from behind and make me purr." she said seductively dropping down to her knees. As the water ran down on her head, she placed his dick in her mouth and began to suck him in a way she knew he loved. Using no hands, she continued to suck him slowly, moaning as she took him deeply as she could. Realizing she had his dick at attention the way she liked, giving it one more lick, she stood up, turned to face the wall placing her back to him, bent over and using her left hand she guided him inside of her. Standing tall and fully at attention, Trey couldn't help but to slap her on her ass, as he pumped away giving her the thrill and satisfaction that he knew she wanted.

After pleasuring each other for a good fifteen minutes, they both decided to wash each other up playfully. Rinsing off, Trey grabbed his towel, dried off and left Scarlet in the bathroom. Closing the door behind him, he couldn't help but smile as he walked down the hall toward the living room listening to her sing. 'I love that woman', he thought to himself, as he sat down on the couch still wrapped in a towel. Grabbing his laptop from off of the ottoman, placing it on his lap, he checked both of his bank accounts first, something he made a habit of doing every day. With only a thousand dollars to his name, he knew that he had to come up with a job quick.

After searching and searching the web for different jobs, and filling out tons of applications from department stores, to grocery stores, he hadn't noticed he'd been sitting in the same spot for a little over 2 hours, until Scarlett emerged from the bedroom fully dressed gathering her things to get ready to leave out, to start her work day. Breaking the silence, she stood above him and spoke, "Baby, you've been sitting here all of this time, what have you been doing?"

"Trying to find me a job, and filling out different applications," he said taken in by the lovely smell of her perfume. Giving her a quick once over, he looked her up and down and added, "Are you sure you're going to work, or do you have a hot date?" She was dressed in a form fitting white dress that came down to her knees, a black belt around her waist, and black high heel booties that came just above her ankle. He was starting to get aroused again noticing she pinned her hair up, and wore her sexy schoolgirl glasses that she knew he loved.

"Aww Poo-Poo, you know you're the only one in my life that I will ever be dating. Besides, maybe we can go on a date when I get off this afternoon that is if I'm not too tired from allowing those residents to drive me insane!"

From the outside looking in, Trey always thought that Scarlett had the easiest job on the planet. She was a property manager for three different condominium complexes, and all she did was sit at her desk in front of her computer and dished out work orders to her three assistants that worked underneath her. "Then a date it will be, if you're up to it baby," he replied walking her to the door to see her off to work. As he opened the door for her and gave her a final hug and kiss before she left, he noticed her butt had an extra jiggle as she walked away which meant she wasn't wearing panties. "No panties?" he called out to her, standing in the doorway still dressed in only a bath towel. Ignoring him, she climbed in her car, turned the ignition, rolled the driver side window down, and yelled out to him, "Who needs any on this beautiful spring day?", and with that being said, she pulled off smiling, waving him good bye ready to start her day. Back in their dimly lit two bedroom apartment with nothing else to do, Trey decided to get dressed and head on out to Panera Bread to eat, surf the web and read today's newspaper. He slipped on a grey V-neck t-shirt, a pair of blue jeans and a pair of white and grey sneakers. He checked his self out in the mirror, while adding on his accessories, which included a platinum necklace with a blue and white diamond **T** pendant that he got from Scarlett on Valentine's Day, along with a gray G-shock watch he purchased on his own. Grabbing his laptop and heading out the door, he thought about how Scarlett hated when he didn't clean the bathroom when he was done, and also how she despised when he didn't screw the top back onto the toothpaste after he used it. Making a mental note to come back and clean his mess, he left out locking the door behind him, and headed to his car. Sitting behind the wheel of his black S550 Mercedes Benz, he turned the volume up on his radio, as he pulled off listening to a song by Rick Ross, featuring the late Michael Jackson. In tune with the music and his own thoughts, he hadn't noticed his cell phone ringing. Picking it up off of the passenger seat, he glanced at it noticing he had two missed calls from Tina. As he redialed her number, he pressed the Bluetooth button so that he would be able to talk to her aloud, hands free throughout the speakers in the car. "Hey Mr.?!" said Tina, picking up on the first ring.

"What's up Tina?"

"Just checking up on you, what are you doing?"

"Driving, on my way to have lunch, alone, and trying to search the web for a job being as though I was fired!"

"Come see me, we can get lunch together, I'll pay for it."

"You got it babe, see you in ten minutes", replied Trey, ending the call with the press of a button. "Tina, Tina, Tina... What am I going to do with you?!" he yelled out, to no one in particular. Placing his phone on the dashboard car holster, he couldn't help but smile to himself as he thought of Tina and her sneaky ways. Being friends with Tina have its advantages, the only downside is when Tina gets drunk, she gets emotional and stresses about being there for him through three relationships and him not ever considering settling down with her. Doing everything together from

12

buying each other gifts, to taking trips to different places, to having sex every so often, but not once wanting to take their friendship to commitment status, which is why them having sex together had been to a minimum. Not wanting to sleep with Tina when she wasn't around came easy because of his relationship with Scarlett, but when Tina came around it was hard to resist her because she was always in a flirtatious state, and she knew how to seduce him to get what she wanted.

Tina taking selfies

Pulling up to Tina's house, Trey decided to give Scarlett a call just to see if she made it to work safely. After calling three times and noticing her answering machine pick up on the first ring, every time, he decided to call her office. "Concorde Management?" answered Scarlett's assistant manager.

"Good afternoon Deb, this is Trey can you transfer me to Scarlett?"

"Oh hello Trey, Scarlett stepped out, but she should be back in an hour, call her cellphone."

"Ok...I will", he replied back, not wanting her to know that he already tried her cell but didn't get an answer. Having a gut feeling that she was up to no good, Trey decided to end the call and go on with his day, noting to remind her that he called whenever she called him back. Stepping out of the car and walking up to Tina's door, Trey walked straight in without knocking or using a key. "I'm home", he yelled out jokingly.

"I'm up here", she replied back from upstairs. As he walked up the thirteen steps, counting each one as he made his way to her bedroom, he knew he was in for a sight. Entering her bedroom and sitting on her futon, which faced her bed, he acted as if he wasn't fazed by the sight of her nude 5 foot 10 inch frame body, sitting on the bed drinking out of the large bottle of Rose Moet Champagne. "Hi", she spoke, well aware that she caught him off guard with her nudity, from reading his body language. "I brought us a bottle of your favorite drink to go with our lunch, come and give me a hug... JEEEESH you're rude! Let me find out Scarlett done pissed you off again?!"

"Not quite", he said rising from the futon. Grabbing the bottle from her, he leaned in to give her a hug as she jumped into his arms playfully, wrapping her whole nude body around his, as he stumbled back against the wall holding on to her as to not drop her. Almost dropping the bottle, they both laughed in unison as she stood and they both released the tight grip they had with each other. Kicking off his shoes, he climbed up on her bed, sat and leaned his back against her king sized headboard. "So what is troubling you friend?" she asked putting on a see through wife beater, before sitting beside him, leaning her back against the headboard.

"I'm broke, I need a job and I think Scarlett's cheating on me", he added.

"So now you need me to come to your rescue...sure I will" she said, "but first thing first. As for your job, I know exactly what you can do that will take your mind off of Scarlett, and you can profit from it!" Looking at her quizzically, he said, "I'm listening."

"You can be a Male Gigolo, where as though you can get paid for performing sexual acts for women and I will help you."

"Thanks Tina, now will you quit playing, because this shit really got me stressed", he said as he took another sip from the bottle.

"Negro, I am serious", she snapped back. "How long have you been thinking Scarlett has been cheating on you? Every time you get caught putting your dick somewhere where it doesn't belong, and she confesses to doing some shit too. I mean, I know you love her and all, and it's been proven that you would do anything for her, which is cool, but it's time you start focusing on you and start doing for yourself. When was the last time she went out her way and done something for you, other than a holiday or your birthday?" Giving what she said some thought, he couldn't help but agree with her. Lately for the last year he has been going out of his way to do everything in his power for Scarlett, only to get little to nothing back in return, even with the insecurities of thinking

15

she was cheating. 'How was it that every time I got caught for doing something wrong, and we talked, she always had a little confession of her own, Damn Tina, you are absolutely right.' he thought to himself. "Yea you right, she is sneaky and always admitting to doing something after I may have been caught or after she speculates that I've done something. But she do for me when she can, it's just lately the bills have been kicking our ass!" Knowing he was making excuses for her as soon as it rolled off of his tongue, and he knew Tina heard it as well. "But then again, you're right Tina. Now tell me more about this bright idea of a job that you have been considering me to do, cause I know this is not the first time you thought of this?!"

"No it's not, but to do it you gotta have mind control, and be able to separate business from pleasure."

"I'm all ears, that's easy, now tell me more!"

"As you know I have been doing this for the past year, and the money is good, but there can be some sick people out there that are willing to pay you a lot of money to do some weird shit. I deal with more men, but I do get a lot of calls and emails from women that ask me all the time do I have a male that can service them, and it's not always all about sex. Some may just wanna talk, some may just want a massage and a kiss on the cheek, and then some may want you to tell them they ain't shit. But, like I said, my experiences are more with the men, although every now and then I may fool around with a woman. I more so get a kick out of the men, because they never cease to amaze me."

Listening to Tina, took Trey back to a childhood place where he witness these same acts first hand with his mom, Italy. Their conversations were so similar, differences are he was now an adult and had to fend and provide for himself. After talking to Tina for more than three hours about this particular job, and going over what he will need to do to start down to the locations, pay, and even her payoff for setting him up with his first client, he decided to go along with it and try it out. He knew he had to tell Scarlett because not only did he want her to trust him, he wanted her to feel like she was a part of something, and that they was a team. Knowing she wasn't going to approve of him sleeping with other women, he decided to make it as if all he was doing was massaging them and leaving. "So are you in or out?" Tina asked, after their long conversation.

"I'm with it, you do what you have to do, and set me up with my first client and I will take it from there." He remarked trying to sound confident.

"So what do I owe you?" Smiling while starting to feel the effects of the champagne on an empty stomach, she added, "Don't worry, I will let you know after you are done with your first client." After spending most of the day with Tina, and still no call from Scarlett, Trey decided to give her another call while Tina was in the shower. After the third ring the phone answered, but no one said hello. As Trey continued to listen he overheard her laughing and fumbling with her phone, telling someone to stop playing and give her the phone, then right before she said hello he heard a woman in the background telling Scarlett she was rude and then a door slammed. "Hello?" she finally said, sounding as if she was out of breath.

"Hey babe what's up, and what's going on?" he asked, annoyed over what he just heard and also from not hearing from her all day.

Tina Holding Trey's Favorite Drink

"Nothing babe, I'm sorry, that was just one of my crazy tenants playing", she lied. "How are you honey, I miss you?"

"I'm good, happy I'm finally talking to you, where have you been, and why haven't you returned my call?"

"Baby I was busy today, I'm sorry, plus I won't be leaving here till around seven instead of five because I have some extra work to do. So, we're gonna have to reschedule our date babe."

"Alright Scarlett, do you want me to bring you something to eat?", he asked, hoping she would say no so he would be able to meet the client that Tina

18

was setting him up with at 6p.m, which was in two hours.

"No, I'm ok baby, just meet me at the house when I get off."

"Okay I will."

"Alright baby, I will give you a call when I get off. I love you and I will talk to you then", she said ready to end the call.

"Alright baby, I love you too and I will talk to you then, goodbye", he replied back ending the call as she said her final goodbye. After hanging up, he felt that strange feeling again that she was still lying and being up to no good. But as quickly as the thought crossed his mind he decided to let it go for now and not let the thought affect him, at least not while he was still in the company of Tina anyway. Fresh out of the shower, Tina emerged wearing a yellow lace see through matching bra and panty set that complimented her golden hazel skin. Approaching Trey, as he laid on her futon in tune with playing Tetris on his cell phone, she handed him a bottle of baby oil gel, turned her back to him and asked that he apply some of the gel to the areas she missed on her back and ass. As he gently applied the gel, he instantly got an erection, but thought against performing a sexual act with her so that he would be fully energized when he went to see his client.

"Oh yeah right there," she said bending over on the bed, enjoying the feeling of his hands as he massaged her ass cheeks.

"Alright I'm done Miss. Temptation", he said smiling as he handed her back the gel.

"Thanks baby, now I need you to give me about an hour to talk back with her to give you all the information and details you will need to meet up with this client. I'm about to head out to run a few errands, you can either stay here and wait for my instructions or you can leave out when I leave out, but it's important that you be there to meet her on time."

Deciding to stay there at her house until she gave him a call, he laid back down on the futon. "I will chill here. What's her name?"

"Candy is all she told me", she answered, "But that's all I know…oh and that she is 5 foot 10, light skinned, about 150 pounds. She is nice looking I assure you, but you don't have to worry about that because remember you are there to perform a service, get paid and then leave. It will be her first time just as well as it is yours, as a matter of fact let me show you a picture of her." Grabbing her laptop from the bed, she sat on his lap as he continued to lie on the futon, with a few clicks she pulled Candy's picture up along with the email that it came in that told Tina some of what she was looking for in a male escort. "Here's her picture along with the emails we sent back and forth to each other", she said handing him the laptop as she rose from his lap. Slipping on a pair of light blue leggings, a tight fitting white V-neck t-shirt, and a pair of white and blue Jordan retro number four sneakers, adding a few accessories along with her lip gloss, purse and keys, she stood in front of him with her arms folded. "Uh buddy, are you done because I'm gonna need my laptop sweets?"

"She didn't really say much," he said handing her the laptop.

"I'll call you with the details", she retorted, giving him a light kiss on the lips before walking away and heading out the door. Listening as Tina exited the house slamming the door behind her, Trey continued to lay in the same spot while playing Tetris, thinking about Candy and the emails she sent Tina, asking for a hot light skinned male escort to drop by her hotel room and give her a full body massage while she was in town for the next three days on a work assignment. After laying there for the next half an hour the call from Tina finally came through. "Hello", he said answering his phone while sitting up.

"Hey boo, I just got off the phone with Candy, she said to meet her at the Sheraton hotel across from the harbor on Charles Street, come to room 498 and bring a bottle of massaging oil. She is gonna pay you $200 for a full body massage front and back, and depending on how the session go she may want to have sex, so bring condoms. Don't blow this, she said if you're good she would be willing to see you again before she leaves and head out of town."

"Ok cool", he said shaking his head up and down as he continue to listen to her speak.

"I'll text you her phone number. She said to tell you to give her a call after you get off the elevator, so she can leave the door open for you. After you are done give me a call when you leave her, so you can fill me in on the details of how things went."

"Ok baby, indeed I will", he replied as he left Tina's house locking the bottom lock behind him.

"Oh and one more thing Trey...smooches." After hanging up with Tina and heading to the nearest CVS to pick up some condoms and massaging oil, the anticipation of meeting Candy was killing him, but also had him excited, along with feeling worried about how Scarlett was going to take to him telling her about his newfound business venture, courtesy of Tina whom she accepted as his friend, but wasn't fond of. Deciding to turn the radio off in the car, he rode to the hotel in silence reflecting on his relationship with Scarlett, wondering where they were going, and how long they would last as a couple before one of them called it quits and walked away. Knowing he would do anything to see her happy, he often wondered if he was going out of his way too much for her and did she appreciate the things he did mentally, physically and financially to keep her happy and satisfied. Glancing at the clock on the car dash, he realized it was 6:35 p.m. and he had twenty five minutes to get to the hotel and find parking.

CHAPTER 2

"Why in the hell would you do that shit?" Scarlett asked, as she entered the bathroom, pulling the shower curtain back to confront her jealous friend. "Because, you are fucking rude! You know, I hate the fact that you are still dealing with him, but then you gonna try and talk to him in my face!" Placing her hands on her hips, Scarlett stared at Ladawn with rage in her eyes, as Ladawn continued to wash up not paying Scarlett any attention. At that very moment Scarlett knew it was time to end their secret weekly rendezvous that only lasted two months. Scarlett knew if she didn't call it off now, then sooner or later Trey would find out what she really was doing at work, and getting caught having relations with a jealous, over emotional woman was not how she wanted her relationship with Trey to end. Grabbing a plastic bonnet off of the back of the bathroom door and placing it on her head, Scarlett stepped her already nude body in the shower along with Ladawn. As she washed in silence, admiring Ladawn's five foot 2 inch, one hundred and forty pound frame. She wished she could have kept her around longer, because she loved the feel of her soft ebony body when they were rolling around sweaty in Ladawn's California king sized bed. As with being her second female partner, she knew at some point that things would have to come to an end, like her on again off again six month affair with Ebony, whom taught her how it felt to be pleased sexually by another woman. Like her, Ebony had a live-in boyfriend as well, whom she was engaged to be married to. He didn't know of her sexcapades with women, just as Trey didn't know of Scarlett's. As Scarlett continued to wash up, she felt that same tingly surge that ran through her body that she did during her first encounter with Ebony.

"So, do you like the model of this condo or do you like the other one?" Scarlett asked, as she showed Ebony the last condo for the day, in hopes that she would choose one quickly so that she could get off work, and rush home to make sweet love to Trey.

"I think I like this one better actually. Which one would you suggest I move into?"

As Scarlett was about to answer her question, her cellphone rang with the tune of Trey's ringtone, she smiled at Ebony and asked to be excused, as she entered the model bedroom closing the door behind her.

"Trey I'm at work baby, what's wrong?" she whispered.

"Baby I got to make a run to Virginia with Italy to pick up a friend and bring her back to Baltimore."

"Okay Trey, so how long do you think you will be because it is already 7 p.m. baby?" She asked feeling disappointed as her plans failed in front of her.

"I'm not gonna be back until about 1 or 2 a.m. at the latest."

"Alright Trey, bye I got to go, I will see you when you get back." As she hung up the phone, Scarlett realized that what she needed was a strong drink and a cold shower. Opening up the bedroom door, she smiled as she approached Ebony, trying to hide her sudden feeling of frustration.

"You look like you could use a stiff one--drink that is." Ebony said, noticing the frustration in Scarlett's eyes.

"Yes I do, girl it's been one long day and after we leave from here I'm goin' to the nearest liquor store and purchase me one!"

"If you like, I have a studio apartment nearby that I converted to an office a few months ago. We can go over there and have a drink together while I fill out the application to move in."

Pondering the offer, Scarlett looked over Ebony and thought how this stranger couldn't have come at a better time, and what harm would one drink with a future tenant be?

"You know what, that sounds perfect!" Scarlett said, leading Ebony out into the hallway as she locked up the condo. "You lead the way and I will follow you."

As they pulled up into a parking lot that set in the back of a small neatly tucked apartment complex, Scarlett was impressed with how clean the outside of the building was. Since the complex was about ten minutes from her office in the heart of Downtown Baltimore, she couldn't believe she had never noticed this complex before.

Stepping out of her car, she followed Ebony inside the building as they rode the elevator up to the seventh floor. As they stepped out of the elevator, Scarlett noticed there were only seven other apartments down the corridor, four on each side. As they entered the studio she noticed there was a queen sized bed in one corner, along with a traditional office setup of desk, chair, computer and a mini book shelf in the opposite corner. The kitchen held a small stove, microwave, Frigidaire and a bar, which contained every kind of liquor you could imagine, from Cognac, to Vodka, to Bourbon and even Whiskey. There was also a green leather loveseat that was against the wall that set between two large windows that looked out to a main road. Removing her black Manolo Blahnik shoes and having a seat on the loveseat, Scarlett pulled the folder that held the condo application and handed it to Ebony.

"What would you like to drink?" Ebony asked, removing the envelope from her hand and setting it on her desk.

"You can give me a double shot of vodka and cranberry juice", she answered, removing her pink blazer while taking in the sight of the color coordinated green, brown and chrome expensive furniture.

Telling herself she had made a mistake coming here with this strange woman, whom she only seen in her

25

office one other time when she was talking to her assistant, and Scarlett was in the other room arguing with Trey about a text message she had read that was sent to his phone by another woman. She figured you only live once and what harm could be done in having a drink with a future tenant in a comfortable private setting such as this one. As the time passed them by, and now on her third double shot, Scarlett knew that the time had come to call their rendezvous quits and head on home before the effects of the alcohol took over her whole being, as it was beginning to do now. As they both sat beside each other still in tune with each other's conversation, Scarlett glanced at her watch, swallowed the remains of her drink, and decided that now was the best time that she should depart. "I'm sorry Ebony, but I do think it's time to call it a night and head on home to my man."

"Oh my, it is getting late," Ebony said, glancing down at her own Movado watch. As they sat beside each other gazing in each other's eyes, Ebony seized the moment placing one hand on Scarlett's exposed thigh, and running her other hand through Scarlett's hair. She gripped the back of her head, pulling her face to hers and kissed Scarlett long, hard, and passionately. Surprised at her body's reaction to being kissed and intimately touched by another woman, the juices between Scarlett's legs began flowing as she craved and fiend for more. As she kissed her back, she allowed Ebony to aggressively take control of her. Pushing her back against the loveseat, Ebony knelt between Scarlett's legs, forcing her dress to her waist, and pulling down her panties all in one motion. Parting her legs open with the help of Ebony, Scarlett pulled her top down, groping and squeezing her own breasts, as Ebony dove head first between her legs. Caught in the midst of the lustful exchange, Scarlett moaned loudly, as she invited Ebony's tongue deeper and deeper into her crevices, as the explosions came back to back from her climaxes. She knew from that point, that a woman's touch had been what she had been missing all of her life, and there would be no way she would be able to go without it.

"It's over between you and me" Scarlett said to Ladawn stepping out of the shower. "I can't do this anymore, so please lose my number, and stay away from me Ladawn."

"Whatever Scarlett", she said, as she continued to lay back on her California king in the nude, flicking the channels on her 47 inch flat screen television.

"Can you lock my door when you leave out please?" Dressed and looking the same as she did when she left the house this morning, Scarlett grabbed her purse along with her cellphone and left Ladawn's house without saying goodbye, leaving the door wide open behind her. As she got in her car, Scarlett never looked back to see if Ladawn had got out of the bed, to close the door.

Stepping out of the elevator onto the fourth floor, Trey dialed Candy's number, and immediately felt butterflies in his stomach when she picked up on the third ring. "Hey sweetie, are you on the fourth floor yet?" she questioned.

"I sure am."

"Well get off of the elevator, make a right and come to the end of the hallway, make the left and come all of the way to the end of the hallway and my room is in the corner on your right. The door will be open for you... Don't, keep me waiting!"

As Trey entered Candy's suite, the first thing he noticed was the flicker of the candle that danced on her nude body, as she laid on her stomach in the shadowy filled darkness, that took over the rest of the room.

"You can start off by getting completely nude" she stated, not once looking up or facing him. "Climb on the bed with me and massage every inch of my body." Doing just that, he closed the door, got completely undressed, and climbed up on the Presidential king sized bed alongside her. Setting the condoms down on the bottom of the bed, he unscrewed the top to the massaging oil, as he poured some up and down her back, ass and legs. Positioning himself on his knees, she turned her head to face him and spoke seductively, "No, no sweetie you are too far away. I wanna feel you, so I would prefer you to sit on top of me while you are massaging me." As he sat on top of her, one leg on each side, he positioned himself just below her butt, as he massaged the oil deeply into her skin.

"So how does it feel to you?" he asked, after about twenty minutes of massaging everything, from her neck, down to her back, butt and legs.

"Your hands are amazing", she moaned, turning over to lie on her back while adding, "Now this side." As he lightly poured oil up and down the front side of her body, starting from her neck down to her breast, her stomach down to her feet, he got an instant hard on, as he took in the beauty of her face along with her flawless body, that was long and curvy in all the right places. Noticing his erection while he massaged her breast, she grabbed his penis with one hand, and played with his testicles with the other.

"That's enough, put a condom on so I can taste you." Ripping a condom pack open, that was already out of the box, and placing one on his swollen erection, he allowed Candy to sit up, throwing him back on the bed and take control as she placed his dick deep into her mouth. "Oh it tastes so good," she said in between slurps. "I'm gonna sit on it, and then I want you to fuck me from behind, and let me know when you are about to cum." As he laid back enjoying the pleasure he was receiving from this beautiful woman, thoughts of Scarlett kept entering his brain, as he wondered if she was doing the same things with different guys, minus the pay. Dismissing the thoughts of Scarlett, Trey laid back as Candy rode his dick, demanding him to rub her oily body, as she came back to back. With every sexual position they performed, it seemed that Candy couldn't get enough. Completing the job that he came to do, Trey knew this wouldn't be the last time he would see her. After ten minutes of showering, only hitting his private areas, using an unscented bar of soap he found in the bathroom that was about the size of his bedroom. He exited the oversized bathroom, and dried himself off as Candy set on the loveseat in a pink see through robe watching, while sipping a glass of Remy Martin that she poured herself. "Would you like a drink?" she asked, as he continued to get dress.

"No, I'm good baby, maybe next time."

"Well I have something for you." she said, handing him three crisp one hundred dollar bills.

"Thanks!"

"No, thank you...Where will you be around noon tomorrow?"

"I'll be free, why what's up?"

29

Taking another sip from her drink she smiled, looked him in the eye and added, "because I want to see you then as well. I will call you around ten thirty with the details on where to meet me. I will pay you for an hour again, even if we don't do what we did today."

"Ok cool." he added, as he walked out of the hotel suite making his way back to the elevator, out of the hotel and back to his car.

As Trey rode home to Scarlett, he decided to give Tina a call to fill her in on the details of how his rendezvous with Candy went. "Hey sweets," Tina answered. "So how did it go?"

"It was cool babe. I went in, gave her a massage, we ended up fucking, she paid me three hundred and then I left."

"So, she tipped you an extra hundred," Tina added feeling a tinge of jealousy, "you must have put it down... so let me guess she wanna see you again?"

Noticing the jealousy in her voice he immediately dismissed it because he felt like he didn't have the energy nor the time to put up with Tina's mood swings. "Yeah, she wanna meet up tomorrow around noon too."

"Ok, I know you gotta go home to wifey, call me tonight when you are free so I can tell you what you need to do to bring in more clients so you can make more money sweets."

"Ok babe," he added. "If I can get away later tonight I will come see you, but if I can't I will still call you and just see you tomorrow."

"Ok sweets, talk to you then." Ending the call with Tina, Trey thought about calling Scarlett but decided against it and figured he would see her when he got home. Turning his music on, he drove home listening to an artist by the name of Trey Songz reflecting on his night with Candy. Smiling to himself, he knew he would be able to do this and get away with it, without Scarlett knowing. It was the extra income he would have to keep her from knowing about unless he lied and told her it was coming from somewhere else. At that very moment while still deep in thought, Trey decided it would be best to get another cell phone, laptop and a discreet location where he could take his clients to keep this new found occupation as secret and discreet as possible. Deciding to make a detour, Trey decided to go to the ATM and deposit the three hundred dollars that he made today. Just as he was depositing the money in the ATM he got a call from Scarlett. Ignoring the call he continued to do what he was doing as another call came in from her. As he pulled off to make his way home he dialed his voicemail to listen to the message that she left him. "*You have one new message.*" replied his voicemail as Scarlett spoke, "Hey baby I was calling to let you know a friend of mines was staying over for a little while until his girlfriend gets off of work because he lost his keys, call me when you get this message baby. Ok, I love you... bye."

"*To save this message, press seven.*" Trey ended the call and redialed Scarlett's number, furious as he raced home to find out who the hell was this so called friend. Getting no answer, Trey ended the call and figured he would confront her when he got into his house being as though he was only two minutes away. Pulling behind Scarlett's car, Trey parked, turned off the ignition, put his phone in his pocket and walked up his walkway to enter his house. Unlocking the door with his key, Trey entered the apartment they shared closed and secured the locks, and headed up the stairs that turned into his living room where Scarlett was sitting on one chair and her "friend" was sitting on the other. Noticing the angry puzzled look on his face, Scarlett rose from the couch with open arms as she embraced him and planted a kiss on his cheek. "Hey baby, I tried calling you, did you get my message?" she questioned.

"Yeah, I got it," Trey answered, staring at the strange unfamiliar face that was sitting on his couch. "Baby this is Vom and he is a good friend of mines. Vom this is my boyfriend Trey I was telling you about."

"Hey Trey, how are you," questioned Vom as he stood extending his arm towards Trey to shake his hand.

"Let me see you in the room real quick," Trey said to Scarlett, walking away ignoring Vom's friendly gesture while leaving him standing there looking confused. "Excuse me Vom," said Scarlett following Trey in the room as she closed the door behind her. "What's wrong with you?"

"What's wrong with me is I don't know this nigga, never heard of him nor have I ever seen him, so you might as well tell him he have to leave because I don't want him here!"

"But baby, he is just a fucking friend who I grew up with and I'm just helping him out!" As she was trying to convince him that everything was innocent and Vom was really just a friend. She decided to get undressed and ignore him. Getting totally nude she knew this would calm him down as she locked their bedroom door and climbed in the bed. "Baby, please come to bed with me," she begged just wishing he would calm down, "I missed you today babe, take off your clothes."

"Baby I'm not about to go to sleep with this..." Before Trey could finish his sentence, Vom was on the opposite side of the door saying he was leaving because his girlfriend was outside waiting for him to come out "Hey S, I'm gone, my girl is outside!"

"Ok Vom", she yelled back."

"Go lock the door and see that nigga out", Trey told her as he began to get undressed. Placing on her blue cotton robe, Scarlett walked Vom down the steps, and to the door as Trey listened to Vom thank her for allowing him to come over and wait. Giving him a light hug, she waited and watched as Vom got into his girlfriend's car, shut and locked the door and came back upstairs to their bedroom where Trey was in the bathroom taking a shower. After about twenty minutes of showering Trey exited the bathroom feeling refreshed and exhausted after such a long day. Turning off all the lights in the house he came to their bedroom where Scarlett was waiting, laying there still nude. He climbed in the bed and laid on his back reflecting on the day's events. "Don't do that no more babe that shit really wasn't cool and the only reason I didn't act a fool is because I trust you and I had to give you the benefit of doubt."

"Ok baby", she replied back. As they laid there in the dark, Scarlett decided to get on her hand and knees and please him orally, allowing him to cum in her mouth as she swallowed all of his semen to the last drop, using her tongue to clean his dick when she was done. Rising from the bed, she went into the bathroom, gargled some mouthwash and came back to bed where Trey had already dozed off to sleep. Joining him, she eventually dozed off while resting her head on his chest.

The following morning as Trey awakened, he opened his eyes to the sight of Scarlett standing in front of him fully dressed in a pair of blue denim jeans that was tight fitting and ripped up and down the front of the thighs and legs, a purple button up shirt that she kept half way unbuttoned to show off her cleavage along with some purple stilettos to match, as she stood staring at him applying her earrings in her ear. "Hey sleepy face" she spoke, kissing him lightly on the lips.

"Hey babe, what time is it," he questioned as he sat up in the bed, "you look nice."

"Thank you babe and its 9:47 a.m. and I'm late, I wanted to eat breakfast with you but you were sleeping so peacefully I would've felt guilty waking you up."

"I know, I was out of it," he said as he rose from the bed and walked to the bathroom, smacking her on her butt along the way. "That was that good head." They both chuckled in unison his humor.

Scarlett

"Whatever boy, I'll call you when I get to work, give me a kiss." She kissed him on the lips passionately as if he didn't just wake up with morning breath, grabbed her purse and walked down the steps to head out the door before adding, "and your phone was vibrating when I woke up, so turn on your ringer and listen for my call."

"Ok", he yelled back watching her leave the house as he exited the bathroom. Trey waited at the top of the steps until she secured the locks from the outside, grabbed his phone out of his pocket and climbed back into their bed. He grabbed the radio remote, clicked the power on and settled with an R & B station. As he laid back checking his phone he was surprised to see he had two text messages from Candy, both coming at 7 this morning saying, *"Good morning"* and another message from Tina that came in at 5 a.m. that read, *"I'm up early thinking about you, call when you wake up boo."* Redialing Tina's number, he listened as the phone just rang until she picked up on the fourth ring. "Hello?" "Tina, what's up?"

"Good morning boo!"

"I see you were up five this morning" he added, "What was that about, and what are you doing now?"

"I'm just laying here high as shit off this Triple Stack I just took, horny as shit and I need to get fucked" she replied back. "So come see me before you hook up with what's her face." Trey just smiled and laughed at her bluntness, he knew how Tina was when she was either drunk or on a pill and it was no limit to what she would do sexually, she just became another person and he knew if he wanted to have any energy for Candy he would have to go and please Tina now. "Alright babe, I'm on my way, see you when I get there."

Trey got up, made the bed and slipped on a grey Louis Vuitton t-shirt along with some matching sweats and sneakers. After he sprayed on some Versace cologne, he grabbed his keys, watch and laptop. Placing everything he was taking with him on the couch, he looked around just to make sure he wasn't leaving anything because he knew he wasn't gonna be back until his date with Candy was over. Taking his time to gargle, brush his teeth and floss before he headed out. He decided to leave Scarlett a note on the bathroom mirror that read, *"I love you baby,"* snatched up everything in one swoop and headed out the door, locking the bottom lock behind him Settling in his Mercedes in route to Tina's house a call came in from Candy. "Hello?" Trey answered.

"Good morning sweetie, are you up?"

"Yeah I am, how are you?"

"I'm fine", she stated. "I was calling because I wanted to know if you can meet at the same place by 1 p.m. this afternoon." Checking his watch, he noticed it was only 10:37 a.m., and one would actually be perfect so he wouldn't have to rush with Tina, allowing him a little break in between the two of them. Digging under his seat, he checked his stash of Viagra, and decided to fuck Tina naturally, but for Candy he knew it would be best to take one so it wouldn't be any complications and also so he could leave a lasting impression, having her feigning for more. Laughing at the thought, as he continued with the conversation they were having, "That's fine babe I can be there by one. Do you need me to bring you anything?"

"No sweetie I'm good, just bring your sexy ass and don't be late."

"Alright babe, see you then." he chuckled at her trying to demand something with her soft voice. Pulling up to Tina's house, he grabbed his phone placing it in his pocket along with his keys, he hopped out, securing the locks with the press of a button from his car keys and entered Tina's house. As always the door was unlocked. Locking the door he called out to her only to be ignored as he climbed the steps. "Tina!" Reaching the top of the stairs he smiled to himself as he noticed the bathroom door shut and the sound of the shower water running from behind the door. He hurriedly walked to her bedroom and discarded everything he had on, throwing all of his clothes in a pile on her futon. Trey rushed to the bathroom and entered the foggy room, shutting the door behind him. He went inside the medicine cabinet and took out two condoms that Tina kept stored for moments like this. Trey pulled the shower curtain back and instantly became erect at the sight of Tina. Standing underneath the shower head, leaning with her back against the wall facing him with her eyes closed and one leg propped up against the soap ledge, she was using one hand to squeeze her breast and the other to insert her vibrator in and out of her. Trey stepped inside with her stroking his dick, as she threw her vibrator on the floor out of the shower, switched positions with him, placing him under the hot water and fell to her knees, orally servicing him.

Staring in her eyes while enjoying the pleasure of her warm mouth, he knew she was really feeling the effects of the pill, because her pupils were humongous and her eyes kept twitching and rolling around. Stood up switched positions again with him as she pushed him to his knees, propping one leg up against the soap ledge, "Eat me baby!" Trey did just that, sending Tina to a height of ecstasy that shook her body uncontrollably, as she climaxed screaming obscenities, "Shit, Fuck, Damn Trey, I love you muthafucka!! Lay on your back" she told him, as she grabbed one of the condoms that he carelessly dropped in the tub when he first entered the shower. Placing

38

one on his swollen dick, she positioned the water to run freely on the both of them as she sat on top of him, bouncing and straddling until they both climaxed together. Too weak to shower, they both stood as Trey flushed the used condom, washed each other up and stepped out of the hot bathroom. They both entered Tina's room holding hands with her leading the way, dried off with the same towel and laid down on her bed. Tina climbed on top of him and whispered in his ear, "I'm so fuckin high." They both laughed aloud together. "When you are done with that bitch, I want you to come back here so we can get you a pill and we can drink something together?!"

"That sounds like a plan" he said, knowing he was gonna be drained and not up to it if Candy demanded the same services as she did the previous day.

"So convince Scarlett you are going out with the fellas tonight" she added, "cause I want you to myself!"

Feeling on her booty as she continued to lay on him, he glanced at his watch and continued to lie there comfortably, realizing that he had an hour and ten minutes to meet up with Candy. "I'll be done with her by 2 or 2:30, ok?"

"Mmhmmm" she moaned, tongue kissing him as he kissed her back continuing to squeeze and play with her butt. Rolling off of him she walked out of the room and headed downstairs where her phone was ringing. While she was out of the room, Trey got up and took that opportunity to get dressed. As he walked down the steps, Tina was on the phone setting up a date of her own for one o'clock that afternoon. He overheard her giving 'the John' her address as she leaned against the door using her index finger to motion him to come to her.

As he stood before her she ended the call, tossing her phone on the couch, and stuck the same index finger inside of her and put it in his mouth. Trey knew how wet she was and knew she wanted another round with him but he killed the urge to have her and knew that business came first. "Hurry up boo and call me when you are done. I got this muthafucka coming over and he want an hour massage. I'm gonna have his ass out of here in twenty minutes!" she said, giggling. Tina opened the door for him, hugged him and watched as he got in his car and pulled off.

Chapter 3

Sitting in the hotel parking lot, Trey decided to swallow a half of a Viagra pill while talking to Scarlett, before heading up to Candy's suite. "So are you gonna be able to come up with all the rent money baby?" she questioned, "because my check is gonna be short and I still gotta pay my car note and insurance."

"Yeah I will have it babe, I got it" he said, as a matter of fact.

"Are you sure?"

"Scarlett, I said I got it!"

"Ok, where did you get money from?"

"Babe, I'm gonna use my check to pay the rent and I'm just gonna make a few moves with my man Tone, so will you be ok?"

"Oh boy, here we go" she said sarcastically, "I don't want you running the streets and getting into any trouble babe."

"I'm not, I won't have to do anything but collect my money. Plus Tina said she has a job I can do that will benefit us really well."

"Doing what", she questioned.

"I don't know, but as soon as she let me know you will be the first to find out" he told her, cutting the ignition of the car off. "I'm supposed to call her back in an hour."

"Ok, where are you?"

"About to meet up with Tone, so as soon as I am done I will give you a call." Stepping out of the car he pressed the lock button from his keys and made his way to the elevator.

"I said, where are you?"

"Baby I'm downtown meeting up with Tone, I just told you" he told her, as he laughed at her audacity to see if he was lying.

"Mmmmhmmm…Alright baby call me when you are done."

"Ok I will call you then."

"Don't forget" she said, hanging up ending the call.

As Trey entered the elevator making his way to Candy's suite he dialed her number to let her know he was there, "Hello sweetie", she answered.

"I'm here sweets, making my way to your room as we speak, so you can unlock the door."

"Its unlocked baby, I'm waiting for you so just come on in"

"Alright see you in a sec" he said ending the call. Trey entered Candy's suite and once again was greeted by the flicker of the candle lights that surrounded her room, while she sat on the loveseat in a purple silk robe, legs crossed exposing a long legged thick yellow thigh. Closing the door and securing it behind him, Trey joined her on the sofa and was mesmerized by her good looks and laid back demeanor. He wondered what was going wrong in her life that made her do what she was doing and why didn't she have a man or a husband for that matter? "So how are you today Trey?" she questioned.

"I'm good babe, you look nice. So how can I be of some assistance to you today?"

"Cute" she said, as she looked him in his eyes from above the rim of her glass, while she sipped on a double shot of Patron Tequila on the rocks. "Well since you put it that way you can start off by taking a quick shower, dry off and join me back here for a drink."

Smiling to himself, Trey couldn't help but think to himself, 'Wow, this woman is interesting, I hope I don't stink.' As he rose to go shower, she stated, "You can undress right here, slowly, I wanna watch you and see what I'm about to get myself into." He happily obliged, fully erected, turned on by her beauty and soft looking yellow skin. Liking what she saw, she watched as he turned and headed for the shower. As soon as Trey was out of sight, Candy rose from the couch unlocked the door to the suite while leaving it open, picked up her cellphone and dialed a number. A woman picked up on the other end and answered, "Is everything in place?"

"Yeah come on up, we'll will be waiting for you!" Candy replied back before hanging up ending the call.

Tossing her phone on the sofa, she walked around the suite blowing out all the candles leaving two lit on opposite sides of the room. She let her robe drop to her feet as she entered the bathroom, cutting off the light as she stepped in the shower with him. As Trey faced her, she grabbed him by the head with both hands, and seductively met her lips with his placing her tongue in his mouth as they kissed slowly, but forcefully. While they continued to kiss, Trey knew he felt someone enter the shower with them, but he was unsure because of how big it was and also because of the darkness, and just as the thought crossed his mind, that is when he felt the hands and lips of another woman stroking and French kissing his dick. Caught in a state of blissful lust as four hands touched and caressed his body, while four lips gently massaged his dick, Trey set back thinking to himself, 'I'm the fuckin man!' Now at full attention with the help from the pill, Trey was ready to take this to the bed just as Candy whispered in his ear, "I hope you like my surprise, you are gonna get paid very well for this so I'm gonna need you to bring your A game poppy!" As the unknown woman continued to suck his dick, Candy cut the water of the shower off and decided to take things to the bed of the suite. As they all exited the shower holding hands, the anticipation of seeing the mystery woman was killing him. Opening the bathroom door, the mystery woman went out first, followed by Candy with Trey exiting last. Climbing on the king sized bed, Tina crawled to the center, turned and laid on her back, legs wide open, propping herself up on her elbows, as she awaited Trey and Candy to join her, while the candle light glittered on the water that ran down her wet body. "Surprise" Tina stated, smiling as she stared at Trey rubbing herself, still feeling the effects of the pill she had taken earlier that day. Candy went around the room, and blew out the last two candles before joining the two of them in the massive bed. For the next 2 hours they each touched, tasted, and performed different sexual acts upon each other. Drained and relaxed from the performance he put on with the two of them, pleasing them both beyond belief, he laid back with them both on opposite sides as they laid on his shoulders sweaty, still rubbing and fondling him. "OMG Trey baby, you fucked me so good." Candy said, kissing him on his cheek.

"I just wanna lay here in your arms like this for the next couple hours."

"I agree baby" Tina said to him joining in the convo picking up where Candy left off.

"That was soooo good both of y'all, but I need to be getting up, making my way home... after I lay here for another 20 minutes." They all laughed in unison.

Tina rose from the bed, hips swaying making her booty jiggle as she walked to the bathroom, and entered the shower. Watching her as she walked off disappearing in the bathroom. Candy and Trey decided to continue on with their conversation. "So what is it you do for a living?" she questioned.

"I was just laid off from a job where I worked as a laborer for the city of Baltimore."

"So, do you do this to pay the bills?"

"Yeah something like that?"

"So, where is your girlfriend" she asked, "and what does she think about you doing this?"

"She's around, but she doesn't know what I do, I keep my business separated from her." Candy rose from the bed refilled her glass with a double shot of Patron, fixing him one as well, then asked, "Do you love her?"

"Yeah I do, but I don't think I am *in love* with her. How about you, what is it that you do for a living...man, kids?" Walking back to the bed she handed him his glass, while setting hers on the nightstand next to the bed to walk back to the refrigidaire. Taking the cranberry juice out, she walked back to the bed where he sat waiting, poured a little bit of the juice in each of their glasses, set the juice down and joined him back in the bed and stated, "I'm recently divorced from my husband of two years, no kids, and I do not work. I'm pretty financially well off from a couple of settlements. One from the divorce with my ex who's a well-known football player, and two others from a car accident that happened a few years ago. This is my first time hiring a, you know...male escort, but I feel like I have known you for quite some time, is that weird?"

"No that is not weird" he told her, "cause I actually feel like I have known you for quite some time as well, maybe it's that good chemistry."

"Yeah I can agree with you on that." As Tina emerged from the bathroom drying herself off, she used the light from the bathroom to see her way around the room picking up her clothes. She looked from one to the other as she got dressed.

"So how was your shower?" Candy questioned.

Letting out a loud sigh she smiled and stated, "It was marvelous, I'm rejuvenated. Now I need a nice drink and a night on the town."

"Well there's the Patron" Candy told her. "There's also some Remy Martin in the fridge. Help yourself, while me and Trey sit back for the next hour or so getting to know each other, if that is ok with you Trey, unless you have other important things to do?" Facing him smiling waiting for a reply, she gave him a kiss on the cheek as she was starting to feel the effects of the Patron.

"No, he'd better not have a problem with that." Tina pitched in pouring herself a drink, "especially since his sexy ass getting paid. Tell her Trey, time is money boo we ain't playing!"

"That's right baby...TIME IS MONEY" he yelled back, smiling at Tina, leaning over giving Candy a kiss back on her cheek. Dressed in a white short sleeved trench coat that came midway to her thigh, similar to a mini skirt, Tina downed three shots of Patron straight without no chaser nor ice. Looked from one to the other and stated, "Well I will be leaving you two love bugs alone, call me later Trey, and Candy girl take care of my baby!" Getting out of the bed still nude, Candy walked over to Tina, hugged and kissed her goodbye and seen her out of the suite. Locking the door behind her she turned and faced Trey walking back towards him, from the bed he walked towards her gave her a hug, embracing her tightly, looked her in the eye and said, "You were telling me how much you enjoy me and love the things I do to you, and how we are gonna be friends for a long time!"

"Well everything you said is true, we can be friends for however long you wanna be. I don't have a problem with that, I like you, I wanna spoil you, and want you to get away with me sometimes. I know you gotta make your money, so what I will do is transfer

46

money to your account when I wanna see you and pay for your flight and travel expenses."

"That will be fine babe" he said, releasing her walking towards his clothes and digging in his pocket to retrieve his phone. Glancing at his phone he saw that he had two text messages from Scarlett saying, how much she missed and loved him, and one from Tina. He stood there responding back to Scarlett letting her know, that he missed and loved her as well.

He smiled as he read Tina message, '*Trey baby don't be all night with her cause I still wanna hang out with you tonight; and make sure you get all of your money boo, TTYL Love ya!!!*'

He texted her back, '*Ok babe, C U soon babe ILY2*'. Placing his phone back in his pocket, he turned back around to face Candy, she handed him a white envelope. "Here baby put that up, it is for you and don't spend it all in one place. When you are done you can come join me back in the bed, and lay with me for another hour or however long you can?!" Accepting the envelope from her, Trey tucked it in his sweats along with his phone, joined her back in the bed, and told her that he could stay for another hour, but thought it would be best he leave after that. She was fine with that and knew he had a life outside of the business, she had already paid him triple for his services, all she really wanted to do was to cuddle and be held, which she told him. "Just hold me for about an hour baby."

He happily obliged holding her as if he was in love with her. As they lay there quietly she broke the silence, and told him that, tomorrow was her last day in town until she flew back to Miami, and how she wanted to see him one more time before she had to go. He just held her and told her, "Ok" as she dozed off to sleep. After about an hour or so Trey awakened still holding Candy with one arm around her nude waist, as she continued to sleep like a baby. He quietly rose from the bed as to not stir her awake, went in the bathroom, washed himself clean in front of the sink and dried off using one of the five towels that were sitting on the ledge of the Jacuzzi, that he hadn't utilized. Exiting the bathroom, he quickly got dressed. When he finished he looked around to make sure he wasn't leaving anything, walked over to her sleeping body, kissed her a few times from her forehead to her nose to her lips, as she opened her eyes smiling while looking up at him.

"I'm leaving baby, I gotta go" he told her, "call or text me when you wanna see me again."

"Ok sweetie, just pull the door all the way closed when you leave out. I'm just gonna lay here a little while longer." She sat up, just long enough to hug him and pull the sheets from the bottom of the bed. As she lay back down, Trey exited the suite and headed to his car. Once inside his car he started the engine and began nodding his head to the music that blared out of the Mercedes BOSE speakers.

Retrieving the thick envelope out of his pocket, he pulled the money out and hopped up and down with excitement, as he counted out two thousand dollars. Taking out his phone, he called Scarlett first as he drove out of the parking lot making his way to her job to surprise her. "Concorde Management," she answered.

Catching the voice he stated, "Hey baby what's up?'

"Nothing baby just a little sleepy, how about you, what are you doing?"

48

"Oh not a thing, just on my way to put something on my stomach, did you eat anything?"

"Yeah I had a chicken salad about an hour ago so I'm fine." Putting the petal to the metal, Trey jumped on the freeway and arrived at her job in less than ten minutes. As he continued to have small talk with her he was able to park outside of her job, purchase three roses from a Mexican woman for $5 that was on the street peddling.

Entering the building, he put his finger up to his mouth to tell her secretary to be quiet. As he entered her office, he walked straight in as Scarlett was sitting at her desk, looking in the mirror applying makeup to her eyes, while speaking to him on speaker phone telling him how much she wanted to spend some quality time with him tonight. "So am I seeing you tonight before I go to bed cause I wanna spend some...Baby you are full of surprises, I'm so happy to see you!" she yelled, smiling from ear to ear and jumping out of her chair embracing him with a hug that showed how much she missed him. As they stood there holding each other, Trey stepped back just enough to hand Scarlett the roses he just purchased for her and told her, "I missed you too baby. I'm supposed to go out with Tony and a few other dudes we cool with to DC tonight, how about you take off tomorrow and we spend the whole day together?" "Thanks baby, these roses are pretty, but as for tomorrow, I may can do that as long as you don't have something come up, cause if you do I'm going with you." She smiled, as she turned and placed the roses in a vase she had that already set on her desk before adding, "So what's in DC and how long you gonna be gone?" He took a seat in her plush leather chair that sat behind her desk, with her joining him sitting on his lap. Hopping off his lap she went to her

49

office door and secured the lock so no one would walk in on them, then rejoined him sitting back on his lap.

"Some lounge Tone wants me to go to with him, it's supposed to end at 2 a.m. so, I should be home by 3. I'm taking my car therefore I don't have to worry about waiting on anyone, and I can leave when I'm ready."

"Ok baby, that's fine, make sure you don't drink too much and I will be calling you or texting so listen out for me." They sat with each other laughing and playing around with each other flirtatiously for the remaining hour, until his stomach started growling reminding him that he hadn't eaten a thing. "I'm about to go and grab something to eat babe, and go holla at Tina."

"You haven't talked to her yet?" she questioned, rising off of his lap.

"No, I'm about to go meet up with her and see what's on her brain."

"Oh alright, I guess I will let you go." Rising from the chair, Trey went into the bathroom that was connected to Scarlett's office, locked the door behind him as he stood checking himself out in the mirror, pulled his money out of his pocket and counted out one thousand dollars. As he put the rest back, he placed the thousand in another pocket, urinated washed his hands and exited the bathroom. Back in her office he stood before her and said, "Oh yeah before I go, here you go babe, that should cover the rent and you can do whatever it is you want with the rest." Accepting the wad of money from him she smiled, thanked him and told him how much she loved him. They hugged and kissed each other as he exited her office with her following behind him walking him to his car. They hugged and kissed one more time before he got in his car. With the money he gave her still in her hand he told her, "Put that money up babe, before I have to hurt one of these fools out here."

"Ok, my macho man!" she said, turning away smiling as he pulled off making his way over to Tina's while Scarlett went back into the office. Sitting at a traffic light while in route to Tina's house, Trey phone rung, just as he grabbed his phone to answer it he noticed a female walking across the street smiling and waving at him, signaling him to pull over, dressed in a yellow Louis Vuitton sweat suit that hugged her body like second skin. Trey didn't realize the light had turned green while he held up traffic with cars behind him honking their horns trying to get by, and Tone blaring through the speakers saying, "**Helloooo**!" for the third time, as he continued to watch the LV printed in white on her ass swaying and bouncing as she continued to cross the street looking at him smiling.

Snapping out of his gaze and back to reality, Trey pressed the gas just making it through the yellow light. "Tone, what's up my nigga?"

"Trey what's up? I was about to hang up, I said hello like four or five times! You didn't hear me?" Continuing to drive to Tina's house, Trey burst into laughter as he said, "Yo, I just seen this phat ass chick walk by me in a yellow Louis V jogging suit, man she was thicka than a snicka!"

"So did you get her?" questioned Tone.

"No, I let her go. I started to though, cause she damn sure was smiling and waving for me to pull over...so anyway fuck her, what's up with you?"

"Nothing, for real, just trying to see what you getting into tonight?"

"I'm gonna be in DC with you and a few other niggas, at a lounge that supposed to end at 2 a.m." Trey told him.

"Let me guess" Tone said, matter of fact. "You told Scarlett that shit? Alright that's cool. Whatever you getting into, make sure you strap up nigga!" With them both laughing together, Trey said, "And you know I am my nigga, I'mma make her think I invented hitting that pussy from the back!" They both laughed while saying their goodbyes promising to hook up with each other on a later date when either one was free. Trey decided to text Tina to let her know that it was ok to unlock the door as he pulled up behind her car in front of her house. While he parked and stepped out of the car making his way to her door, she sent him a text back, letting him know it was okay to come in. When Trey entered, Tina was sitting there in the living room Indian style, on the black and white loveseat with nothing on but, some yellow lace boy shorts while typing away on her laptop.

"Come have a seat and look what I have been working on."

Securing the locks on the door; Trey walked past her and stated, "gimme a sec, I'm hungry as shit!" As he searched through the refrigerator, she came behind him and pulled his shirt up and off his body, tossing it on the kitchen table. Settling for some leftover spaghetti she made the previous day, he warmed a plate of the pasta up and sat at the table and ate as if he hadn't in weeks. As Tina set across the table from him, she produced two yellow starred X pills, as he reached behind her into her opened fridge and grabbed a bottle of Ciroc and Cranberry juice. Drinking the Ciroc out of the bottle followed by the Cranberry juice, Trey past the bottles to her and asked, "So what did you wanna show me on the laptop?"

"Pill first!" she told him, as they both laughed at each other.

As Trey swallowed one of the pills with Tina swallowing the other one, he chased it down with a swallow of the Ciroc, while Tina swallowed hers down with the juice and stated, "Well I just got off the phone with the city paper, and I placed an ad in there for you, also I posted a couple profiles of you on a couple websites as an escort for a woman. They both are websites for affluent woman, some married, some divorced, some single, but they are all looking to pay top dollar for some male companionship. I have a phone that you will be able to use just for this, and when they call your number, you will just have to set the date up, they already know your rates, but if they don't, just let them know what they are for the hour. Come on in the living room with me so I can show you." They both rose from the table, Tina grabbing the drinks, Trey rinsing the plate off, setting it back on the dish rack where he found it as he joined her back in the living room, sitting next to her on the loveseat. Tina showed him the two websites, explaining and showing him everything he needed to know about how to be successful at becoming a good escort. When they were done talking about the business, Tina gave him the phone he was gonna be using, letting him know he was responsible for paying the bill every month, as well as keeping it away from Scarlett and not letting her get ahold of it. With the effects of the pill starting to kick in, Trey looked at Tina and questioned, "So,

53

what are we doing tonight, cause this pill and drink is starting to kick in?"

"You already know I got us boo. Now take off them sweats and let me see that dick, while I make this phone call to our destination for tonight!" As Trey stripped off the remaining of his clothes, he sat his phone on the ottoman that sat in front of the other couch in the living room. Tina was on her phone calling one of her girlfriend that lived down the street to come over, and drive with her and Trey to DC, while gesturing Trey to come stand in front of her. She began sucking his dick as she made the call, waiting for Shay to answer. As she sucked his dick while talking to her girlfriend Shay, Trey received a call from Scarlett.

Taking the call while presuming the act allowing Tina to continue, Trey spoke with Scarlett as she told him, she was off from work and was going out to a club in D.C. as well with a couple of her girlfriends. Ending the call with Scarlett, and tossing his phone back on the ottoman, he laughed to himself as the sensation from what Tina was doing to him, as well as over how the pill and liquor took over his body, putting him in a good mood. After about twenty minutes, Shay was knocking on the door. Rising from the couch, Tina answered the door letting Shay in, as Trey went in the kitchen grabbed three glasses and returned back to the living room catching Shay off guard, with the sight of him naked walking towards her and Tina, handing both of them a glass each.

"My goodness, damn Trey you are looking good enough to eat," said Shay, "I heard so much about you, I don't know if I should hug you, or strip down and fuck you. Damn Tina, bitch you said he was fine, but you ain't tell me he was this fine!" They all laughed in unison, as they all took a seat on the couch, with Tina sitting next to Trey and Shay on the ottoman in front of them, taking glances between his legs while sipping on her second drink that she made herself, all liquor with no chaser. Tina looked at Trey and said, "So are you wearing what you had on today, or are you gonna change your clothes?"

"Do I have that Christian Louboutin shit upstairs that I bought last week?"

"You don't have to, but yeah its upstairs, I'm gonna go up and slip something on then we can be on our way and get out of here" she said, "I will bring it down when I come down, just give me a sec!" Tina kissed Trey on the cheek, rose from the couch and blew Shay a kiss as she made her way up the steps. Approaching her bedroom she yelled out to them, "You Perv's can talk, kiss, screw...do something while I'm gone ok?!"

"Ok" Shay said, yelling back up to her rising from the ottoman and sitting down beside him.

"So, what's up?" Trey asked her, when she plopped down in the chair beside him. Crossing her legs in a tight green mini dress that left little to the imagination, she reached over grabbed his dick and began wiggling it around, before adding.

"You are what's up, so when am I gonna get a chance to feel this?" Noticing she was feeling good on whatever drugs she was on. Trey felt underneath her dress and told her.

"Baby I'm high as shit right now, how about you give me a sample of what that pussy is like tonight, when we get to where ever we going, or better yet when we get back." She giggled allowing him to continue to

55

play underneath her pantiless dress. Feeling horny and turned on, she leaned over and wrapped her lips around his dick and began sucking him, rising up and wiping her mouth she looked at him and asked, "So how did you like that sample?"

Trey rose from the couch and said, "Yeah, that was good, you gotta good head on your shoulders" while walking up the steps he added, "Yeah, I'm gonna get your lil ass, I be back!" As he approached the top of the steps, he overheard Tina in the bathroom on the phone, "**Just make sure you come, and no he won't figure it out, as long as you don't do anything stupid...Ok and I miss you too, bye!**" Just as Tina was ending the call, she exited the bathroom still looking down in her phone, and bumped right into Trey as his hand was reaching for the bathroom knob to enter. "Baby" she said startled, "you scared the crap out of me, come on put your clothes on so we can get out of here." Grabbing him by the hand and leading him to the bedroom, she tossed her phone on the bed, pulled his clothes out of the closet, sitting them on the bed beside him. While she went back to the closet to retrieve his shoes, Trey took that time to look in her phone at her last call, noticing it was gone which evidently meant she deleted it. "So, who is meeting us at this place?" Trey asked, as she handed him the box that his shoes came in.

"Nobody, I was just telling my girl to get a nut out of her boring sexual romp with her man, and fake it to perfection, jeeze Boo, you got some good ears!" His inner gut feeling told him that Tina was lying, he let it slide though, simply because he really was starting to feel the pill and the drink and he really wanted to have a nice time with her and Shay tonight. After getting dressed, the three of them gathered their belongings and headed out of the house, taking Tina's Range Rover, with Shay driving, the three of them flirted, joked and played with one another the whole ride to D.C.

CHAPTER 4

Finally arrived in D.C., Scarlett set in the parking lot across from the lounge watching, as Tina's truck pulled up on the side of the lounge. As Tina, Trey and another female whom she couldn't recognize exited the vehicle laughing and playing, they made their way inside the crowded building. Choosing that exact moment to make her grand entrance, Scarlett exited her truck stopping traffic in a short white mini sequin skirt with a matching white top that resembled a bikini top. She walked past the long line flashing her front of the line pass, and entered the packed lounge as a waiter handed her a glass of champagne from his tray. As the DJ played the latest pop music, the whole lounge was filled with dancing, while some sat at the bar having drinks and dancing in their seats, others were either engulfed in a conversation with the opposite sex, or in their own world making the best of their night. Scarlett made her way to the restroom ignoring guys as they tried to get her attention. Once in the bathroom, she pulled out her phone and began texting Tina, to let her know that she was there where she needed to be. After about five minutes, leaving Shay and Trey on the dance floor to tend to themselves, not letting them know where she was going, she entered the restroom where Scarlett was leaning against the wall, alone waiting for her.

"Hey sexy" Tina said, as she walked up to Scarlett kissing her passionately. Both women hugged, feeling each other bodies and continued to kiss ignoring a real light complexioned girl that came out of one of the stalls.

"So, does he know I'm here?" Scarlett questioned, referring to Trey.

"Not even a clue baby." She answered.

"So, what time are we getting out of here cause I want you!"

Tina looked her in the eyes and said, "Well, how about I leave him with my girlfriend since they are all over one another, leave them my car keys, tell them I have a date, and meet you at your car and we can go!?"

"Sounds like a plan, I'm parked directly across the street in the parking lot, meet me there and don't take long!" Scarlett said. As they both exited the restroom, Tina squeezed Scarlett on the behind as she made her way back to Trey and Shay, with Scarlett making her way to the parking lot.

It took Tina all of ten minutes to find them, when she did they were in the VIP area making out with Shay sitting on his lap.

"There you two go!" She said, as she sat beside them. She whispered in Trey's ear letting him know that she was going to be heading out with an old friend whom she just ran across. She handed him the keys, before leaving she kissed both of them goodbye, winking as she walked away blending in with the crowd, making her way to a waiting Scarlett who sat in the parking lot patiently for her to come on. As Scarlett waited, she reflected on the dreadful day her and Tina met, a day she wished she could take back.

Listen Al, I am really taking a chance by letting you in my home while Trey is at work, cause I really don't want to hurt him, and if he catches us here he is gonna be pissed, and I really don't feel like the drama!!" Scarlett said, letting her ex-boyfriend Al into her home. Knowing how she felt about being caught by Trey in their home, the home Scarlett and Al once shared. Usually under no circumstances would Scarlett allow another man to come into her household that she shared with Trey, but being in desperate need of money to get her car fixed and also to go on a weekend trip to Miami with some of her girlfriends, she didn't know anyone else to call. While waiting on a cab to come drop her off to work, Scarlett received a text from Al saying he was in the neighborhood, and just wanted to say hello. Wondering what he was up to, being as though she hadn't heard from him in almost a year, she decided to respond back saying, "*Hello.*" Taking that as a sign to continue to converse, he sent another message to Scarlett asking, "***R u ok and do u need anything?***" Pondering the question, she knew she didn't need for anything, and she really didn't wanna open up old wounds-- seeing as though she was happy in a new relationship, but desperation had a way of taking over, and she figured fuck it why not. Responding back to his message, she laid it all out on the line flatly. "***I'm ok, besides the fact that, I need a thousand dollars to fix my car and another five hundred to go on my trip next week, why, are you gonna give me the money?***" Regretting having sent him the message, she cursed under her breathe when her phone rang and she realized it was him calling her back instead of responding to the text.

"Hello?"

"So where are you?"

"I'm in the house waiting on my cab so I can go to work."

"Are you alone?" he questioned.

"Yes, but what are you thinking?" she questioned, back.

"Well I see your boyfriend isn't there, cause I don't see his car, but how about if I step in for a few minutes and give you this money."

"So what do I have to do, cause I'm not tryna be caught up with you, especially not in the home where my man rests his head!" she said, matter-of-factly. Taking that as a sign of weakness, he knew he had her where he wanted her, "I promise I won't be in there long, and you can just pay me back when you can, in fact, I will even drop you off at work."

"No thanks but come on in and hurry up!"

Ending the call, Scarlett allowed Al to hurry up and come in, before one of the neighbors spotted him. As soon as he entered they went upstairs to the living room. After exchanging hugs, she allowed him to go use the bathroom, which she just shook her head knowing that was another mistake. When he exited the bathroom he handed her the cash, as they made small talk on why she didn't think it was a good idea that he be there, he began to kiss her, catching her totally off guard, as he began to pull her dress up. Turning her head away from his kiss, she continued to tell him that it wasn't right what they or better yet what he was doing. "This is not right Al, we are not supposed to be doing this!"

"It will be over before you know it Scar," he told her, as he had her panties down to her ankles.

Dismissing the pain and allowing the pleasure to take over her being, she allowed him to push her on the couch, as he kissed and licked her pussy, tenderizing her clitoris, bringing her back to the pleasure he used to give her when they were together. Somehow being caught in the moment, she hadn't noticed he had slipped on a condom and was now thrusting inside of her, as she laid back begging for more. Allowing him to flip her over on her stomach, she never heard the front door open and close, as she was on her knees, allowing him to pump in and out of her from behind. As Tina stood at the top of the steps, catching Scarlett being intimate with another man in the home that she and Trey shared, she thought of turning back around and leaving out. As that thought entered her brain, she quickly dismissed it, pulling out her cellphone and recording the whole scene.

After they were done and starting to stand up, Tina decided to choose that moment to make her presence known, "Awwwww.....What a nice performance!" said Tina, clapping, startling the both of them as they both clumsily scrambled to fix themselves, knowing they were caught. "Don't worry, I'm just here to drop off Trey's car to you Scarlett, he doesn't have to know about this if you don't want him to" she said to her, looking from one to the other, as they both looked back at her dumbfounded while fixing their clothes. Before Tina turned to leave, she just shook her head and smiled adding, "Call me when you wanna talk and oh, don't forget to wash that kitty. MEOW!" When Tina was gone, Scarlett raced to the window watching as Tina entered another vehicle with an unknown female passenger, watching as they pulled off. Picking the money up off of the couch that Al had given her earlier, she threw it at him as it splattered everywhere. She told him angrily to get out and leave and never to call her again. He tried to talk to her, but gave up when she lashed out at him again. Leaving the money on the floor where it landed, he quickly dismissed himself out of her house and out of her life for good for the last and final time. After he left, Scarlett called her job letting her receptionist know, she wasn't going to make it in today. She laid on her couch for hours in a fetal position and cried her heart out. After several hours went by she decided to get up and gather the money up placing it in her purse, cleaned up the condom as well as the wrapper that he carelessly dropped on the living room floor, flushing it and soaked her body in the tub where Trey later found her, with a flower and teddy bear in his hand as a gift for her.

Entering Scarlett's vehicle, Tina leaned over and gave Scarlett a quick peck on her cheek, "Damn, what took you so long?" Scarlett snapped, finding herself annoyed thinking about how much she did still care and love Trey, knowing she was deceiving him by not being faithful and also by sleeping with his friend Tina. Hating Tina, she wiped the lipstick of hers off her cheek, while looking her in the eyes.

"So where to?" asked Tina.

"I was thinking the nearest hotel. I'm emotional and need a drink and I need my kitty licked!" Scarlett told her as they drove out of the parking lot. Tina told Scarlett, where the nearest liquor store was. They stopped, paid a guy that was sitting outside of the store to go in and purchase them a fifth of Ciroc vodka, along with a fifth of Rose Moet and headed to the nearest Hilton hotel they came across which was three miles away from the lounge. Once inside they booked a room on the fifth floor overlooking the city. Scarlett poured herself a drink, mixing both the liquor and the champagne, as Tina followed suit. They both stripped naked, sat opposite each other on the massive king sized bed, with Scarlett leaning her back against the headboard with her legs agape, and Tina sitting between them. "I am happy to see you, I was starting to feel neglected" Tina told her.

"There's no need for that Tina, you know I ain't going anywhere, besides you have me under lock and key with that juicy tongue you got" Scarlett told her, laughing aloud as the words rolled off of her tongue. Flicking, her tongue out her mouth rapidly.

Tina took another sip of her drink, taking Scarlett's out of her hand, and setting both glasses on the nightstand, and orally serviced Scarlett in a way she knew would blow her mind. They enjoyed each other bodies, with both being opposites on the receiving end. After they both made the other cum, they went back to sipping on their drinks, laughing in unison and complimenting each other on their cunnilingus techniques.

"Boy I'm ready to get out of here. I'm high, drunk and my juices are flowing between my legs!" said Shay, whispering in Trey's ear. After dancing and tiring one another out for the past two hours in the packed lounge, they decided to leave the club and find a hotel in D.C somewhere. Settling for the closest one of which was the Hilton, they end up booking a room on the fifth floor right next to the elevator. Trey was intoxicated, and also feeling the effects of the pill but had no desire to be with Shay any longer. After calling Scarlett for the fifth time, and not getting an answer, only to get her answering machine, he was surprised her phone had picked up after the eighth try, "Hello...Hello?!" Ready to give up and end the call, he sat and listened as he began to hear a conversation with what seemed to be Scarlett and another familiar female voice "so why did you introduce him to that? Come on Tina, I know ya'll are supposed to be friends but that is still my man."

"I know Scar, I just figured he needed the money, being as though he lost his job, and besides he is not doing anything with the women but massaging them...Geeeeshhh!! You act like he is fucking them!" she lied.

"Well is he?"

"No Scar, at least not to my knowledge he isn't."

"So what about what you saw, that you sneakily recorded, when you uninvitingly walked in my house?"

"I told you that as long as you give me what I want, you don't have to worry about me telling him, and you can get what you want as well." The more Trey listened the more he was becoming irate, and the drugs definitely did not help! Placing his phone on mute, he looked down at Shay. Realizing he had been standing there in tune with listening, he hadn't realized she had undressed, and was on her knees in front of him unbuttoning his pants.

Smacking her hands away, he told her, "look I'm not for this shit right now, put your clothes back on, we are getting out of here and I'm dropping you off!" Getting angry, Shay jumped up, defensively and grabbed hold of his collar. "No you not, you gonna fuck me!" Tossing her on the bed followed by a smack to her face, he snatched her back up and let her know he wasn't in the mood to be fucking around with her, and either she was gonna put her shit on and leave with him or he was gonna leave her there. Shay jumped up holding her face. Grabbing the lamp that was still plugged into the wall, she snatched out the cord and threw it at his head. Just missing his head, Trey decided to leave her there. Storming out of the hotel room, Trey quickly got on the elevator as it was halfway closing, shaking his head at the sight of Shay in the hallway naked, yelling obscenities and saying how she was gonna get him arrested for putting his hands on her.

People came out of their rooms watching her make a fool out of herself, she cursed at the onlookers as well, calling them a bunch of nosey mother fuckers. Having heard the commotion, Tina jumped up and ran to the door looking out of the peephole. Realizing her phone was answered and had been for the last twenty minutes with Trey on the other end, Scarlett quickly hung up and knew she was in for a long fucked up night. Wondering just how much he had heard, she decided right then to not bring it up unless he did because he might have not heard anything.

"We need to go," she told Tina. Just as she was climbing out of the bed she noticed Tina run out of the room with only her mini skirt on, and came back in the room with a crying Shay who was also nude. Scarlett decided, this was too much, grabbed her belongings and went in the bathroom to clean herself up, locking the door behind her.

"What happened?" Scarlett overheard Tina, questioning the girl.

"He fucking put his hands on me" she continued to tell her, still screaming, "and I'm gonna get his ass arrested!"

"Calm down and tell me what happened" Tina asked calmly, while sitting her down on the chair holding her as she waited for a response.

"I don't know, we was ready to fuck and he just went crazy and started slapping me, and throwing me around the room. I just wanna go home and get out of here. I don't even know where I am!"

"Well, what room are you in?" Tina further questioned.

Shay gave her details of where the room was, and the best way she could remember to get there in her stupor. Tina decided to call the lobby attendant, and explained she had locked herself out of her room. After arguing with the attendant that everything was under control, they finally sent someone up to unlock Shay's room. While Tina got dressed and headed to Shay's room to gather all of her belongings, Scarlett emerged out of the bathroom, looking on at a drunk Shay asleep on the couch. It took everything in Scarlett not to stomp Shay with her four inch Christian Louboutin heels, but she decided against it. After Tina came back, she and Scarlett fought to put Shay's clothes on as they gathered everything they came with and struggled to carry Shay out of the hotel to Scarlett's truck. Throwing Shay onto the backseat, she curled up in a fetal position and again was sound asleep.

Scarlett took her time driving back to Baltimore, because she knew she had to get her thoughts together, and putting up with Tina was not in the plans. She knew she had to play her close in order to get the video, but she also knew that it was time to just be honest with Trey about the secret life she had been having with Tina.

"So, where does this Thing on my backseat live?" Scarlett questioned Tina, as they drove down 295N making their way closer to Baltimore city. Tina gave Scarlett   Shay's address   as   she punched   the information into her GPS.

After driving about thirty minutes from DC, it took them another twenty minutes to arrive at Shay's house. Scarlett sat behind the driver seat of her car and never once turned around to check to see if Tina needed help getting Shay out of the truck, she couldn't stop thinking about Trey and wondering what was he doing, where he was, and what was his mood now that he had heard what he heard…if he actually heard anything at all. It didn't take Tina long to get Shay with her belongings in her house. Once inside Shay got herself together, taking off her clothes and laying on her couch. Shay thanked Tina for helping her get home, and it only took Tina twenty times before Shay realized she was home. Locking Shay's bottom lock on her front door, Tina got back in the car with an angry look on her face, while Scarlett wore a devilish smile on her face to hide the way she was really feeling. "Are you okay, Scar?" questioned Tina.

"No I'm not okay Tina. I know Trey heard part of our conversation earlier when we were in the room right before you darted out the room and came back with your little friend!"

Looking at her puzzled, Tina asked her, "What do you mean he heard us?" "Bitch, I looked down at my phone and somehow my phone picked up, and the call lasted 20 minutes! When I realized it, instead of saying hello I just hung up and ended the call!"

"Well maybe he didn't hear anything."

"Yeah right Tina, I know he had to have heard something cause, he was blowing my phone up. He must have called about ten times before it magically picked up, so I know he heard something. I just don't know what, and how much." Scarlett told her, matter-of-factly.

"Well call him and see how the conversation goes and take it from there. We will figure something out!"

Scarlett looked at her, and burst out laughing and told her, "yeah the truth!" On her way to Tina's house to drop her off, Scarlett decided to call Trey when she was alone.

"Shit!" Tina said aloud interrupting Scarlett's thoughts.

"What's wrong?"

"Trey, got my fucking house keys, they are on the same ring with my car keys."

"So, what now?" Scarlett questioned.

"Let me give him a call first, and see where he is" said Tina. As they sat outside of Tina's door, she noticed his car was gone along with her truck. She called his phone about ten times, only to get his voicemail after the first ring which meant he either cut his phone off or the battery had died.

She gave up on trying, after leaving him text message after text message, along with several voice messages. She decided to call one of her favorite clients who had been trying to reach her all night, and decided to have Scarlett drop her off at his house.

"If you see Trey or speak to him before I do, please have him to call me ASAP." Tina told Scarlett. After dropping Tina off, Scarlett decided to go home, on her way she decided to give Trey a call. She left him a long voicemail saying how much she misses him and needed to see him. When she arrived at their home she noticed Trey's car was parked out front along with Tina's truck. Parking behind his car, she had a gut feeling when she got in they were going to feud and fight, so she sat there for a moment trying to prepare herself. Exiting her vehicle, she entered their home and was caught by surprise to walk in and see him sitting on the living room couch dressed in a pair of pajama pants and a tank top watching TV as if everything was cool.

"Hey baby" he said to her, tapping on the seat next to him. "Come here, bout time you're home! I missed you!"

Stepping out of the elevator, Trey was furious over the conversation he just overheard between Tina and Scarlett. Then with Shay, she was a crazy bitch. 'I'm glad I didn't fuck that bitch', he thought to himself. Walking through the lobby still feeling the effects of the pill he had taken earlier, he felt he was in the mood to get laid and take his frustrations out on someone's daughter or someone's mother. Waiting on the valet to pull up with his vehicle, Trey couldn't believe the conversation he had heard between Scarlett and Tina.

Especially since Scarlett acted as if she couldn't stand the mere thought of Tina.

Tipping the valet driver when he finally arrived, Trey decided to give Scarlett's receptionist a call, as he headed out of the city in route to pick up his car and leave Tina's parked.

"Hello?" Deb answered, picking up on the second ring.

"Hey Deb, what's up? What are you doing up this late?"

"Trey?" she questioned.

"Yeah it's me," he told her.

"So, you finally decided to call me I see, it took you long enough. So what are you getting into, do you want to stop by?" Knowing he really wanted to sleep with Deb and knowing how much she wanted him he decided to drive to her house and pick her up. Along the way there he told her how he needed her to drive his car to his house and once that was done he would go back with her to her place. After arriving back in Baltimore doing 70 mph the whole ride back, Trey decided to play it cool with Scarlett and Tina and act as if he didn't know anything of their secret relationship.

Picking Deb up, he caught an instant hard-on when she exited her house and walked to the car dressed in a plain tight fitting white V-neck t-shirt without a bra, allowing her nipples to stand out behind the fabric, and a green pair of leggings that showed a perfect Coca-Cola bottle figure.

"Hey boo" she said, as she entered the truck, "this truck is nice." He thanked her explaining to her that it

70

belong to a friend of his. The whole ride to Tina's house they conversed about any and everything that came to mind. Deb confessed that she had been interested in him for a long time, but was too afraid to say anything being as though her boss was his girlfriend. They continued to flirt as they both made each other comfortable. The whole ride they were touchy feely with one another. Once at Tina's house, Trey ran in and grabbed a bottle of Rose out of Tina's stash and headed back to her truck after locking her house back up. As he pulled off, Deb followed him. He decided to turn his phone off so he could think, as well as entertain Deb. Once they pulled in front of his house, he allowed Deb to park his car in front of his door, after she was done she got back in the truck with him. Trey drove off, and pulled the truck in a school parking lot not far from his house. Once there, he turned the car off and popped the bottle of champagne. As he took a sip out of the bottle, he told her, "I'm horny, let's fuck!"

Smiling from ear to ear, Deb unzipped his pants and began sucking his dick. When she was done, he found a condom in Tina's glove compartment, placed it on his long dick while leaning the driver seat back as far as it would go.

Pantiless, Deb came out of her green leggings, and climbed on top of him, straddling him in ecstasy as they both came together. Once they were done, Trey got out of the truck, grabbed a t-shirt that was on the backseat, poured some of the champagne on his dick and wiped his self-clean with the t-shirt. Tossing the shirt on the ground, they both laughed and talked while taking sips of the champagne the whole ride back to Deb's house. After pulling up and parking, they exchanged hugs and promised to stay in contact with each other. They both knew it was wise to not allow Scarlett to find out, it was something understood that did not need to be discussed. Driving back home, Trey continued to sip on the remains of the alcohol, finishing the bottle as he pulled in front of his door. Once inside his house, Trey immediately took a shower and slipped on a pair of pajama bottoms and a tank top while settling on the living room couch watching cable. Reflecting on his whole day, all he could do was sit there and smile to himself over how crazy things can go. As he laid there thinking, he wondered what time was Scarlett gonna arrive. Just as the thought crossed his mind, she was walking through the door. As she stepped in the living room, he noticed she had a weird air about her mostly because she knew she was caught and that he knew something. "Hey baby, come here, bout time you're home I missed you!" Throughout the whole night Scarlett was doing everything in her power to be extra affectionate, caring, giving and pleasing. Something that Trey noticed, but was fine with. He knew some of her catering to his every need was from the heart, but he also knew the majority of it was done out of guilt. Sex with Scarlett that night was the best they had in a long time. She did things that she vowed she would never do, like anal. In the beginning she was very hesitant and jumpy to the feeling of him inserting it in, although she wanted and begged for him to put it in. But once it was in, she was like a ravishing tiger begging for more and not wanting him to take it out or stop while insisting him to pump harder. Surprised by her actions, he happily obliged giving her everything she asked and begged for. She did splits, squats, and even positioned her body on her neck on the floor and allowed Trey to dip his dick, balls deep, in and out of her. When they were finally done after an hour of nonstop intimacy she sucked everything out of him and swallowed all of his semen down to the last drop.

They both slept like babies throughout the rest of the morning. The following morning with Trey awaking first, he crept out of bed quietly and went into the living room and grabbed his phone. While powering it on, he sat on the couch and watched the number of voicemails and text messages start to add up to a total of 10 between the two.

There were three voice messages from Tina, telling him to call her when he awoke, cause she needed her vehicle along with her keys. She also sent him three text messages saying how much she missed him and hoped he wasn't ignoring her. The other four remaining messages were voicemails from two female clients who had said how they had seen his ad online and was looking to setup an appointment for later on that day. They both left their numbers where they could be reached. Calling Tina first, she picked up after the first ring, "Boy, bout time you called, where are you and why have you been ignoring me?"

"I wasn't ignoring you, I've been busy and had my phone off, plus I'm home and your car is here along with your keys." he told her.

"Well, I'm home" she replied, "but I do need my car so if you don't mind I will just come through and pick it up?!"

He told her that if she was coming then come now because he had a few things to do within the hour. She took a long pause and then asked, "So how are you and Scarlett coming along?"

"Everything is as good as they are gonna get under the circumstances" he snapped back. "Why, how should we be coming along?" Waiting for her response, he knew exactly what she was referring to but figured he would play her game and pick her brain, to see if she would touch on what he had overheard between her and Scarlett last night. Taking the bait and falling for his trap, she came right out and admitted her guilt and her role in the private affair they were having.

"I'm sorry Trey, I know I shouldn't have been sleeping with her behind your back, and when I walked in on her and her ex having sex in y'all living room, instead of recording the shit and blackmailing her to sleep with me, I should have just told you." Shocked over the information he was hearing he wanted to go and slap Scarlett awake.

He felt deceived and betrayed by the both of them, and really didn't want either one in his life at that moment. Cutting the conversation short, he told her that it was okay for her to come and get her keys along with her truck, and they will discuss whatever when she arrived. Accepting what he said, she told him she would be over in an hour and ended the call. Just as he was about to call the clients back, in walked Scarlett, hair all over her head from not wearing a scarf the night before.

"Hey boo?!" She spoke, smiling as she joined him on the couch, still nude laying her head in his lap. "Hey" he spoke, nonchalantly.

"So what's on your agenda for today, besides spending part of it, if not all, with me?"
He smiled at her audacious tone, partly because he knew she was dead serious, but also because after

hearing what he had just heard from Tina he knew he had no plans to hang out with her for the next few days. He figured he needed time to digest all of the bullshit, and space was the best way to put a plan in motion on how he wanted to handle everything. Playing Scarlett out of position, and lying to her came easy, but he really wasn't in the mood for games and lying. He explained to her that he had to make a few runs with Tone, and he was leaving out with Tina when she arrived and he didn't know when he would be back. Kissing her on the lips, he promised her that he had a surprise that he knew she would love, but it was going to be a couple days before it came through. She happily accepted what he said, but pouted and explained to him how uneasy she was feeling that they couldn't spend any time together. He slipped on a t-shirt and some sweatpants, brushed his teeth and washed up in front of the sink, while she followed his every move going from room to room being overly affectionate. When Tina called to let him know she was out front, Scarlett answered his phone knowing he despised when she did that, but she did it anyway, knowing that was how she would get his attention, since she was feeling ignored. "Hello?"

"Hey Scarlett, can you let Trey know that I am out front?"

"So where are you taking my husband Tina? Cause he is punished and needs to be back home before the sun goes down!" Just as Scarlett was waiting on a reply from Tina, she felt a sharp bite on her neck as Trey snuck up behind her taking the phone out of her hand. "Ouch baby!" She screeched, facing him while grabbing her neck. "Can you kiss it and make it better?"

Placing the phone to his ear, he told Tina he would be out in a sec. He tongue kissed the spot on Scarlett's neck that he just bit, and put his tongue in her mouth, as she happily accepted and reciprocated. He gripped her nude butt cheeks and told her he would call her when he was done for the day. He turned and left out the house to an impatiently waiting Tina, who was standing at the door alone frowning. She followed him to his car, and told him to follow her to her house. Trey knew he was in for an ear full, but an ear full was exactly what he needed, especially from being betrayed by the one person he thought he could trust.

He just sat back in his car, listening to a CD by the late Luther Vandross and cruised in silence the whole ride to Tina's house.

CHAPTER 5

Sitting in his car, before going inside of Tina's house, Trey made a call to the two female clients that had left him voicemails looking to set up dates. The first one he called was a Dominican woman, age thirty by the name of Consuela. After speaking with her for the next twenty minutes, he agreed to meet her at her place in Columbia right outside of the city at 4 p.m. that day. He told her his rates were $200 for the hour, and anything besides the massage was going to be extra. Consuela assured him money was not an object as long as he delivered like he was supposed to. After getting her directions and flirting back and forth they ended the call assuring one another they would be pleased by the other. Just as Trey was about to make the second call, his phone rang with Tina's number popping on the screen. "Hello," he answered.

"Are you coming in, or are you gonna sit in the car all damn day?!" She stated, sarcastically rather than asking.

"I'm coming!" Just as she was letting him know the door was unlocked he hung the phone up in her ear in mid-sentence.

Dialing the second client's number, another call came in and this time it was the number that he just began dialing. Answering the phone he spoke, "Hello."

"Is this Trey?" questioned Demi.

"Yes this is me, how may I be of some assistance to you Demi?" he questioned. Taken aback by how he knew her name, she then realized she had left him a message when she tried to contact him that morning.

"Well, I will be alone tonight on my yacht here in Canton, and I was wondering if you could swing by and stay a few hours and make me happy? I read your fees online, so I am fine with the cost, but I must say you have a lovely body, but before we connect, would you mind sending me a picture of yourself to my phone for reassurance?" Trey's first thought was to not send it, because he felt with Scarlett knowing what she knew she could have been playing a trick on him to set him up. But quickly he dismissed the thought, because he knew when Demi had first sent him a message, he and Scarlett had been lying in bed together and it was a little too soon for her to try to pull some shit on him and besides, she was the one that was in hot water not him.

"Sure I can do that, I promise you won't be disappointed though and oh don't let the Baby Face fool you!" he told her, meaning every word. She giggled before they hung up. Demi explained to him where to come to and what to bring. They both sent each other a picture of the other while they were still on the phone chatting it up. When Trey finally hung up he told himself he needed to be at Demi's yacht at exactly 6:59 to tear her half Chinese and half Hawaiian looking ass up. Stepping out of the vehicle and entering Tina's house, he closed and locked the door behind him. He went up the stairs to meet a crying Tina that was sitting on her futon, looking and feeling guilty about what she had been doing behind Trey's back to deceive him. Trey sat next to her, as she gained her composure, "So what's up with you and Scarlett?" He questioned her, as he laid a hand on her bare inner thigh. Trey already had it in his mind that he was gonna forgive Tina for her actions, but it was gonna cost her big, little did she know. He figured he would listen to her blabber and sit through her excuses, as to why she did what she did, but truth be told he just wanted to see the video of Scarlett and Al, to see how she crossed him and also he wanted to know of any other dirt she may have known. After that he decided he would come up with a plan on how he would eventually deal with Scarlett. Tina told him everything, from when she first caught Tina and Al, to the few times she and Scarlett had slept with one another at different hotels. She also explained how she was always the aggressor, and how Scarlett liked being with women from time to time, but she really only have love and desire for him. Trey just listened, and began caressing Tina's inner thigh. The more he listened he kept thinking, how he wanted to fuck Tina really hard and aggressively partly because he knew it would turn her on, but mostly out of anger for her deceit. And also just for the fuck of it. After realizing Tina was starting to repeat herself, he made her show him the recording of Scarlett and Al. After seeing the video with his woman and her ex, Trey's heart dropped into his stomach, and he could not believe what he was seeing. Not only was she allowing another man to pump her from behind, but she was doing it in the living room that they shared. After seeing it in its entirety, Tina tried to take up for Scarlett by letting Trey know how hurt she was to have let that happen with Al, especially in the home they shared together. Trey just sat there listening in a state of shock, but also in a state of disbelief. After setting there for a few moments deep in thought, he hugged Tina tightly and told her not to sweat it, and how he forgave her for creeping with Scarlett while reminding her that it couldn't happen again, and if it did then there would be consequences, and he wasn't going to fuck with her again. Happy that he had forgiven her, Tina squeezed him tighter around his neck, thanking him and letting him know, that she would never deceive their trust again. He thought she was going to knock the wind out of him until she finally let him go. Without another word or hesitation Tina must have been reading his thoughts, because she dropped to her knees on the floor, tugging his sweatpants down and took his mushroom shaped head into her mouth. She made love to his dick with her mouth knowing it would drive him crazy. She did things she knew he would love, from moaning while deep throating him, to licking his testicles while deep throating him and sucking all around it sloppily but with perfection as if she was trying to leave hickeys on it.

Standing at attention, Trey rose from the futon and lifted her up from the floor, aggressively bending her over on the bed. He grabbed the KY Jelly from her nightstand, where he knew she kept it, as she waited patiently bent over on the bed fingering herself. When he came behind her, he lubed her real good with the jelly and entered her anally. He took his time with her at first but   after a few pumps her ass got wetter and wetter. While craving more, he pumped hard ravishing her as she moaned and cried out in ecstasy, coming multiple times. When he felt he was about to cum, he pulled out of her, put her on her knees, and shot his load all over her face and down her throat, pumping in and out of her mouth allowing her to not only taste him, but to taste herself as well. Trey couldn't help but think how good of a whore Tina was, and despite what she had done behind his back and creeping with Scarlett, he realized at that moment while she was beneath him looking up into his eyes, how much love he still had for her. After they were done, Tina sat there on the floor wiping his cum from her face, and put it in her mouth. She finally rose from the floor, took his hand and walked him to the bathroom. Once inside, she ran the shower and told him to take a shower with her. He knew she wanted more, and more was definitely what she was gonna get. Fulfilling each other's sexual needs and wants and bringing each other to a state of sexual bliss beyond belief, that they both knew only they could bring out of the other, what no one else could. They both gave it their all, as if nothing or no one else mattered. Trey held her in the air in his arms against the shower wall, pumping in and out of her as the shower water sprayed down on their heads, and he felt himself about to cum again. He couldn't help but think how good she felt without a condom. Dismissing the thought of Tina giving him a STD because he knew how careful and strict she was when it came to protecting herself. He continued to pump in and out of her rhythmically. She begged for him to cum inside her, "Please cum inside me Trey baby, I wanna feel all of you! Oooooh…Oooh, keep it right there, I'm cummin'!! Cum with me baby!"

Just as the thought of him impregnating her crossed his mind, he quickly dismissed it and exploded his load inside of her until he went soft and felt he had given her all of him.

"Damn that was so good baby!" she protested, as he put her down.

"You were good too baby" he said, grabbing two towels from behind the door handing her one, "Now let's get out of this bathroom and get to the money. I need you to set me up some dates with these clients. If I work the women and you work the men, there is no way we can fail!" he looked her in the eye as he helped her out of the tub. She sat on the toilet, as she felt him starting to leak out of her. He leaned over and kissed her, then added. "What am I gonna do with you? I will see you when you come into the bedroom." After the steamy episode Trey had with Tina in the shower, he leaned back on her bed with his arms folded, legs crossed and thought of Scarlett's deceitful acts not only with sleeping with Al in their crib, but with sleeping with women also, both things he never thought she would do. He figured he could forgive her for sleeping with other women seeing as though he was doing the same, but her sleeping with Al in their house was unacceptable, something that she would have to pay for. Trey just laid there and figured he would deal with Scarlett when the time came, because for now he would focus his attention on making money through his clients, and also with Tina. Once Tina exited the bathroom, she noticed Trey laying on her bed deep in thought. She knew he was probably thinking about Scarlett. She also knew how much she cared for and loved him, so she figured she would do everything in her power to keep his mind focused on her, and not on Scarlett. Tina dropped her towel on the floor on the side of the bed, climbed on the bed and crawled on top of him with tears streaming down her face. "I'm sorry Boo for doing what I did to you" she told him as she leaned down, hugging him, wrapping her arms around his waist and laying her head on his chest. "I hope you can forgive me and Scarlett for being so stupid?!" As he hugged Tina back, he told her first things first he needed her to go back online and put the business phone number up, because she must have made a mistake rushing and put his regular cell number on there. Then he explained to her how they were going to use her house to bring the male and female clients to, and that all the money they made they were going to put in a safe, and how they would only take some out if they really needed it or if it was an emergency. Tina just set on top of him and listen saying, "Ok" between every sentence, letting him know that she understood and was willing to do everything he was telling her he wanted them to do. She grabbed the laptop from the bottom of the bed, and sat it on his stomach. With a few clicks, she changed the old number to the correct one and checked both of their email accounts and answered some emails from clients that wanted to see the both of them on later dates. When she was done she sat the laptop down on the side of the bed and looked Trey in his eyes. As he was stared back up at her she wondered what he could possibly be thinking. "What?" she questioned him.

"You need a haircut" he told her, smiling from ear to ear. She smiled and punched him lightly in his chest, then said, "Don't talk about my hair. I'm gonna let your barber give me a number 1 with the grain and you're gonna pay for it, Punk. Matter of fact, we can go together cause you need one too... now." As they both laughed at each other's jokes about the other ones head, Trey had to admit he loved the way Tina wore her hair, not allowing it to grow past a number 2 while keeping it shaped up and changing the color from time to time to match different outfits, or to compliment however she was feeling that day or week.

With a serious face changing the subject, Trey told her, "I want you to set it up so we can have a Ménage a Trios with Scarlett. I want it to be soon like sometime this week." "How am I gonna do that Trey?" Tina questioned, giggling because she knew how serious he was.

"I don't care how you do it, just make it happen. Trust me she will be with it, even if she don't think that it's a good idea."

"Ok Trey, I got you Boo and I will make it happen!"

Trey's phone began ringing in his sweatpants pocket that was on the floor. Tina climbed off of him, as he got off the bed and grabbed the phone from his pocket. Knowing by the ringtone that it was Scarlett, he answered, set down on the futon smiling as he looked at Tina who was lying back on the bed winking her eye at him smoking a joint of blueberry weed she had rolled in some TOP.

"Hey Baby!"

"Babe I was just calling to tell you that I love you and also that Maya will be in town for the next few days and she will be staying with us."

"Ok babe that's cool, when will she be here?" He questioned.

"She's gonna meet me at the house by 8:00 tonight, then I am supposed to ride to Annapolis to my mom's house and drop her off some money. I was gonna ask if you wanted to go with me?" Scarlett asked.

"Babe, I'm gonna be busy until about 10 tonight" he told her.

"Alright well, I'm just gonna go up there by myself and depending on how I feel I may just spend the night. However I do wanna see you sometime today before I leave, if that's possible, and I will just give Maya your cell number in case you aren't back by 10 and in case she needs to leave out for any reason." Trey just sat there listening to see if she would say anything more. Once he realized she wasn't, he told her that it was cool and to just give Maya his number and that he would call her back in the next few hours when he was free so they could meet up somewhere. He told her how much he loved her and they both ended the call on that note. Tina just laid there on the bed high, smiling as she played in her own cell phone. Breaking the silence as if reading his thoughts, Tina asked, "You are gonna fuck Maya, aren't you?" Trey threw one of the futon pillows at her, as she caught it and stated, "No, I'm not gonna fuck her. I really don't like the bitch honestly; because she sneaky as fuck and I know she really don't want me and Scarlett together."

"Well at least she is not the only one!" Tina said, letting her emotions for Trey show. Catching on to Tina's sarcasm, Trey knew what Tina had said had some truth behind it. He knew she really wanted to be with him, something he was considering but just couldn't commit to as of yet, because of the love he still had for Scarlett. Trey glanced at the time, and realized it was time he left Tina, and started making his way to Consuela, his first client for the day. Trey changed his clothes and put on one of the many outfits he kept at Tina's house. Settling for a Louis Vuitton polo shirt and L.V. sneakers to match, he walked over to Tina as she lay on her side leaning on one arm watching him. He kissed her on the lips as she turned over and lay on her back grabbing his face with both hands and planting another kiss on his lips. He explained to her where he was going and what he had planned for the day, and as he was about to exit her house she took a duplicate key to her house out of her drawer and handed it to him. "Here, this is my house key. The safe is in my other room closet." She gave him the combination and assured him that no one besides the two of them held the combination.

They hugged one another once more before he headed down the steps to leave. She followed behind him and locked the door when he left out. Back in her room, Tina text Trey letting him know how much she really cared about him, and she hoped in due time that things could get better for the two of them mentally, physically and financially. She then called a client she had been texting when Trey was on the phone with Scarlett, and told him that it was ok for him to come to her house now for an hour session. Trey read the message Tina sent him and smiled as he made his way to Consuela. He sent her a message back saying, *"likewise"* followed by another message instructing her not to say anything to Scarlett about the conversations they had earlier. He also informed her how he didn't want her to know that he knew of her infidelities, as of yet, and that he would let her know that he knew when the time was right. She messaged him back saying *"ok"* and that *she loved him.*

Trey pulled up at a dirt road that had a mailbox with the address Consuela had given him engraved on it. His GPS brought him to this location and when he looked around all he could see was trees. He called Consuela as he drove down the winding dirt road, looking for a house to appear. As soon as she answered, Trey was mesmerized as he pulled in front of a gated brick mansion that looked like a castle from the outside. "Hey Trey sweetie, I see you found me. For a second I thought you was gonna turn around at the beginning of the road".

Trey laughed and then asked, "Wow, so you saw me when I first pulled up at the mailbox?"

"I sure did," she told him. As she opened the gate she told him to drive around the massive statue of the naked woman that stood in the middle of the waterfall that was in the middle of the grounds in front of the front entrance.

"You can pull up in front of the doors, where my driver will be waiting for you. Give him the keys to your car, and he will park it for you. Come on in the double doors and I will be waiting for you."

He told her he would and ended the call. Trey dug into his stash and swallowed a half of Viagra pill, like he said he would, put the pills back up and was again taken aback at the beautiful sight of the statue and its features. Noting that it had to cost a pretty penny to have had it made, he said to himself out loud, "Damn that's a pretty ass statue, I would like to fuck her!"

Trey pulled up in front of the two massive doors of the mansion, where her driver was waiting just as she said he would be. As soon as he hopped out of the vehicle her driver opened his door for him, allowed him to step out as he stepped in telling him he would take it from there. While informing Trey that Madam Consuela was waiting for him in the foyer 'Madame Consuela?' he thought to himself, as he made his way in the humongous house where Consuela was approaching him with open arms. "Hi Trey baby, I'm glad you could make it!" She said, as she gave him a hug and kissed him on the cheek. "You are so handsome!" As she moved past him to close and lock the doors, her expensive heels clicked what seemed to be a fine tune on the white and gold marble floor. Trey was in awe of how beautiful Consuela was and how the purple silk long flowing strapless dress, that came down to her ankles, hug to every curve on her body. Her ass was nice and round, as he watched it jiggle as she glided toward the doors to lock them. At that moment Trey realized it was her face and body that the statue out front was made to resemble. She smiled, took his hand and told him, "Come with me." As they made their way to a side room, that looked like a huge living room with a massive book shelf. She pushed one of the books in and a small bookshelf on their left side opened up. They went inside the walkway of the bookshelf behind them and entered an elevator that took them upstairs to her master suite. Trey kept quiet while taking in everything, and knew he would have to bring his A-game to win her over. He vowed to find out everything he could about her, to see what her story was and why she was interested in dealing with escorts. As they reached the top floor, and came out of the elevator Trey noticed they had exited one of the mirrors that were aligned with the rest of the mirrors on the wall. There was a massive in ground hot tub made to seat four, along with a sauna, his and her toilets and sinks. They walked hand in hand through another door that opened up to her master bedroom while making small talk; or what she thought was small talk about different parts of her house, and how she had it built from the ground up. Entering the room, she quickly discarded her shoes and signaled him to do the same, while they stepped onto the white wall to wall mink covered floor.

There was an extra-large presidential king sized bed that sat in the middle of the room made into a canopy, a 75 inch television that hung on the wall and another Jacuzzi tub that was made for four in one corner of the massive bedroom. The Jacuzzi was filled with bubbles, and the steam that was coming from the water let Trey know that, that was where they were going to end up. As Trey continued to scan the room, he noticed none of the windows bore shades or curtains and, he immediately assumed that she was an exhibitionist. As if reading his thoughts, she sat down on the steps of the hot tub and said, "yes as you can see I don't like shades or curtains, it gives me a thrill to bare and show all while wondering if there is somebody out there staring, with lust in their eyes at this 5 foot 11 inch exotic Dominican pussy cat!" They both burst into laughter, while Trey knew he would be doing the same thing if he were on the other side of that window. "So are you a cop or do you have anything to do with the law?" Consuela asked, catching Trey off guard with the unexpected topic. Trey stopped laughing, and instantly became offended with what she had asked him, showing it all over his face and body language. "Hell no, is you?"

"Don't take it personal Trey" she told him, and then added, "I have to ask these things because I'm not trying to do a walkthrough on soliciting prostitution!" "Well, to answer your question, no I am not a cop. Cops stink!"

"But before we move any further there is one more thing I need to do, and that is see your license to make sure you are not a minor, and of age."

Trey couldn't help but burst into laughter at her audacious request. He handed her his license, she quickly scanned it and handed it back to him. "Anything else you wanna know?" he asked her, sarcastically. She stared him in his eyes, as Trey took in the beauty of her navy blue eyes for the first time. She stood up and let her silk dress drop to the floor, leaving her standing there in the nude, like Trey had expected, with the prettiest pink perfect round areolas he had ever seen. Along with a phat, bald, smooth shaven pussy that also had pretty pink lips that hung between her legs giving her a nice gap between her thighs.

"No not at the moment, but we will get to that in a second, in the meantime take off your clothes and join me in the hot tub." She watched him undress, and they both entered the tub, allowing the warmness of the water enveloped their bodies.

"Would you like a drink?" she asked, sitting across from him using her right foot to rub his chest, "Champagne, wine, liquor, beer, water?"

"Champagne is fine?" he told her. Consuela stood in the hot tub and turned her back towards him, bent over, giving Trey a full view of her yellow perfectly heart shaped round naked ass, pressed a button and began telling her butler to bring them a bottle of Ace of Spades Rose in a bucket of ice along with 2 flutes. She giggled underneath of her breath, as she looked back at him admiring her ass, as the water glistened and ran down her legs. She turned and faced him, sat down as the jet streams in the water danced on her skin. Within seconds a tall white man entered the room, dressed in nothing but a bowtie, and a matching pair of black slacks. He sat the bucket of champagne on the side of the tub, filled both of their flutes and sat the champagne back in the bucket, leaving as quietly as he had come closing the door behind him. "So what is it that you do and why do you live in this big ass house alone, without a husband or a man?" Trey asked, as he took a sip of champagne.

She grabbed a small mirror, that was on the side of the hot tub that Trey hadn't noticed before, grabbed a rolled up hundred dollar bill, and sniffed two of the four lines of powdered Cocaine; one in each nostril, before offering him some. "No thanks babe, enjoy yourself." Consuela sat the plate down and grabbed her glass of champagne, took a sip and began caressing his dick with her feet underneath the water.

She sat her glass down then stated, "I'm a realtor, and I own my realty company. I have been selling houses and property since I was 22, and I just turned 30. I have made a fine living for myself, without the help of a man. But do I want one? Yes! Am I lonely? No!" She took another sip from her glass, refilling both of theirs to the rim then added, "I live my life happily single, on the edge and that is why whenever I feel the need for companionship, I hire an escort to give me that or whatever else I need taking care of. It's better that way, no strings attached!" Trey felt his dick pulsating and standing at attention, something she noticed as well, while continuing to run both of her feet against it.

"If the right one comes along" she continued to say, "then I will be happy to commit to him forever, and give him half of everything I got. I don't care if he is rich or poor." After sitting in the hot tub for a little over a half hour; talking about her likes, dislikes, wants and needs. She arose from the tub, took his hand and they walked over to the bed. She handed him a towel as they both dried off. She walked around the bed and undid the strings of the canopy curtains, climbed on the bed and told him to get in the bed with her. He happily obliged. She lay on her stomach on two massive black towels, handed him a bottle of strawberry scented edible massaging oil and clicked a button on the large remote that was within hands reach at the foot of the bed, as the sounds of water on a beach with crashing waves exited the surround sound speakers throughout the entire room. As he began to massage her, she turned the tables and began asking him about his life. "So what brings you to this business, honestly?"

"Well, I had lost my job working as a laborer for the city, and I needed some income besides unemployment, and since I love making beautiful woman like you feel good, I figured why not?" he answered as he dug deeper in the arch of her, enjoying the moans of satisfaction she began to cry out, letting him know she was enjoying what he was doing to her.

"So how about you come work for me and become my personal assistant?" she asked, as he began massaging the oil into her ass cheeks.

"And what does that consist of?" he asked.

"Doing what you're doing now and then some." she told him, then added, "Unless of course, I am asking for too much?"

Moving down her legs to her feet, Trey was enjoying touching her soft flawless skin as much as she was enjoying the touch from his manly hands. Consuela turned and laid on her back as Trey began massaging her arms then down to her breast where he studied and took his time. As his hands slid back and forth over her areolas and nipples, he noticed how her nipples became erected by his touch.

"No that's not too much to ask, I am just a phone call away babe." He told her, meaning every word. As he moved down her stomach and began rubbing her thighs and legs, Consuela spread her legs giving him a full view of her wet shaved pussy.

After massaging the oil down her legs and feet, Trey came back up to her shaved pussy and began to gently rub his fingers against her clitoris with one hand, and using his other hand to rub her moistness, he began sliding his middle finger in and out of her. Squirming around with satisfaction, Consuela took his throbbing dick and began stroking him with some of the edible oil she poured in her hand.

"I want you to reach under the pillow and grab the blindfold along with those black gloves you will see. Put the gloves on, blindfold me and climb on top of me. I want you to choke me and fuck me as hard as you can!" she told him, as she used both of her hands massaging the oil into her own breasts. Trey watched as she arched her back, reached back without taking his eyes off of her watching as she squirmed full of lust, grabbed the black gloves along with a magnum condom, and the black blindfold. Positioning himself between her legs, he ripped the gold pack open and rolled the condom down his dick and began to lick her oily stomach, tracing his tongue down her hair line

92

below her navel tasting the strawberry oil, as his head went lower until his tongue reached the hood of her clitoris. Grabbing his face before he could get any lower, he looked up at her wondering what she was doing. As their eyes locked and her face became serious as if she was turned off, and said in a serious but demanding tone, "Do as I say Trey, and we can go a long, long way. Now blindfold me, choke me and fuck the cowboy shit out of me, as if I killed your best friend!" Releasing the tight grip from his face, Trey was caught off guard, but smiled at her aggressiveness and gave her exactly what she demanded. Consuela cried out and moaned at the top of her lungs from the pleasurable pain Trey was giving her with every thrust. Wrapping her legs around his head, she used her hands to part her ass cheeks, inviting him to pump deeper.

Her light complexion made her face become red, and her eyes rolled in the back of her head underneath of the blindfold, and with as much air her lungs would allow her to give under the tight grip he had on her neck with both hands, she managed to scream out.
"I'm cummmmmin'! Oh yes Trey!! Don't stop...Don't stop!!! Oooohhhhhh Yesssssss!" Releasing his grip from around her neck and putting her legs down, he continued to pump in and out of her with long deep slow strokes as her body shook uncontrollably. She brought him to a height of ecstasy, which reminded him of his wild tryst with Tina. The tingly feeling he once felt in the head of his dick was now a sensitive sensation that seemed to last for hours, as he came inside of her. He felt as if his soul was coming out of his dick head, as Consuela worked her pussy muscles, squeezing and draining everything out of him until the last drop. "Damn, you were sooooo great Trey!" she said to him.

93

They both laid side by side with chests heaving, both out of breath from wearing each other out. Consuela sat up, leaning on one arm and began rubbing her index finger up and down his chest. "C'mon, let's get you showered and cleaned up." she told him. She pulled the jizz filled condom off of his dick, rose from the bed and said, "Come with me so mommy can clean you up." He happily obliged.

CHAPTER 6

Tina stopped orally servicing the skinny, tall, red haired white man that laid on her futon before her. She stood up looking down at him nude, arms folded with all her weight on one leg and said, "Look Sam, you've been here an hour and twenty minutes to be exact, and I have been sucking on your dick for the last half an hour, you've only giving me $150! My hands hurt, my jaws hurt, and unless you are about to come up with another hundred dollars, I am sorry but your time is up!"

If looks could kill, then Tina's eyes would've been two rocket launchers firing down simultaneously on Sam's body at close range, two inches away. Noticing the hard and angry look in her eyes, Sam didn't try to persuade her to continue like he usually did every time they got together. Knowing she wasn't going to bend, he rose his 6 foot 3 inch frame from the futon, placed his shirt, pants and shoes on, got on his knees and kissed both her left and right foot like he usually did. Got up, headed down the steps and exited her house, with Tina tagging behind and locking the door behind him. Tina just shook her head smiling to herself as she climbed the stairs and entered her bathroom. While she washed her hands and began to brushing her teeth, she wondered what the hell Sam did with the condoms he used after he left. Even after ejaculation, he would never allow her to throw them away. He always took them with him when he left, something she always thought was weird. Tina exited the bathroom, entered her bedroom and laid across her bed. She decided to give Scarlett a call, while she surf the web on her laptop.

"Hey Scarly-poo," Tina spoke, when Scarlett picked up on the second ring.

"It's you again," Scarlett answered, in her usual sarcastic tone. "Are you done corrupting my man?" "Well you know, I've never given it any thought, but now that you mention it how about we both corrupt him?!"

"Meaning!?" Scarlett asked, wondering where Tina was going with this.

Thinking carefully before she spoke, Tina paused for a few seconds, and replied with, "I was thinking how about the three of us get together and ménage?"

"Tina, have you and Trey ever done anything sexually, honestly?"

"No, and why is it that every time I ask you a question, you ask another instead of just answering my question Scarlett? You do that shit all of the time, if you haven't noticed."

"Because, Tina, I need to know. I mean, I see how close you two are and it has been on my mind for some time now."

Tina closed her laptop, and laid her head on her pillow, growing bored with the conversation. She sighed loudly and said, "I'm just saying Scar, if I wanted him,

I could've had him, but I never went there. Now that I do wanna go there, I figured why not have both of ya'll at the same damn time, instead of sneaking behind each other's backs and doing it." Tina knew she had Scarlett right where she wanted her, and it was no way she was gonna tell her no. Just as the thought crossed her mind, Scarlett began to give in, "How do you know he would even be game for that? I mean Tina, him and I have never done that type of thing before, and he may look at me differently if he found out I like to be with women sexually every now and then." "Scarlett," Tina said, pausing before she spoke, "He is a man and all men fantasize about being with two women. You have to live a little Scar, trust me he will enjoy it, just be yourself!"

"Alright, I will think about it, but if we do then it's gonna be about pleasing him, and I mean focusing on him only!" Tina chuckled, as she let Scarlett continue, "I'm serious Tina, and it is not funny! I hate you!"

"Well, I love you too Scarly-poo, just give it some thought. And no, I did not tell him about you and me. I will let you do that."

"Bye Tina, this is Trey beeping in on the other line, so we'll have to finish this convo up some other time, okay?"

"Smooches," Tina replied back, as she ended the call.

Scarlett hugged Trey as they stood outside of her car, stepping back and looking him from head to toe she smiled and stated, "Mmmmmm…you smell good. You didn't leave out with that on this morning?" Placing her hands on her hips, she put on a serious face and continued in her usual sarcastic tone, "So, who is she, and when and where did you change your clothes nigga!?"

Trey smiled, hugged her around her waist and leaned his body weight against her making her lean back against her truck. "Whatever Scarlett, you know you are the only one for me. When and where I change my clothes, shouldn't make a difference, what you need to be worried about is where I'm leaving them when I'm done wearing them!"

"Whatever boy, play with me if you want to and I will kill that bitch!" she said, wrapping her arms around his neck smiling from ear to ear.

"So, what time you gotta meet your homegirl again?" he asked.

"She text me again, saying that she should be here by 7pm, so I'm gonna be on the road as soon as I let her in, or I can just leave the door unlocked for her cause I'm trying to be at my Moms house by 8pm." Releasing his grip on her, he stepped back allowing her to rise from leaning on the truck, letting her know whatever she was gonna do was fine by him. He also reminded her that he had to be somewhere with Tone by 7pm, and to have Maya call or text him if she needed anything. With a little over an hour to meet up with Demi, Trey decided to kill a little time with Scarlett even though he was still vexed over her infidelities. Playing it cool with her came easy, partly because of his wrongful doings on how he now made a living and mostly because of the love he still held for her. Because of the lack of trust and intimacy, Trey felt like the love they shared was slowly dwindling. Something he knew she was well aware of but never really spoke on. Never being the confrontational type, whenever a situation arise that she didn't like or agree with when it came to her and Trey, she either hint on it when it became too much to bare or beat around the bush when saying what she really wanted to say. Driving herself into an emotional wreck, full of frustration and doubt causing her and Trey to fuss and fight for weeks. As they wrestled around their living room playfully, a tear streamed down her right eye as she pinned Trey down to the floor, sitting on top of him while looking down into his eyes. Trey asked, "Baby what's wrong?" Not being able to hold it in any longer a few more tears rolled down her cheeks.

Wiping her face, she just smiled and answered, "Nothing Trey, I just love you that's all!" Lifting off of him, Trey rose from the floor, hugged her and reminded her that, he loved her as well. While they continued to embrace Trey felt his phone vibrate in his back pocket. Releasing her from his grip, Trey retrieved his phone from his pocket, hesitant about pulling it out at first. Forgetting that he left the business phone in the car, and not wanting to get in a discussion with Scarlett on why he had two phones. Realizing it was Tina calling him, he hit the ignore button sending her call straight to his voicemail. Placing the phone back in his back pocket, Trey informed Scarlett that it was getting close to the time he had to meet up with Tone. Not wanting to question him, Scarlett kissed him lightly on his cheek and let him know she would be home for a little while until Maya called, but she planned on being at her mom's house by 8pm. Trey watched her ass sway from side to side, as she excused herself and went into the bathroom, closing the door behind her. With her out of earshot, Trey pulled his cell phone out and dialed Tina's number back, as he scanned the frigidaire looking for nothing in particular. "What's up T?" he asked when she picked up.

"Where are you?" she questioned.

Trey informed her he was in the crib with Scarlett and was about to leave out in any minute. Picking up on the hint that he couldn't really talk, she told him to just call her as soon as he was able to talk without discretion.

Tina

Ending the call and placing the phone back in his pocket, Trey closed the fridge and headed for the bathroom to let Scarlett know he was about to leave. Just as he raised his hand to knock on the door, Scarlett was opening the door with a smile spread across her face. "What are you smiling about?" he asked,

99

reaching underneath her shirt and fondling her left breast.

"What, I can't smile when I see you?" She asked then added, "Plus I had a feeling you were gonna be outside the bathroom door when I opened it."

"Oh really?"

"Yes really!"

Trey hugged and kissed Scarlett letting her know he was leaving and would be waiting for her and Maya to call. She kissed and hugged him back, while walking him to the door she kicked him in his behind playfully. Trey tried to turn around and grab her but she slammed the door, locking it and burst out into laughter. While sitting in his vehicle ready to pull off, Trey laughed thinking about Scarlett and the things she did that kept him smiling and loving her through everything. Pulling off, he called Tina back as he made his way to Fells Point to meet up with Demi. When Tina picked up, she told him about the conversation she had with Scarlett earlier, "So Trey all we have to do is find the right time and place to do the threesome boo!"

"So was she excited when you mentioned it, or did you have to do a lot of talking and persuasion for her to agree to do it?" he asked.

"Well she was hesitant at first, and she didn't say yes she would do it, and she damn sure didn't say no either! But she did make a point to say if we do it, than the focus needs to be on you and only you." Trey smiled, as he thought about the conversation him and Tina was having. He knew Scarlett would be game for the ménage, and he also knew it was best to continue to let Tina focus on getting it done, rather than him. He knew if he mentioned it then she would opt out and swear that he and Tina had something going on. Ending the call with Tina, Trey parked his car in the lot that sat in front of the water, where all the yachts and small boats were docked. With 15 minutes remaining before he was scheduled to be here, he decided to call Demi and get a better description of her boat, and to let her know he had arrived. He looked from left to right out of his car window at the line of boats that were docked. Grabbing the cocoa butter gel, along with the KY jelly and box of magnum condoms from underneath the seat, Trey exited his vehicle when he spotted the boat she told him to look for that had the words "**Wett Kitty**" engraved across the side, in bold pink lettering. Walking toward the yacht, Trey was taken back at the size of the yacht, as he got closer. 'Damn this is a big ass boat,' he thought to himself as he spotted her standing on the deck of the yacht in a short pink silk robe, looking on as he approached. Trey flashed a million dollar smile and waved, watching in awe as she turned her back, stepping down the steps slowly, letting the spring breeze lift her robe up exposing her yellow and pink trimmed panties that hugged her perfect round apple bottom cheeks. She opened the door to the yacht, smiling as he stepped on board. They embraced before she closed and locked the entry. Trey was taken aback, by the smell of SJP perfume by Sarah Jessica Parker that she wore, reminding him of Scarlett since that was one of his favorite scents she wore. Turning to face him once the locks were secure, she told him to follow her to the side of the yacht. They made their way through another door and down some winding crystal made steps that opened up to a massive room that he was impressed with. Picking up the remote off of the white bearskin rug that lay on the floor, Demi clicked a button to close the blinds on the window, dimmed the lights and clicked another button to allow some jazz music to play low and softly from the surround sound speakers throughout the entire room. "So how are you Trey, with your handsome self?" she asked, dropping the pink robe she had on, letting it hit the floor. She sat down on one of the white mink adorned chairs that hung from the ceiling, crossing her oily yellow legs, she grabbed a half hit blunt from a solid gold Lion head ashtray, along with her gold lighter. Lighting the blunt, she inhaled deeply and looked on at Trey seductively as he removed his shoes and began to speak.

"I'm good Demi, glad to be in the presence of your sexy exotic ass. I see you're smoking good, what's that you smoking on?"

"Something I brought back from the islands," she told him. "Why, you want some?"

"Naw, I'm good babe, but enjoy yourself." Trey sat back in the other mink adorned chair in front of her watching as she opened and closed her legs exposing her fat pussy print.

"Get comfortable Trey, and take them clothes off, I wanna see what I am paying for!" she insisted, while blowing the exotic smoke from the marijuana filled cigarillo in his direction.

Putting the blunt out in the lion head ashtray, eyes halfway open, she looked him up and down as he got undressed and stood before her nude. "Nice," she exclaimed, licking her glossy juicy pink lips. Getting out of her seat she walked towards him, allowing her exposed perky breasts to jiggle with every step. "So, you like what you see huh?" he questioned her, as she stood her 5 foot 7 inch frame directly in front of him, allowing her hard pink nipples to rest on his chest. Ignoring his question, Demi wrapped her arms around his neck, as he lowered his face to meet hers and began kissing her passionately, allowing his tongue to meet hers and dance in her mouth. She let out a soft moan, as their bodies inched closer. She then wrapped her hands around his dick, between his legs. Breaking their lip lock, she turned her back walking away from him, and looked behind her back and told him to grab the stuff she requested, and come with her. Grabbing the KY jelly, oil and condoms, Trey followed behind her as they made their way to a massive circular shaped bed.

Clearing the bed, of its many cheetah print decorative pillows, Demi crawled on the bed on her hands and knees, arching her back as she slid down on her stomach, slowly allowing her ass to poke out in the air giving him a good view of her pussy lips as they peeked from the sides of the thin lace material. "Mmmmmmm help me out of these panties Trey baby and give me one of your intoxicating massages from head to toe," she moaned. "And then I wanna feel your juicy tongue inside of my wet kitty!" Trey removed her panties, and began pouring the oil up and down Demi's back, butt and legs. Starting with her shoulders he massaged them deeply, then he made his way down to her back, applying the well needed pressure to her muscles as she moaned out softly, enjoying the feel of his strong hands. Working his way down her lower back to her butt, Demi parted her legs and told him, "Yes Trey baby...Damn that feels good. Your hands feel so good on my booty!"

Massaging the oil deeply into her butt, one cheek at a time, Trey felt himself begin to get aroused when he began working his way up and down her legs, never taking his eyes off of her fat yellow kitty.

Positioning himself between her opened legs, Trey worked his hands back up her butt allowing his rock hard dick to set on her ass cheeks, when he reached her back and shoulders once again. After about 30 minutes of lying on her stomach and being turned on from his touch, Demi turned her body over and laid on her back smiling from ear to ear at the size of his dick, as it stood fully at attention pointing in her direction. Still positioned between her legs, Trey applied the oil to her front, starting from her neck down to her feet. Once he was done, she begged him to eat her. "Please eat me Trey, I need to feel your tongue inside of me." Trey dove in head first, orally pleasuring Demi to ecstasy. While lapping his tongue against her clitoris like a starving dog drinking water for the first time in weeks, Trey began to get irritated when he heard his phone ring loudly four times back to back from the other side of the room, where it was in his pants pocket. Ignoring Scarlett's ringtone he continued to orally service her as she began shaking uncontrollably, gripping the back of his head with her hands, while gyrating her hips. After his phone began to ring for the seventh time, Trey rose from the bed ignoring Demi when she demanded that he just let it ring. Rushing to retrieve his phone from his pocket, Trey thought to himself, 'this shit better be important!' Answering his phone, Scarlett interrogated him on what he was doing and why was he ignoring her. He lied to her and told her he was using the bathroom and his phone was on the charger in another room. Once he realized that nothing was wrong and she was basically calling to let him know she was on her way to her mom's house and Maya was left alone in the house, he became pissed.

Trey began to raise his voice a little letting her know not to ever call him back to back unless it was an emergency. Demi just rested her body on her elbows laughing loudly and watching as he turned the tables on whoever he was on the phone with.

"Who is the fucking female laughing in the background Trey?" questioned Scarlett.

"That's some fucking kids laughing at some shit on the television."

"Whatever Trey, you are a fucking liar and you think I'm stupid and don't know that you are up to no good!" Just as Trey was ready to end the call and hang up, Demi became frustrated and threw 2 of the cheetah printed pillows that she swept to the floor earlier at him, and began speaking loudly so that whoever he was on the phone with could hear.

"Trey, miss kitty is waiting!" Putting his index fingers to his lips to tell Demi to be quiet, Trey began to tell Scarlett he would call her back when he was done doing what he was doing. Trey hung the phone up in her ear when Scarlett began to yell obscenities, questioning him about the same female voice she just heard again. He turned the ringer off on his phone, and put it back in his pocket, before heading back to the bed where Demi was lying there smiling waiting for him.

"Let's get one thing straight Mr. Trey, when you are with me you belong to me, and Ms. Kitty don't come second to no bitch!" Tilting his head to the side and raising his left eyebrow, Trey cut her off in mid-sentence letting her know he was in control of his actions, and nobody told him what he could or couldn't do. After checking Demi and putting her in her place for being rude, Trey gave up talking when he realized, him standing his ground was turning her on by the second. Demi rose on the bed and crawled to him on her hands and knees and began sucking his dick, as he stood before her at the foot of the bed. Trey became erect in her mouth and began to grind his dick in and out slowly, closing his eyes to enjoy the pleasure she was giving him. For the next 45 minutes they enjoyed one another's bodies sexually. Tackling every position they could think of, Demi was pleased with Trey's sexual performance and the multiple orgasms he gave her. After they showered together, Trey got dressed and looked on at Demi who slipped her pink silk robe back on, and lit up another blunt. Demi opened the drawer that was on the wall and took out some bills. Letting the blunt rest between her lips, she counted out $250. After she handed him the money, they then walked up the winding crystal steps hand in hand with Demi leading him out the side of the yacht, and back on the deck. Never once tying the strings on her robe, she didn't care that her yellow perky twins and swollen pussy was exposed for anyone walking by to see. She hugged him lightly, planted a kiss on his cheek, and told him she would call him in the near future when she wanted to experience him again. Unlocking the latches on the back entryway of the boat, Trey exited the yacht and made his way back to his car.

Trey sat back in his car shaking his head at how wild Demi was. He knew she was a cool female, but he also had seen her type before and knew just how she was. She was just another rich girl from the hills of Montgomery County that tried her best to fit in with those from the hood. A beauty she was, and all Trey could do was think about all the women he came in contact with lately, and how they all were a financial gain for him to get rich, and possibly never work a regular job again in his life. While thinking of a way to better his future, Trey gathered up all the money he had made throughout the day with his two clients. He counted out $750, placed the money in his glove compartment, and pulled off from the parking lot making his way to Tina's house to stash the money in the safe like they agreed upon. He picked up his phone, checking his missed call log and saw that he had four missed calls from Scarlett, two from Tina, two from Tone and one from an Atlanta number who he figured was Maya. Trey called his voicemail, pressing the Bluetooth button allowing the audio to come out of the BOSE car speakers. The first three voicemails were from Scarlett, hanging the phone up when the answering machine picked up, on the fourth message she spoke, "*Okay I tried calling your fucking phone four times. I don't know why the fuck you are ignoring me all of a sudden, but two can play that game!! I heard the bitch in the background, and I know your sneaky ass is up to no good!!! I know what you are up to Trey, so do you, and don't worry about me, cause I will be surely doing me!!*" As Trey continued to drive he smiled as he replayed Scarlett's message, thinking he would call her later when she cooled off and calmed down. The next message was from Tina letting him know that she was just checking on him and to call her when he got a chance. Listening on, there was a message from Tone, "*Yo, call me back playboy. Scarlett has called my phone twice, and I'm not gonna answer it until I talk to you, cause I know you probably told her that we was together! But hit my phone when you get a chance pimp, I'm out.*" The last voicemail was from Maya: "*Hey Trey, this is Maya, Scarlett gave me the number. Just wanted to let you know that I am at the house, bored out of my mind, where is the liquor in this camp? Anyway call my number back when you get this message, maybe you can bring me something back on your way in. Alright, talk to you then."*

"*YOU HAVE NO MORE MESSAGES.*" Trey ended the call to his voicemail, leaned his leather seat back, and dialed Scarlett's number while he continued to drive toward Tina's house.

◊◊◊

Scarlett pulled up to her mother's apartment building, grabbed her phone and thought twice about answering it for Trey. Letting the phone ring until the call went to her voicemail, she pressed the 1 on her speed dial to get her mother's number. Mrs. B answered on the third ring sounding sleepy, "Hello?"

"Hey mom, I'm out front. Do you need me to come up to bring you this money or are you coming down?"

"C'mon up Scarlett baby cause I don't have anything on and I had dozed off to sleep."

"Ok, that's fine mom, I'm not staying anyway so just meet me at the door so I can head on back to Baltimore."

Ending the call, Scarlett exited her car and raced up the three flights of stairs where Mrs. B was at the door waiting for her. Scarlett handed her the envelope and hugged her mom goodbye as she raced back down the same three flights, and hopped back in her car, never once turning the ignition off. Throwing the car in drive, Scarlett turned her radio on, and headed for the highway making her way back on the hour long drive back towards the city.

◊◊◊

Trey pulled up to Tina's house laughing aloud as he conversed with Tone on the phone letting him know, about the time he had with Demi. "Tone, homey when I say she was a bad bitch with some good pussy, trust me on that homie cause I ain't never lying!"

Tone laughed along with him and added, "I believe you my nigga, and you gotta put me up on one of them bitches and let me see what it's hittin on."

"I got you my nigga," Trey added. "We gonna hook up tomorrow, and I'm gonna take you with me so you can meet the next one, and afterwards we gonna hit the strip club and go crazy in that bitch, how we usually do it!"

"Alright Trey, make sure you carry your ass home tonight, before Scarlett kill your ass."

"I got that nigga," Trey said. "That's my bitch, so I will handle my business like I'm supposed to. But I'm gonna get up with you tomorrow my nigg!"

"Alright, pimp be easy!"

Trey ended the call and grabbed the cash out of the glove compartment while stepping out of the vehicle, and made his way into Tina's house. Using the key she had given him, Trey entered her house locking the door behind him. As he made his way up the stairs, he stopped halfway up the steps, as he heard female moans coming from Tina's room. Tiptoeing up the pitch black dark staircase, so he wouldn't be heard, Trey smiled to himself at the sounds of Tina having sex. Ignoring the sounds, Trey walked past Tina's room, and entered the second bedroom quietly closing the door behind him. Trey used the light from his cell phone to enter the combination to the safe. While placing the money in the safe, Trey noticed Tina had money already stacked in the safe. After he closed the safe back quietly, he listened on as the feminine moans grew louder. After listening closely, he knew whoever was in the room getting fucked wasn't Tina, cause he definitely knew what the sounds of Tina's cries and moans were from anywhere, and it wasn't her! Trey exited the room and figured he would barge into Tina's room, just to be nosey and see what was going down. Trey cut the bathroom light on and opened Tina's door and was instantly turned on, but not surprised at the sight of Tina on the bed on her knees with a strap-on hitting Shay wildly from the back. Tina looked Trey in the eyes never once stopping her stroke, as she continued to pump in and out of Shay while she cried out in ecstasy. With Shay facing the opposite direction crying out with her eyes closed, she never once looked up or even knew she was being watched. Trey chucked Tina the deuce sign with his fingers, smiling as she did the same, closed her bedroom door back, turned out the bathroom light and headed down the steps and out the door. Locking the door behind him, Trey got back in his car and drove home. As he drove, it dawned on him that he should call Maya back. When he dialed her phone she answered and told him she was in the crib a little tipsy and needed a drinking partner, demanding that he come join her since Scarlett was missing in action and nowhere to be found.

Tina feeling some kind of way 💻

He told her he would be there shortly, ended the call and continued his drive to his house. Pulling in front of the house, Trey dialed Scarlett's number back before exiting his vehicle.

"Yes Trey?" she answered, picking up on the first ring. Hearing the anger in her voice, Trey figured he was too drained from the day's activities to fight with Scarlett.

"Baby what's up, how are you?"

"I'm fine Trey, I just have a problem with you lying and ignoring me."

"Scarlett, when will you be back home, I miss you and I don't wanna fight with you."

"I don't wanna fight with you either Trey, but I'm gonna be hanging out with some friends tonight out Annapolis. So depending on how I feel, I may just stay at my mom's house because I really don't feel like hitting the highway and coming back down there tonight."

"Alright Scarlett babe, enjoy your night and we will just talk when you get back baby."

"Why can't we talk now Trey?" she asked him.

"Well first off, I'm tired baby and I'm about to go in the house and get some rest."

"Uh huh, Whatever Trey, I will call you later and let you know if I decide to come home or not."

"I love you Scarlett" he told her, ready to end the conversation that he could see was going nowhere fast!

"I love you too Trey!" Trey ended the call with Scarlett, exited his car and locked it with a press of a button on his key ring. When Trey entered his house he looked at the top of the stairs, realizing just how drunken Maya was with every single light on in every room of the small townhouse. Taking two steps at a time, Trey walked up the staircase cutting off every light as he made his way to the kitchen where there stood Maya with her back turned dawning a thong, too small t-shirt with no bra, pouring Patron tequila out the bottle and into her glass. Maya with her back still to him, felt his eyes dancing all over her body broke the silence, "So are you gonna stand there behind me looking at my ass all night?" Turning to face him, Trey couldn't help but smile, knowing he had been caught admiring Maya's perfectly rounded brown complexioned phat ass that swallowed the leopard print thong she wore. Setting the bottle and her glass on the countertop, she walked around the counter that separated the kitchen from the living room, with her arms opened and smiling walking towards Trey and said, "Hey Trey baby, how are you I'm glad to see you!" Trey knew that if he didn't correct this situation it wasn't going to end right, especially if Scarlett walked in and saw them hugging in the middle of the living room, with Maya pretty much fucking naked.

"Whoa, whoa Maya, Are you drunk?" he questioned her, releasing his embrace on her and stepped back to get a better look at her.

"No boy I'm not drunk, I'm a little tipsy but nowhere near drunk!" Sitting down on the chair and kicking his shoes off, Trey grabbed the TV remote that went to the 47 inch flat screen that hung on the wall, clicked on the fireplace channel, closed his eyes and enjoyed the crackling of the wood burning and the sight of the fire as it illuminated the living room wall resembling a real fireplace. Maya walked over to where he was sitting, and sat on his lap, facing him while twirling the glass around in her hand that was filled to the rim with Patron on the rocks. Placing the glass to his lips, she told him to drink up. Trey did just that, drinking the liquid in the glass down to the last drop all the while looking Maya in her eyes as she continued to tilt the glass up to his lips. Setting the glass on the floor, Trey looked at Maya and asked, "What are you doing on my lap?" Looking at him seriously, she tilted her head to the side and burst into laughter and said, "Quit being a pussy Trey, I'm riding your dick, that's what I'm doing." Maya continued to burst out into laughter as she hopped up and down as if she was riding and bucking on a horse. Trey just shook his head, because he knew he was in for a long night fooling around with this girl. "I've been thinking Trey, with all the stories Scarlett has told me about how you put it down in the bedroom, I'm curious. How about I dance for you, than you can show me what you are working with, and then show me how you can work this?!" Maya said, patting on her pussy while giving him a full view pulling the front of her thong to the side. Trey rose from the sofa lifting Maya up with him, bringing her to her feet. He turned his back on her and walked to his bedroom with Maya following behind him. Discarding his clothes, Maya leaned in the bedroom doorway, licking her lips watching on as Trey changed out of his clothes and into a pair of thin blue POLO pajama pants with no shirt or nothing underneath of them.

"Damn your body is banging boy, you got my pussy wet as shit looking at your sexy light skinned freckled faced ass!" Trey continued to look serious and kept his cool as he walked toward her.

He knew she was impressed with his body, cause shit, he was even impressed with it when he looked in the mirror. He also knew that working out in the gym and running on the treadmill had paid off. Trey knew it wasn't a good idea to fool around with Maya in the house that he shared with Scarlett, but being so tired from his full day with Tina, Consuela, and Demi he just wanted to chill in the house and the effects of the Patron were starting to kick in. His inner gut feeling told him not to fool around with her, and that it was a bad idea, especially if Scarlett decided to come home and caught them. He told himself he would be careful and wouldn't take things too far with her, and probably only allow her to suck his dick if nothing else. "Fix us another drink," he told her, smacking

114

her ass as she smiled back at him walking towards the kitchen.

"Boy don't start nothing you can't finish!" she told him. Turning the knob on the radio to click it on, Trey played with the IPOD until he found the tunes that best fit his mood. Settling to an artist by the name of Rick Ross, Trey sat back slouched on the living room sofa, rocking his head up and down to the music. Maya handed him his drink while taking a sip from her glass.

"I got something for you Trey, I hope you like it," she told him, setting her glass down on the table. Moving the small glass table from out of the middle of the floor, Maya began to snap her fingers and dance seductively to the sound of the music, with her back towards Trey. Trey continued to slouch down on the chair, with one hand in his pants stroking his quickly growing dick. Maya began to shake her ass cheeks like a stripper in the club, and he was mesmerized by her moves, and the way she made her ass clap. Trey sat there holding his dick with one hand, and sipping out of his glass with the other. Maya came out of her too small t-shirt exposing some perfect 38C cup breasts, and swollen rock hard nipples that looked as if they were sitting in the freezer, before coming out of the leopard print thongs she wore, and twirled them around her fingers, before throwing them at Trey. Sipping the remains of her drink, Maya continued to dance for Trey for the next twenty minutes, doing any and everything from standing on her head and rocking her ass and pussy back and forth, to crawling on her hands and knees, and using her pussy muscles to make her pussy open and close, all the while making her ass cheeks jump one at a time to the continuing sound of the beat. Crawling over to where he sat, she began to rub his dick, through the thin pajama material pants he wore. With his hands behind his head and eyes closed, Trey sat there enjoying Maya's touch, as she pulled his swollen dick out from behind the fabrics, and began to suck him slowly. Deep throating his ten inch dick down to his testicles and back up to the tip of his mushroom shaped head, Trey was speechless as he let out a low moan.

"Damn this muthafucka tastes so good, me and Scarlett are going to have to share this!" she said, as she continued sucking and slobbering on his manhood with perfection, as if she possessed trophies in dick sucking!

CHAPTER 7

It had been 3 days since Scarlett had been home. She made sure she talked to Trey every day at least four times a day, giving him the excuse that her mother was badly ill and she needed to stay with her, something Maya knew was a lie. Many times Trey had insisted on coming to her aid, but telling him she was ok and her mom was getting better, and she would be home that day, was her excuse.

Scarlett stepped out of the shower using a towel to dry her hair. It was 9am on a Friday morning, and Trey was beginning to believe she was once again lying. He questioned Maya about her whereabouts but Maya kept Scarlett's infidelities a secret from Trey, mostly because of the money she had paid Maya to seduce and sleep with him and also for the bigger reward of having him to herself, if she succeeded with the plan. Maya knew she was playing on dangerous grounds, because she knew that Scarlett still loved Trey, but being loyal to her friend came first and then the greed for the money and possession of something she had always wanted: Trey.

"I don't know Scarlett, you are my bitch and I will do anything you ask of me, but I don't wanna be the cause for you and Trey to break up."

Scarlett

Scarlett sat on the sofa next to Maya with $2,000 in one hand, and taking sips of the Patron out of the glass with the other hand, with one of her eyebrows raised. "Maya you have to do this for me, you are the only one

I can trust to do this and besides that, Trey and I are having major issues! I know he is fucking around on me, making his money by doing, "Special Favors" for different women, something he doesn't know that I am aware of! So, are you in or are you out?"

Snatching the two grand from Scarlett's hand, Maya agreed with the plan and told her she owed her another grand if she succeeded, and she was only doing it because she was her girl, but after it was done not to ever put her in another situation like that again. They hugged on the couch in Scarlett's living room, with Scarlett thanking her best friend and agreeing to pay the additional thousand after the deal was done and over with. Rising from the couch, Scarlett grabbed her purse and phone and exited the house. Once inside her truck, Scarlett called Trey's phone to let him know she was on her way to her mom's house. After calling four times and then arguing with him about ignoring her and overhearing the woman's voice in the background, she called Maya's phone. When Maya picked up, she reminded her that she would be gone for a week and if Trey questioned her about her whereabouts to just tell him that she was at her mom's house, as planned.

Scarlett stepped out of the shower using one of the hotel towels to dry her hair. Glancing at the clock on the stand next to the king size bed, she cursed aloud when she seen it was 11:53 a.m., seven minutes until check out time. No wonder the phone kept ringing earlier, as well as she knew she heard someone knocking on the door. "Fucking room service," she said, aloud to no one in particular. Winding the towel up in her hand and snapping the towel back with full force, Scarlett burst into laughter cracking the bare ass cheek of Tone, who laid on his stomach snoring, sprawled out on the massive king size bed. "What the fuck!" Tone cursed aloud jumping out of the bed grabbing his gun off of the nightstand. Realizing what had just happened he stood up, joining in on the laughter with Scarlett, still clutching his gun in one hand and rubbing his stinging ass cheek with the other. "Alright I got you, you think it's funny that shit hurt like a mother fucker! I thought I was shot!" Setting the gun back on the nightstand, Tone walked up to Scarlett hugging and palming her soft ass cheeks. "That was for fucking me like a maniac this morning nigga." She told him, wrapping her arms around his neck. Separating from their embrace, Scarlett walked over to her suitcase and began to get dressed, as her eyes followed his ass as he walked into the bathroom.

"You did it, you are the one who was begging for me to fuck you harder. *Fuck me harder Tone!*" He said mocking her.

"Don't flatter yourself buddy!" she yelled back to him. Exiting the bathroom still nude with a towel wrapped around his waist covering his bottom half, Tone began getting dressed.

"I'm gone. Call or text me later boy." said Scarlett, clutching the handle of her suitcase heading towards the door.

"So, will I see you later?" he asked, before she headed out the door. Ignoring his question, Scarlett exited the hotel room and entered the elevator and headed down to the first floor of the Quality Inn hotel. Stepping out of the hotel, Scarlett entered her vehicle, throwing her suitcase on the back seat and let a tear roll down her left cheek, thinking about how she slept with Trey's closest friend and how she put him in a position to sleep with hers. Driving out of the parking lot, Scarlett was bombarded with emotions as she drove home thinking about how wrong she was. She knew she shouldn't have allowed Tone to come see her at the hotel and lean on her shoulder about the issues he was having with his girlfriend, knowing she was vulnerable and upset over the drama and issues she was having with her boyfriend, whom she loved dearly and didn't want to lose...or did she. The anger and feeling the need for some attention mixed with the Patron she had been drinking before Tone got there had her brain clouded and her body open to be comforted by Tone. He happens to be there at the wrong time, and for the right reasons. As the tears continued to stream down her face, she couldn't stop reading the text messages Maya sent her telling her how she had been fucking Trey for the last four days, along with the pictures she sent her showing them naked in the bed that Scarlett and Trey had shared. Not to mention the couple videos she managed to get of Trey visible face not knowing he was being recorded while she sucked his dick.

Through with all of the drama that her and Trey was going through, her emotions turned into anger as she contemplated going home to set Trey down to put everything on the table, and iron out their differences after she beat Maya's ass, and sent her back where she came from. Pulling in front of her job, Scarlett decided to stop at her office to pick up some notes from her receptionist. Parking her truck in front of the office, Scarlett exited the vehicle, walked through the doors and was actually happy to see a familiar face. "Hey Deb, you looking cute in that dress boo!" Deb rose from her chair and walked from around her desk with her cell phone glued to her ear and did a full 360 spin, giving Scarlett a full view of the white and pink mini body skirt with the same color 6inch heels to match.

"You like?"

"Hell yeah I like, girl you look nice. So are you on a date or are you at work?" They both laughed in unison at Scarlett's wit. Settling back behind her desk, Deb handed Scarlett a manila envelope telling whoever she was on the phone with to hold on, while letting Scarlett know that everything she needed was in the envelope, and making sure she didn't need any further assistance. She grabbed her cell phone, getting back to the conversation she was having as Scarlett told her, she was fine and headed upstairs to her office. While she walked away, Scarlett overheard Deb on the phone telling someone she was in need of some more of that front seat action, along with some more Rose. Stopping at the top of the steps, still eavesdropping on Deb's conversation, she could have sworn she heard her say, "Trey you are crazy!"

Entering her office, she closed her office door and sat behind her desk and dismissed the thought that Deb was talking to 'her' Trey. She figured she would store that in her mental bank for a later date in case something came up later in the future, but until then she was just gonna take it as she was tripping with all the craziness that had been going on with her and Trey. For the past two hours Scarlett sat at her desk doing paperwork and entering future tenants' information in her computer, along with rent payments for two of the three condominium buildings she ran. Tired and drained from the two hours of work she had just done, Scarlett made sure everything was in order in her office, grabbed her purse and her files and headed down the steps to leave out of the two story office building. Noticing Deb had already left for the day, she punched the security code in the alarm on the wall and exited the building locking the door behind her. Once in her car she called Trey phone, as she pulled off making her way home.

"Hey babe, what's up?" he questioned, answering the phone.

"Hey Trey, where are you?"

"I'm in the house watching Scarface, about to step out and take care of something in a few, how about you babe, what are you doing?"

"Nothing, on my way to the store to get me something to eat because I am starving," she told him pressing on the gas to get home quicker. "Where is Maya?"

"She's sitting right here with me, doing the same thing, why you want to speak to her?"

"No thanks, just tell her I will call her later. Plus when I get back I wanna talk to you about something, nothing major, but I should be back sometime tomorrow." she lied. They conversed for another ten minutes about how her trip was with her mom, and he told her about how his days had been long and lonely since she been away tending to her mother. They ended their conversation with telling one another how much they couldn't wait to see the other, and how much they loved and cared for each other. Ending the call on that note, Scarlett drove in silence making her way home deep in thought.

◊◊◊

"Who was that, Scarlett?" Maya asked, lying back on the sofa looking up at Trey with her head resting in his lap. Trey sat there in his gray POLO boxer briefs texting Tone, letting him know he needed to see him sometime today to catch up on their future business dealings. "Yeah that was her, she said she would be back tomorrow." Trey told her, waiting patiently for Tone to text him back, while glancing back and forth from the action on the television to his cell phone to her nude body, that had his dick standing tall fully erected underneath her head. Maya raised her head from his lap, grabbed the remote for the TV and turned the volume up, making it sound as if the action that was on the screen was actually in the house. "What are you doing?" Trey asked her, watching as she stood in front of him. Maya took his cell phone out of his hand, and set it on the living room table, grabbed his right hand and told him to get up and come with her. "Where are we going?" he asked, rising up from the sofa. Still holding his hand, she guided him to the bathroom. Closing the bathroom door behind them she sat on the toilet seat and pulled his briefs down, causing his throbbing hard dick to spring free. She took him in her mouth and began to lick all around his dick. Maya stood up and kissed his cheek and told Trey to get in the shower, and wait for her to return. Doing just as she said, Trey got in the shower, making the water and bathroom foggy and steamy hot and waited patiently underneath the water for her to return. Maya returned holding two bathroom towels, a gold pack Magnum and a bottle of *Astroglide* anal lube from out of her suitcase. Shutting the bathroom door so that the steam from the hot water would stay locked in the room, Maya climbed in the shower with him, setting the condom and lube on the huge window seal that set before them.

Wrapping her arms around his neck while pressing her erect nipples against his chest, she whispered in his ear, "I need you to fuck me good and hard baby, I want you to cum in my ass!" Resting his palms on her soft brown ass cheeks, Trey caressed, rubbed and spread them apart. Dropping her arms from around his neck, she got down on her knees and began sucking his dick until it was rock hard to her liking. Trey grabbed the back of her head and began pumping in and out of her mouth, biting down on his bottom lip as the pleasure her mouth was giving him took over his whole being. Maya grabbed the condom from the windowsill, ripped the pack open with her teeth while placing the condom in her mouth, and using no hands she applied the condom on his dick using her lips to roll it all the way down to his testicles. Trey was turned on by the sight of what she had just done with the condom and her lips, impressed that she never used her teeth nor did she accidently nip him with her teeth.

Maya stood up slowly, using her tongue to make circular motions on Trey's six pack abs, up to his strong Pecs, to his neck and deep down his throat. She grabbed the anal lube from the windowsill, without breaking their tongue wrestling she continued to kiss him, as she pulled a handful of lube on his dick with one hand and stroking the lube around it with the other. She poured some more of the lube in her hand and began rubbing it in between her ass cheeks and in and out of her ass using her middle finger. When she felt like she applied enough of the lube in and out of her, she removed her lips from his and set the lube back on the windowsill next to the empty condom wrapper and turned her back towards him. Bending forward, she spread her legs as far apart as she could in the small tub made for two, reached down between them grabbing his ankles. She told him to take his time and put it in her ass. "Put it in Trey, go slow putting it in, than once it's in FUCK ME, Ouchhhhhh!!" She cried out, as Trey entered her from behind. Taking his time, Trey pumped in and out of her, picking up the speed when she demanded him to pump harder. "Yes Trey, it feels so good in my ass…Fuck me harder!!" Pulling up next to Treys car, Scarlett parked, stepped out of her truck and grabbed her suitcase from out of the back seat. Closing and locking her doors, she walked past Trey car and begin walking around it looking inside of his windows and noticed a phone on the floor lighting up as if it was ringing. With her spare key, Scarlett leaned her suitcase on the back passenger door, unlocked his car doors and hopped in the passenger side, grabbing the ringing phone off of the floor. Pressing the talk button, Scarlett stood there with one leg on the ledge of the door with the door setting open, with the phone to her ear waiting for whoever was on the opposite end of the line to say something.

"Hello," the female voice answered finally breaking the silence.

"Yes how can I help you and who are you looking for?" Scarlett asked, with one eyebrow raised waiting for the caller's reply.

"Well hello sweetie, but yes, you may be able to help me. This is Consuela, and I'm looking for Trey, is he around?"

"Consuela is it? So how is it that you know my cousin Trey?" Scarlett asked, getting angrier by the second. 'So this sneaky mother fucker got the nerve to have another cell phone with bitches calling him, oh hell no, I'm gonna kick his ass!' She thought to herself, almost saying it out loud. As Consuela continued to speak, "Oh I am a very good friend of his, and when he gets to his phone, cousin, can you have him to give me a call as soon as possible."

"Friend huh," Scarlett said, holding her composure ready to explode on Consuela. "When you say friend you mean as in *fucking* friends?"

Consuela laughed aloud at the audacity of this so called cousin, and since she asked she figured she might as well tell her, "Uhhh yes as in *fucking* friends, let's just say he is my boy toy and he does a damn good job with making me his freaky Latina bitch...*Cousin!*" With hearing enough, Scarlett slammed Trey's car door shut, locked the doors back, grabbed her suitcase and walked to her front door. Not wanting to hear anymore, Scarlett told Consuela she would let him know that she had called, ended the call and with her keys unlocked the house door and entered. Setting her suitcase down she locked the door and headed up the steps, where she was greeted by the loud sounds of Scarface playing loudly on the living room television. As she reached the top of the steps, she noticed the bathroom door was closed. Ignoring the loud sound of the TV playing in the living room, Scarlett angrily burst into the bathroom ready to curse Trey out and drill him about his infidelities and also to let him know she knew about him and Maya fucking around while she had been gone, and give him a dose of what she had been doing also. Entering the bathroom, Scarlett was engulfed with the steam that was locked in, making it hard for her to see, but what she heard was enough to make her step back with both hands to her face as a single tear streamed down her face. Knowing the two of them never heard her enter the bathroom, Maya and Trey continued their act totally oblivious of Scarlett on the opposite side of the shower curtain.

Built up with rage, Scarlett ran to her bedroom, kicked her heels off and put her sneakers on, grabbed her baseball bat out of the closet and bolted back to the bathroom swinging wildly into the shower curtain. The sound of the baseball bat cracking against the head of one of the silhouettes in the shower was loud enough to hear over the loud sound of the shower water, as well as the loud television in the other room. Trey jumped back, slipped and fell into the shower curtain, hitting his head against the sink as he fell out of the shower wrapped in the curtain trying to jump to his feet and take the bat away from Scarlett's grip while she continuously swung the bat wildly at him and Maya. Pushing him out of the way and making him slip and fall to the floor again, Scarlett dropped the bat and charged after Maya and began to beat her with her fists. Maya still dazed from the initial blow of the metal bat tried her hardest to fight her way out of the small bathroom, but to no prevail as Scarlett continued to beat on her. She kicked Maya in the face and stomped her face into the floor when she finally fell over Trey. Trey was able to get to his feet and grab Scarlett around her waist, locking her arms down to her side. "Get the fuck off of me Trey!" she screamed out at the top of her lungs. "I can't believe you would do this shit to me, get the fuck off of me!" Trey continued to hold onto Scarlett while watching Maya get to her feet and run out of the bathroom soaking wet and bleeding profusely from the mouth, nose and forehead.

"Baby, please calm down, I'm so sorry," Trey pleaded, walking her to their bedroom with her still in his tight grip. Once inside the room, he released her and immediately closed the bedroom door, locking them both in the room alone together. Scarlett put her hands to her face and began to sob uncontrollably, leaned back against the wall until her legs gave way and she slid down onto the floor and laid in a fetal position. Still nude with the condom swinging from the tip of his penis, Trey got down on his knees before her and tried his best to apologize and plead his case, but no matter what he said to her it was as if he was talking to a wall, because Scarlett continued to cry and push him away when he tried to reach out and embrace or touch her. Realizing he still had the condom on, he jumped to his feet removing it and headed to the bathroom closing the door behind him, leaving Scarlett in the room to cry on the floor alone. He flushed the condom down the toilet, turned the shower water off as it flooded and soaked the bathroom floor. Grabbing the Astroglide and empty condom pack from the floor, he threw the empty wrapper in the toilet, flushing it as well and walked out of the bathroom with his head down. When Trey raised his head Scarlett was standing in the bedroom door with tears in her eyes pointing a 45 automatic at his chest. Trey stopped in his tracks, looking from her to the barrel of the gun and then back to her. "Baby, please don't do this!"

"Shut the fuck up nigga, and get your shit and get the fuck out of my house!" Trey walked towards her slowly, Scarlett fired a warning shot at his head, which flew past him and hit the bathroom door just missing his head. Maya cried out from the bottom of the steps, begging Scarlett to calm down. Just as Scarlett turned to point the gun away from Trey and out the door towards the bottom of the steps where Maya was standing, Trey charged after her causing her to lose control and drop the gun. Trey hurried to his feet and picked the gun up off of the floor where it laid. Ignoring Scarlett, he went back into the bedroom, pulled on a pair of blue POLO sweatpants and a white V-neck, tucked the gun in his dip and put on his white RETRO Jordan #4's and grabbed his car keys and phone and headed down the stairs. Walking past

Scarlett, who was now in the living room yelling obscenities to both him and Maya, telling them to get the fuck out of her house! Trey grabbed Maya by her arm and pushed her out the door, slammed the door closed and locked it and took her to his car. Pulling out of the parking lot, Trey looked at Maya who was holding a t-shirt to her nose trying to stop the bleeding and began to question her, as they drove heading towards the nearest hotel.

"Do you have anywhere to go?"

"No," she replied, looking back at him. "Trey, I'm so sorry. I didn't mean to fuck up things between you and Scarlett, but she paid me two grand to sleep with you." Taking his eyes off of the road, Trey looked at her with a confused look on his face.

"What? What do you mean she paid you, and you went along with it!? You are a treacherous ass bitch! Get the fuck out of my car!" Pulling over on the side of the road, Trey jumped out of the car, leaving the driver's side door open and walked around to the passenger's side where she sat, opened the door, and snatched Maya out of the car.

"Please don't do this Trey! I'm so sorry!" Maya said, falling to the ground. Grabbing her purse from the passenger side floor, he threw it to her feet, where she set on the ground begging him not to leave her here like this. Consumed with frustration, Trey slammed the door and walked back to the driver's side, closed the door back, threw the car in drive and pulled off leaving her on the ground, not giving a damn how she got where ever she would end up. As Trey sped down the road with nowhere in particular to go, he decided to give his homie Tone a call and vent to him about his wild night, in which Scarlett had caught him and her best friend in the shower. Trey pulled into a liquor store parking lot and dialed Tone's number, parked the car and exited the vehicle making his way into the store to get something to sip on to numb the bullshit he had just endured. "Trey, what it do pimp? Talk to me!" Tone answered, in his usual greeting.

"Man, you ain't gonna believe what the fuck just went down, but I need to holla at you like yesterday cause I done fucked up homie!" Trey told him, entering the store. Walking straight to the counter, he told the clerk to give him a fifth of Patron silver, a sprite soda, 2 cups and a 12 pack of twelve ounce Moet Rose. While the clerk rung his order up, Trey was explaining to Tone where to meet him. He paid for the alcohol, ended the call with Tone and made his way back to his car. Trey leaned his seat back, closed his eyes and rested his head against the black leather headrest. As he sat there in silence it dawned on him that he didn't have his other phone, and knew that if Scarlett got her hands on it then that would be some more bullshit that he didn't need. He began searching the car, checking everywhere from the glove compartment, to underneath the seats, to in between the seat, but to no prevail. Getting out of the car, he searched the insides of the car thoroughly, but it never turned up. Settling back in the car, he cracked open one of the bottles of Rose and took a sip and set the bottle inside of the cup holder. Pulling away from the store parking lot, Trey decided to head to the spot where he was supposed to meet Tone. Grabbing his phone he dialed Tina's number, and pressed the Bluetooth button, and her phone began to ring through the BOSE surround sound speakers throughout his Mercedes.

"Hey boo." Tina said, answering on the first ring.

"Hey Tina babe, I got a situation and it's a lot going on tonight, but I misplaced the business phone and I need you to call it from a different number and see who has it."

"Not a problem baby, are you alright though? Scarlett called my phone and left a message on my answering machine talking about, *'my boy done fucked up, and I hope you have a place for his trifling ass to stay'*". Tina burst into laughter, then added. "So what's good, I hope she didn't catch you up with that bitch Maya or got her hands on your phone and talked to one or all of your clients!" Thinking about what Tina just implied, he told her the first part she said was true concerning Maya, but not wanting to really get into it now he told her he would explain everything to her later. She agreed that that was a good idea, and that she would keep calling the phone and find out if Scarlett had it or not. Ending the call with Tina, Trey sat in the Valentino's restaurant parking lot waiting for Tone to arrive. Just as he was going to pick up the phone to check the time he had a text message come through. It was from Scarlett that read: ***"You are a triflin' good for nothing rotten ass nigga Trey! I can't believe you would fuck with my friend in our home. You are a pig and I don't live with filth, so you need to remove your junk from my home, before I trash it or better yet burn it. O and BTW, I know about your little get rich quick schemes with your Consuela's and Demi's and all the rest of them bitches that pay you to sleep with them!! What goes around already came back around and since you fucked me you have been fucked back, just ask your homie Tone!! I love you too boo!"*** Trey sat his phone down, deep in thought over what he just read, and although he knew Scarlett was pissed, he didn't know what she meant by '*Just ask Tone*'. As the thought crossed his mind, Tone was pulling up beside him in his old Ford Taurus station wagon with "Jesus Saves" stickers all over the back window, and dressed in a cheap pinstripe suit which Trey knew could mean one of many things; either he had just made a drug deal or was about to go make one and that he was carrying his favorite gun named Mr. Rogers in the glove compartment with him. Trey looked down at his ringing phone and seen it was Tone. "Hello" Trey answered.

"Yo take a ride with me to pick up some laundry." Tone told him.

"Alright, follow me to go drop my car off around the corner, cause I don't wanna leave my shit here and they end up towing my shit. Fuck that, I done had enough excitement for the night as is!"

"Alright cool, let's go." Trey pulled away from the parking lot on his way to Tina's crib, with Tone following behind him. Each time he looked back at Tone through his rearview mirror the thought of Scarlett's message danced across his mind, wondering what she meant by '*Ask Tone*' had him on the edge. Dismissing the thought, he figured he would deal with that situation later when he and Tone conversed because he was sure to let him know what she had said. Maybe the two of them conversed about something, who knows, but he was sure to get to the bottom line of what she meant. Trey parked his car in front of Tina's house, got out locking his door behind him and entered Tone's vehicle bringing his alcohol that he had just purchased with him cause he knew this was going to be a long ride. "What it do pimp?" Trey said shaking Tone hand. "I see you dressed in your, 'I'm a country ass deacon attire!'" Tone burst into laughter, looking from his friend to the road.

"Yeah nigga, the cops don't fuck with a nigga when you are on your deacon shit! But enough about me, what's going on with you?"

Trey handed Tone a bottle of Rose, but he declined the Patron, saying, he had to be alert when he made a pick up.

"Man I fucked up homie." Trey told him.

"How?"

"One, I got caught fucking Scarlett best friend from Atlanta in the fucking shower." Trey went on to telling him everything, from when, Maya first arrived to when he came home and she was standing there in the kitchen in her panties, tipsy and throwing herself at him. Even down to Scarlett being out of town with her mom, to him putting Maya out of his car for confessing to him about her and Scarlett setting him up by paying Maya to fuck him in their home.

"Damn my nigga, you really did fuck up! So where is Scarlett now, and what the fuck you gonna do?" Trey leaned his seat back and took a sip of his Patron, then chased it down with a swig of the Rose and said, "Man I gotta give her some time to get over this shit, and I'm gonna make it right with her. I just gotta talk to her my nigga."

Tone grabbed his ringing phone, answered it and told the person on the other end of the line that he was pulling up now. Setting his phone in the cup holder, Trey watched as Tone reached underneath his seat and pulled a black desert eagle handgun from beneath it and placed it in the front of his pants, buttoning his suit jacket to conceal it. Tone grabbed a small duffle bag full of money from the floor behind the passenger seat.

Opening the glove compartment, Tone showed Trey Mr. Rogers and told him if anything was to go wrong he knew what to do. Trey smiled and shook Tone's hand saying "Already, handle your biz!"

Tone pulled up behind a black Cadillac Deville with tinted windows, got out of his car grabbing the duffle bag of money and disappeared in the backseat of the Cadillac, closing the door behind him. As Trey sat back in the car waiting for Tone to finish up with his transaction, he opened the glove compartment, grabbed Mr. Rogers examining its chrome beauty, checked to see if it was loaded and placed it back where he found it when he realized it was. Taking another sip of his drink Trey grabbed Tone phone as it began to ring. Confusion was written across Trey's face, as he recognized Scarlett's number appear on the ID as it continued to ring. When the phone stopped ringing Trey began looking through Tone's phone at all the times and days that he and Scarlett had been conversing. Anger took over him when he went through their text messages and seen that they had not only been seeing each other behind his back but they had actually slept together and had been flirting and talking dirty to each other right before Scarlett came home and caught him in the act with Maya. "You no good mother fucker!" Trey yelled aloud to no one in particular. "So that's what the fuck you meant by, ask your friend Tone!" Downing the remains of Rose out of the bottle, along with the last bit of Patron he had left in his cup. Trey sat Tone's phone back where he found it, grabbed Mr. Rogers out of the glove compartment, cocked the hammer and just as he was about to step out of the vehicle three shots was fired from inside the Cadillac taking him by surprise. Trey rushed out of the passenger side leaving the door open to rush to Tone's aid. Even though he was about to jump out of the car and kill everyone in the Cadillac, including Tone for betraying him, loyalty had him helping his friend out of the sticky situation he was now in, but revenge would have him deal with him later. Tone fell out of the car clutching his smoking desert eagle in one hand and two black duffle bags in the other. Jumping to his feet he tossed Trey one of the bags, yelling at him out of breath, "Get in the car homie, let's get the fuck out of here!" Trey jumped back in the passenger seat slamming the door behind him, holding on to the bag and Mr. Rogers as Tone hopped in the driver's side. Just as Tone was about to pull off, the driver of the Cadillac got out holding his shoulder with one hand and pointing an UZI machine gun with the other at the direction of Tone's car. Before he could let off a shot, Trey was already out of the car firing shots at him, hitting him twice in the head. As he fell to his knees Trey ran towards him, stood over top of him and placed another bullet in the back of his head, making sure he was dead. With his shirt, Trey opened the back of the Cadillac and emptied the rest of the shots inside the cab making sure no one was left alive. "Come the fuck on!!" Tone screamed from behind the wheel. Getting back in the car, they pulled off leaving a bloody mess for the cops and coroner to deal with.

CHAPTER 8

Keisha pulled up in her driveway, parking next to Trey's car. Still a little tipsy from just leaving the club, she grabbed her purse from off of the passenger side floor, kicked her heels off, and got out of the car barefooted. Leaving her dress as is, exposing the black thong she wore that did little to hide her shaved vagina and allowing her ass to be on full display to whoever was still up in the wee hours to see her. As she walked to her front door, she pulled her phone out of her purse and glanced at the time and wondered why Trey's car was parked in front of her door at 5:17 a.m. Tossing her phone back in her purse, she retrieved her keys and let herself inside, locking the door behind her and headed up one of the double stairways that lead to the upstairs where she slept on one side of the massive 5 bedroom, 3 bathroom mini mansion and her parents slept all the way on the other. Dropping her shoes and purse on her all white thick carpeted bedroom floor, she wriggled herself out of the tight navy blue and black striped Nautical inspired Christian Dior dress she wore that had risen with every step she took to get to her bedroom. Making her way down the hallway dressed in nothing but a black strapless push up bra and matching black thongs, Keisha opened her parents door, peeked in and saw them both in a deep sleep snoring loudly as if one was trying to out snore the other. Shutting their door back quietly, she then went back down the stairs searching the house to see if she spotted Trey asleep anywhere, cause a surprise was what she had in store for him. After searching the whole second floor with no signs of Trey anywhere, as if a light bulb glowed above her head, it dawned on her where he may have been hiding. Opening the door to their humongous soundproof basement that had the layout of a studio apartment, she locked the door so no one could come down without calling down on the intercom that set on the wall next to the mirror tinted glass window in order to gain entry. She walked her five foot seven, 158lb. frame down the steps with the hopes that when she got to the bottom and walked around the corner he would be there. The anticipation was killing Keisha with each step, as the effects of her night were still evident. To her delight, Trey was laying on one of the red butter soft couches asleep.

Keisha smiled from ear to ear and walked over to the makeshift bar and made herself a glass of Jack Daniels and Coca-Cola with two ice cubes. Stirring her fingers inside the glass to mix the contents up, with her back towards him, she never heard him creep up behind her. Smacking her right ass cheek playfully, Keisha jumped almost having a heart attack at how scared she was, all the while holding her drink. Turning around to face him, she put her free hand to her chest and said, "Trey, boy you scared the shit out of me!" Punching him in his chest, she joined him in the laughter and added, "I owe you one for that buddy. Fix a drink and come sit with me." Trey put his index finger to his lips while looking Keisha in the eyes with a serious face and in a low tone saying, "Shhhh, girl be quiet before Tone or Crystal come down here and catch us!"

"Anyway, Trey they are both in bed sleep, I looked in their room before I searched the house for you when I saw your car out front!" She told him adding, "and besides the room is soundproof, they couldn't hear what is going on down here if two fire trucks were blaring horns and ten thousand people was screaming at the top of their lungs! Another thing, I'm 24 years old and therefore a fucking adult, not 12 with milk behind my ears. So if you are worried about them coming down, don't, cause I locked the door from the inside so they would have to call down on the intercom and one of us would need to let them in!" A devilish grin spread across his face, then he asked, pointing to the door that led to the back yard, "So, what about this door right here?"

"Shit!" she mumbled aloud to no one in particular, walked over to the door and applied the 3 deadbolt locks. Facing him, she asked, "Satisfied?" Trey walked over to the bar and grabbed a shot glass filling it with two shots of the Patron Silver tequila, and walked towards the red loveseat where Keisha was sitting waiting for him to join her. Plopping down on the chair, Trey closed his eyes and put his head back resting it on the chair.

"You look beat, like you had a long day. What's the deal with you?" she asked, downing the Jack and Coke in two or three gulps. "Come here and let me make you feel better." Keisha sat her glass on the triangular smoke red glass table that sat in the middle of the floor, got down on her knees in front of him and began unfastening his belt along with his pants. Trey pulled his phone out of his pants pockets before she pulled them down to his ankles, checked the time and seen that it was now 6 a.m. and he had 9 missed calls from Scarlett. He sat the phone down on the arm of the chair and decided he would deal with Scarlett later. Pulling his boxer briefs down, Keisha didn't waste time wrapping her lips around his semi hard dick and began sucking and slurping until it was rock hard the way she wanted it. While she continued to suck him, she managed to remove her bra and thong as Trey rose to his feet and began fucking her mouth in a slow rhythmic motion. Removing him from her mouth Keisha rose to her feet, and walked towards the couch where they were once sitting, dug in the cushion and came out with a gold Magnum condom. Handing him the condom, Keisha climbed on the couch with her back to him and her knees planted in the couch in a doggy style position so he could enter her from the back. Trey applied the condom to his rock hard dick, looking her in the eyes as she looked back over her shoulder watching him entering her. "Yes, Trey baby hit it! I've been wanting this for so longgggg, hit it boyyyy...YESSSSSSS!" She screamed out. As Trey

138

continued to pound Keisha from behind all he could think of was how this was sweet revenge at Tone's expense for fucking his girlfriend. 'You fuck my bitch nigga, I'mma fuck your daughter and I hope that pussy is as good' he thought to himself. "Is it good bitch?" Trey asked, as he began pumping harder and harder feeling himself about to explode. After twenty minutes of pounding his friend's daughter, Trey was standing in the bathroom of the basement washing his genitals so he could depart Tone's house and make his way home to try and talk with Scarlett. As he exited the bathroom, Keisha walked up to him covered in a pink towel and asked, "Well, will I see you again?" Handing him his phone, Trey told her he would see her again as long as she was able to keep quiet about their dealings. Keisha laughed and removed the towel that was wrapped around her and began drying his testicles and groin area. Once she was done she told him to store her number in his phone, while asking her for the digits she dropped down on her knees and with each digit she gave him she sucked him that many times until the number was complete and stored. Rising to her feet, Keisha pulled his underwear and pants up, kissed him on the cheek and told him, "Don't be a stranger and make sure you call me later Trey, cause I want some more already!" Trey smiled and smacked her ass lightly as she walked past him and got in the shower. Fixing his clothes, Trey told her he would hit her up later and walked to the top of the steps, unlocked the basement door and let himself out of the front door, locking the bottom lock behind him. During the whole drive to his house Trey reflected on how his night began and eventually ended, with an extra eighty grand in his pocket that Tone had given him for being there for him during the Cadillac boys' incident. Trey knew a vacation was needed, as he laughed to himself when the thought of Tone damn near setting his self on fire when they torched the 'Deacon mobile' for fear of someone witnessing the car at the scene of the crime. "Stupid mother fucker," he said aloud as he continued to drive in silence. Knowing he wanted to kill both Scarlett and Tone for crossing the line and sleeping with one another behind his back, he just couldn't seem to stay mad at Scarlett for what she had done because of the sneaky shit that he was doing constantly behind her back, and he figured getting caught with Maya evened the score. Even though Scarlett paid Maya to do it, he knew she had a thing for him a long time ago, which didn't make it difficult for her to make the decision to come along for a free trip out of town, along with the sexual fling and the money to top things off. As for Tone, he couldn't see himself killing him because they had been through too much together over the past 15 years, and not only that, he knew how deep down in his heart he couldn't kill him over a woman, even if it was Scarlett. But he had crossed the line and his phat ass daughter and wife was gonna pay the price for his mistake, not even caring if he found out. Trey knew going to war with Tone was not an option, but it was something he was prepared to do and making both Keisha and Crystal fall for him was going to be a quick karma, one that if Tone found out he would have to live with forever. "Karma's a bitch!" Trey said aloud, laughing to himself. Breaking him out of his trance, Trey grabbed his phone from his pocket as it rung. Knowing who the caller was from the sound of the ringtone, he smiled as he answered, "Hey my beautiful favorite lady in the world!"

"Hey Trey, my son, what are you up doing early this morning?" asked Italy, as she sat in her living room smoking a cigarette.

"On my way home to get some rest, I've been out all night, but enough about me, how are you and Ronnie loving life in Puerto Rico?"

Inhaling and exhaling her cigarette, Italy smiled at Trey's question and said, "Puerto Rico is nice baby, you gotta come visit sometime."

"Tell Trey I said what's up!?" Ronnie yelled out, leaning over the couch where Italy laid and kissed her on the cheek.

"Tell Ronnie, I said what's up? And I will be up there to see y'all both very soon."

"Ok, Trey boy, tell my baby Scarlett I said hello, and tell her I said call me sometimes!"

"Ok mom I will tell her."

"Oh, I meant to say thanks for the edible arrangements, it was so pretty I didn't want to eat it," Italy said, smiling from ear to ear taking puffs from the cigarette.

"You're welcome mom, I'm glad you liked it."
Pulling in the parking lot next to Scarlett's truck, Trey continued to talk to Italy as he wondered what Scarlett could have been doing. Ending the call with his mom, Trey smiled to himself when he thought about how much he missed his mother and made a mental note to book a flight to Puerto Rico to not only visit her, but take a plunge into their night life over there that he had heard so much about. Getting out of his car, Trey locked his doors and walked to his house. Just before he entered he received a text message from Deb,

saying how much she missed him and would love to see him today being as though she was off of work. Trey replied back telling her that sounded like a plan and he would call her later when he could get away from Scarlett. Placing his phone in his Louis Vuitton holster that was attached to his belt Trey entered the house, walked up the staircase and noticed Scarlett had packed all of his clothes and shoes neatly in bags. Looking through the bags Trey laughed to himself at the thought of him moving and not living in the same household with her. With eighty grand in his bank account and money he had saved in the safe at Tina's, he knew where ever he moved he would be very comfortable. Unaware that he was home, Scarlett exited the bathroom in a see through silk pink robe that he had purchased her for Valentine's Day that did little to cover her ass cheeks. Entering the bedroom, she jumped, startled when she seen him sitting on the side of the bed. "Trey you scared the shit out of me! Why do you have your shoes on in my house?" she asked. Giving her a questionable stare, Trey patted the bed beside him and told her to have a seat. Folding her arms, Scarlett leaned her body's weight onto one leg and said, "For what, I don't wanna sit next to you, and I would appreciate if you would get your dirty clothes you are wearing off of my bed! On top of that your stuff is neatly packed in the living room waiting for you to take them with you wherever you gonna live!" Standing up Trey stood in front of Scarlett looking her in her eyes, close enough that he could feel her breath on his top lip. "First of all, you packing my shit was really all for nothing because I'm not going anywhere. Second you are gonna sit down on this bed and like I said we are gonna get to the root of our problems, then together WE will make the decision whether I stay or go, is that understood?!" Scarlett looked Trey in the eyes and never before had she seen him so serious. On one note she felt like she did want to sit down and work through their problems but on another she really felt like space is what they needed because the shit they were going through was really too much to bear. Not able to hold his gaze, a single tear escaped her right eye as she put her arms through his and began hugging him tightly as the rest of the tears began to fall and damping the black V-neck POLO t-shirt that he wore. Wrapping his arms around her body, Trey squeezed her back, running his hands up and down her back as the thin silk robe clung tightly against her skin making her body feel softer than it normally was under his hands. Letting go of the embrace, Scarlett grabbed his head putting both hands on opposite sides and pulled his face to hers and began to kiss him passionately. Trey untied the strings on her robe, exposing her naked body from behind the silk lace fabric. Still locked in a tongue wrestling kiss Scarlett fumbled with his belt, full of lust, trying desperately to unfasten it. Once unfastened, she moved to his pants as she unbuttoned and then unzipped them pushing them down to his ankles. Doing the same with his black Ralph Lauren boxer briefs she pushed them down, grabbing a hold of his rock hard erection and allowed her robe to fall to the floor she began backing up to the wall with him inside her hand. Once Scarlett's back was against the wall, she hoisted up her left leg as he held her leg up while palming her buttocks and guided his dick inside of her as he began pumping in and out of her still locked in an orgasmic toe curling tongue wrestling kiss. Unlocking lips, Scarlett moaned out in pleasure as Trey filled her womb with his massiveness and lifted her legs up and palmed her other ass cheek while continuing to plunge in and out of her pussy. "Yes baby, give it to me it feels soooo good!" she moaned

143

in his ear. Still cradling her in his arms, Trey turned around moving from against the wall and tripping over his pants that were still around his ankles and laid her on the bed on her back while still deep inside of her. Whispering in her ear, Trey told Scarlett how good she felt and how much he loved her, "Damn baby, you feel so good! This pussy is mine and I need you!" Scarlett arched her back and with both hands she cupped and squeezed her breasts while turned to one side, with her mouth open and ass hanging off of the bed she gave Trey full control of her as he held her lower half of her body in his hands while she began to shake uncontrollably from the earth shattering orgasms she had back to back. "Oooooohhhhh" she cried out as the last orgasm shook her body until she was calm again. Trey felt her explode four times on his dick as he continued to pump in and out of her, feeling himself bulge up and ready to explode. He was taken aback as Scarlett pushed him off of her and stood to her feet. Looking at her quizzically, Trey let out sigh and yelled out, "What the fuck are you doing babe, I was just about to cum!" Reaching down Scarlett grabbed her robe off the floor and placed it back on, leaving it untied so that her front was totally exposed. "Well, I got mines and I'm sorry you didn't get yours. I'm pretty sure you have someone to help you with that. I'm going to take a shower and when I'm done I expect you and your shit to be gone out of my house and out of my life!" Mouth wide open, Trey stood there in disbelief with his erect dick still in his hand, boxers and pants still around his ankles, watching as Scarlett rolled her eyes and walked off to the direction of the bathroom, slamming the door when she got there leaving him standing in the floor frustrated. Trey pulled his briefs and pants halfway up, holding them with one hand just above his knees. Walking like a duck with his pants halfway up, Trey thought to himself, 'this bitch can't be serious', frustrated with Scarlett for the foul way she had just tried to play him. Checking the doorknob of the bathroom door, his anger began to rise realizing she had locked the door from the inside. Trey smiled as he tried to plead with Scarlett to open the door so they could continue or he would be able to clean himself up and go about his way. "Scarlett baby, open the door please! How are you gonna do me like this babe? I'm so horny for you, open the door babe so I can at least wash my dick!" "Trey, please go away! I have to get ready for work and I need time to get over this bullshit you got me going through!"

"So you are just gonna fuck me, get your nut and tell me to get the fuck out?" Tears streamed down her face as Scarlett leaned over the sink with her hands looking at herself in the mirror. Wiping her tears away, Scarlett let her robe drop down to her ankles and turned toward the shower, turned on the shower water adjusting the temperature and got in allowing the steamy hot water to envelope her body. "Uhhhh yes, Trey I was horny and in need of your touch and to have you near, now that I came I'm good for now, but I need my space from you." Walking away from the door, Trey went inside the hall closet and grabbed a bar of soap and a wash cloth, headed to the kitchen sink and began washing his genitals. Once he was done, he fixed his clothes buttoning his pants and belt and grabbed 2 of the 6 humongous trash bags that Scarlett had filled with his clothes. He stormed down the steps and exited the house, walked down the walkway and sat his bags on the ground leaning against his trunk. Going back and forth into Scarlett's house and grabbing the remaining 4 bags, two at a time, Trey stuffed 3 of them in his backseat and the rest fit perfectly in the trunk of his Mercedes. He climbed in the driver's seat, pulled out a pen and paper and scribbled a small note: *"This is for you to take care of whatever you need to take care of! I hope it is enough, enjoy your days Scarlett. No need to thank me. Trey"*.

Once he was done writing the note he reached in his glove compartment and grabbed $10k, exited his car with the money and the note and headed back to the house. Once inside, he walked upstairs to the kitchen, opened the frigidaire and set the money and note inside of it on the top shelf. Scarlett was sure to find the money there. Closing the frigidaire, he walked through the house checking to see if there was anything else he wanted to take along with him while Scarlett remained in the bathroom still taking a shower. Checking the bathroom knob again, he realized that she had still had it locked. As he turned to leave the thought of him leaving his key on the floor and locking the bottom lock crossed his mind but he thought against it and left out the house locking both the top and the bottom locks and got back into his car. Settling inside of his car he turned the volume of the BOSE sound system up a notch listening to an artist by the he continued to drive his phone began to ring over the car speakers breaking him out of the comfort zone that the music put him in. Not recognizing the number on his caller I'd he pressed the button on the steering wheel and answered the call, "Hello".

"Hi boo! I see you got your phone back." said Consuela.

"Uh yes, but who am I speaking with?" Trey questioned. He knew it had to be a client because that was the only phone he had misplaced and now as he listened to the deep accent on the line, he realized it was Consuela he was speaking with. After a quick thought, he realized that he didn't recognize the number was because it was stored in his other phone and made a mental note to go and pick up another phone but quickly dismissed the thought when he realized he could just call his service provider and get another line on the phone he already had. Listening in on Consuela as she continued to speak, Trey turned the radio volume up so he could hear her more clearly as he continued making his way to Tina's house.

"So, I just so happened to be riding to Chevy Chase Maryland to do a little bit of shopping and I needed some company to come along, being as though you are my new knight in shining armor I feel obligated to take you shopping and lunch with me. It's a beautiful Saturday afternoon, so how about I come and pick u up around 5pm sharp?"

"Ok Consuela, sounds like a plan. I will give you the address to where I am around 3pm, is that cool?"

"Yes Trey, I will see you then." she said ending the call on that note. Once the call ended the music began playing again and Trey smiled at the thought of having a woman spoiling and showering him with gifts. As he continued the drive to Tina's house, thoughts of Scarlett invaded his mental again. All he wanted to do was fix the issues they were having before they got out of hand and irreparable. Knowing that separation could only do one of two things and that's bring them closer making them realize that they needed each other or make them grow all the way apart and never be able to rekindle or get back together. He knew he would sit her down and have conversation with her to fix things, 'maybe I will take her to Puerto Rico with me and rekindle our love and get things back the way they used to be down there' he thought to himself as he pulled up behind Tina's Range Rover.

CHAPTER 9

Trey sat beside Tina eating spicy buffalo wings dipped in ranch dressing, one of his favorite appetizers, while sitting on her futon in her bedroom. After bringing his 6 bags of clothes and shoes in her house and placing them in her second bedroom that she never used, they conversed about the status of their massaging venture that they were both knee deep in. Tina went into the safe and showed him all the money they were accumulating together, as they both sat on the floor counting the money together.

Counting up $26k they both smiled at how much they had made in such a short period of time. Tina informed him that for the remaining twenty-eight days in the month of July, they both were booked with clients. It seems as soon as their ads went up on the numerous online sites, they both had clients calling and emailing them from everywhere looking for their services. While they sat there on the futon continuing to finish off eating the remaining buffalo wings, Trey started to explain to Tina the events that occurred between him and Scarlett that morning that had him feeling as if he had *blue balls*. Ready to pounce on Tina as if she was a medium well done filet mignon and he was a starving lion that hadn't been fed in two weeks. As she sat next to him, naked with only a pink G-string that barely covered her pussy, she looked him the eye while sucking the sauce and the ranch off of her fingers slow and seductively one at a time. "Awwwww, poor baby! Do you need mommy to make you feel better?" she questioned laughing aloud at what Scarlett had did to him while teasing him as if he was an infant baby.

After applying the hand sanitizer that set on the nightstand next to Tina's bed, Trey wiped his hands clean with a napkin to get the gritty sauce off of them from the wings they just ate. Trey gathered up the trash standing up and tossing the hand sanitizer at her with intentions on hitting her lightly with it for teasing him, but she caught it with both hands still laughing at her own joke. "Pull ya pants down Trey and stand right here!" Doing exactly what he was told after tossing the trash in the can, Trey unbuckled his belt pulling his pants and briefs down with one tug as he stood in front of her. Scooting up off the floor and onto the futon so she could be face first with his shaft, Tina took the sauce from wings she just ate and ran it all around his shaft and then down to his ball and began devouring him. She sucked and slurped him, going from the tip of his shaft to underneath his balls while licking the sauce from her hands and fingers at the same time. While holding him in one hand she grabbed her phone and dialed a number with the other and placed it on speaker so she could talk 'hands-free', she continued to suck him as a female voice answered. "Hey Tina!" Shay spoke.

"What are you doing?" Tina questioned while still slurping him as he stood erect above her with his head back and eyes closed.

"Nothing, in the house bored as shit. Why, you want me to come over?"

"Yeah, I have a surprise for you and don't wear any panties!" Shay giggled, told her okay and she was leaving out now. Hanging up the phone, Tina tossed the phone on the futon and continued to suck him like a vacuum. As if realizing she forgot to tell her something, Tina picked up the phone and called Shay back letting her know that the door was unlocked and she would be in her room waiting for her with a big surprise, "And lock the door back behind you!"

Shay answered, "Ok, I will be there in 5 minutes." After hanging up with Shay, Tina rose from the futon and told Trey to get naked and leave the sauce from the buffalo wings along with the ranch dressing on his dick and testicles while she ran downstairs to unlock the door for a special guest. When Tina left the room Trey was out of his clothes in a split second standing exactly where she left him when she returned. "When she comes I want you to fuck her like she stole something, cause she deserves it after she embarrassed you the way she did in that hotel that night in front of me and Scarlett!" she told him as she sat back down in front of him on the futon. Wrapping her lips around the head of his penis without using her hands, Tina deep throated his penis until the head was down her throat and her tongue was licking the dressing from the wings off of his testicles. Trey leaned his head back and closed his eyes in ecstasy while his mouth fell open from the way Tina worked his dick with the warmness of her mouth and tongue. Reaching her hands behind his back she grabbed hold of his ass cheeks and pulled him closer to her trying to devour more of his hard penis down her throat. Releasing his ass she held his penis with both hands and licked her saliva and the remaining sauce off of it, working her way from his testicles to the mushroom head where she licked the precum that oozed out of his dick head. "Mmmmmm, mmmmmm, mmmmm boy you got some good dick," Tina stated looking from his penis to his eyes as a tear fell from her watery eyes. Trey smiled at her as he looked in amazement at how she cleaned his dick and balls without a trace of sauce left,

"Babe that's you with that good ass head on your shoulders, that shit felt like I was in some wet warm pussy." They both laughed in unison as they felt someone's presence in the room behind them, causing them both to turn and looked back. Shay was standing in the door nude rubbing her pussy with her right hand and using her left hand to squeeze and massage her left nipple, smiling as if she had just been caught doing something wrong. She looked from one to the other as Tina put up her hand was holding onto Trey's still erect shaft. Shay walked across the carpeted bedroom doing as she was told until she was inches in front of them both. Tina looked her in the eyes, with the same index finger she used to motion her to come to them with was now pointing to Treys dick as she told her, "Bitch, get on your mother fucking knees and obey this dick! First I want you to kiss it as if you speak French fluently and get it nice and wet, then while he lays back on the bed I want you to ride it and make it disappear in that sweet pretty ass of yours!" Without saying a word Shay was on her knees kissing and sucking on his hardness as if her life depended on it. She moaned softly while making loud slurping noises as she took him in and out of her mouth. Feeling his dick pulsate in her mouth letting her know at any moment he was about to cum, Shay closed her eyes as Tina felt the same as she continued to hold onto his throbbing penis with one hand. Removing him from Shay's mouth before he came, Tina told Trey to lay down on the bed while Shay ride her juicy tight ass on his dick. Trey laid back on Tina's bed on his back as Tina stood from the futon and retrieved a gold magnum condom and some lubricant from the nightstand next to her bed. Opening the condom pack and removing it from the wrapper, she place the condom on his erect mushroom head and guided it down his dick until it couldn't go down any further. She then squeezed the lubricant out of the bottle onto him with one hand and stroked him with the other until she felt as though she had applied enough of it. Rising off of the floor Shay climbed onto the bed and sat atop him backwards with her back to him as Tina squeezed more of the lubricant into her hand and applied it between Shay's ass cheeks, while she inserted a finger in and out of her ass. Removing her finger from inside of her, Shay sat down on Trey's swollen dick and began bouncing up and down riding him anally. Tina sat back on the futon with her vibrator and watched on as Shay rode him and cried out as if she were in pure ecstasy. "Ohhhhh, damn nigga you fucking my ass so good, I'm about to cummmmmmmm!! Riding this dick in my ass hurts so good babyyyyyy!!!! Yes Treyyyy, I'm cumming, I'm cumming, Ohh shit I'm cummmmmminnnnng!"

For the next forty-five minutes Tina watched as Trey had his way with Shay, not once joining in. After getting herself off with her vibrator she just sat back on the futon with her legs crossed and enjoyed the live show they were putting on in front of her. Only getting up once to go downstairs and retrieve a fresh bottle of Moet Rose, just to return and sit back in her same spot, legs crossed with a smile on her face. She loved the way her man handled and took control of Shay. After he was done releasing himself on her face, he rested his body on his knees in front of her while she laid on her stomach with her head up and her eyes closed waiting for him to finish cumming on her. Tina began to clap and say to them both, "Marvelous, Marvelous! Now the two of you need to change my sheets, after buying me a new pillow top mattress of course, and hop y'all sweaty cum dripping asses in the shower!"

"Trey boy you got that shit running down my face and my damn ass is killing me," Shay told him as she rose from the bed. With her face held high looking toward the ceiling, she held her hands to her face so she could stop the cum from dripping onto Tina's floor before they owed her new carpet as well. Watching Shay make her way to the bathroom, Tina put her hand out to Trey as he walked towards her. Looking at her as they smiled at each other, he placed his hand in hers as she slapped his hand, giving him a masculine handshake. They both burst out in laughter. "Boy you fucked the shit out of that hoe, like a G." She told him handing him the bottle of Rose then adding, "here take a sip and cool your sexy Hercules dick having ass down! When you done sipping go and wash my dick off cause from now on that muthafucka belongs to me!"

After popping the cork on the champagne and tipping the bottle up to his lips for a swig, he never once took his eyes off of Tina as she stood before him grinning with her hands on her hips with all of her weight leaning on her left hip. "Your dick huh? So when did you decide that this dick belonged to you and when were you gonna tell me?" he asked her smiling from ear to ear handing the bottle back to her. Accepting the bottle back from him, Tina took a swig from the bottle and said, "I'm telling you now boy, and please don't play with me. Oh and Miss Scarlett has been blowing your phone up, calling back to back at least three times in a row!"

"I'm not thinking about her, she play too many games and I'm over it." he told her grabbing his phone off of the futon and seeing that he did indeed have three missed calls from her, as well as two text messages. Checking his messages he read the first one which was

153

from Scarlett saying how much she needed him and still loved him even though she hated him for the hurtful shit he had done to her. She also explained that although she had done some things herself, she was willing to put it all on the table and start fresh by putting all the pain and drama behind them and start anew. Trey just stood there smiling to himself thinking Scarlett was a very confused woman, but he would give it some thought, after he gave some time to see what his life would be without her. Moving on to the second message he noticed it was a message from Tina telling him how handsome he was. Quoting her message aloud he looked at her and said, "You're so handsome!" Catching her off guard with the statement, she blushed as she took another sip of the champagne. "Yeah, boy you were looking sexy pounding that thing out, I wanted to tell her ass to leave and jump on you myself but I refrained because I needed to see you terrorize that hoe!" Glancing down at his still semi hard dick, she took it in her index fingers and exclaimed,

"Ewwwww boy, you are leaking and still dripping on my damn carpet!"

"Hell yeah, let me go and hop my ass in the shower and get cleaned up." Turning away from Tina about to go join Shay in the shower, she grabbed his arm and told him how there was no way she was gonna let him go and shower with her, then added, "so you might as well let that bitch finish so she can leave, cause I'm tired of her stank ass already! Matter of fact, come here and let me taste it before all of that nut drips on my damn carpet." Getting down on her knees in front of him, Tina placed the head of his penis in her mouth and worked her lips up and down the neck of it, sucking the remaining cum from out of him. When she felt that she got it all she rose from the floor as Shay was exiting the bathroom. "Damn, y'all are still at it?" Shay questioned entering the room using one of Tina's pink towels to dry off the remaining droplets of water that was running down her right arm. "Ummmm Shay don't you have something to say to Trey?" Tina questioned her then added, "and bitch what did you come over here in? Where are your clothes?" Shay smiled at Tina while dropping the towel on the bedroom floor and walked up to Trey. She gave him a hug then reaching up, she gave him a kiss on his cheek, stepped back with that same grin planted on her face and placed her right hand on her chest. "I just wanted to apologize to you for my actions that night in the hotel. I usually don't act like that but I was drunk and...." Before Shay could finish apologizing there was a loud bang on Tina's door as if the police was knocking, startling everyone as they all got serious looking from one to the other. "Who the fuck is knocking down my fucking door like the police?" Tina said walking to her window trying to see if she could recognize who it was from the window by the vehicle. As the banging continued, she spotted Scarlett's truck and knew exactly who it was and why. Turning around to face them, she looked at Trey and said "It's your bitch, Scarlett!"

Trey looked at Tina and told her, "Oh well, let her ass knock, I ain't fucking with her right now."

"I agree baby, but if she continues to knock on my door like that one of my neighbors will call the cops!"

"Oh well, what's gonna happen? Nothing. Man fuck her, I'm about to take a shower and you can deal with her." he told them both looking from one to the other as he walked out of the room and into the bathroom leaving them both standing there looking confused, closing the door behind him.

"You want me to answer it and tell her something for you?" Shay questioned as Tina walked past her and waved her hand in the air as if to say 'whatever'.

"Hell no, you can just see your way out the door and be on your way because I got shit to do and I'm not thinking about no damn Scarlett, that's his bitch!" Before entering the bathroom with Trey she turned and faced Shay and told her to make sure she lock the door behind her. Shay just looked on at the bathroom door that was basically closed in her face and thought to herself, 'Oh no this bitch did not just slam the door in my face and speak to me as if I'm some weak mother fucking bitch! Fuck her and that bitch ass nigga, shit, I got a trick for both of their asses. I'm still pissed that he put his fucking hands on me at that hotel that night anyway, with his big dumb dick having ass!' Shay scanned the room for something to put on, noticing Trey's clothes in a pile on the floor. Walking over to the pile of clothes, she grabbed his shirt, smelled it and was impressed by how good it smelled and put it on. She then walked over to Tina's dresser and opened one of the drawers finding a pair of gray sweatpants and placed them on as Scarlett continued to bang on the front door. While rummaging through Trey's pants pockets she took the $200 he had in them and began looking through his wallet as his phone began to ring. Tossing the wallet on the floor, Shay grabbed the ringing phone off of the futon and answered it when she seen Scarlett's name flash across the screen. "Hi, Scarlett." Hearing a different woman's voice other than Tina's had Scarlett puzzled and fuming mad cause she just knew she was being toyed with. "And who is this and why are you answering my man's phone?"

"Oh it's me, Shay. You remember me, don't you?" She questioned while walking back and forth, stuffing the money in her pockets, making her way down the stairs. Before Scarlett could answer her she said, "Oh and if you are looking for Trey, he can't come to the phone cause he is in the shower with Tina letting her wash that big ole dick of his that just came out of both of our pussies!" The anger in Scarlett was building as she listened to Shay, letting her words sink in. After Shay was done talking, all Scarlett could think was, 'I am about to go to jail if what this bitch is saying is true!'

"Bitch you need to put Trey on this phone or open this door before the fuck I break this bitch down, NOW!"

"Okay hun, gimme a second I will let you come in and see for yourself. Girl if that is your man, you need to get rid of his ass cause he don't give three fucks about your ass!" Shay grabbed her car keys and then the trench coat that she had worn over there and removed the phone from her ear as Scarlett began yelling obscenities. Opening the door with her car keys in one hand, her trench coat under her arm with Trey's phone in her other hand, she handed Scarlett his phone and commenced to walk past her as Scarlett stood in the doorway with her arms folded filled with rage as she looked at Shay as if she wanted to rip her throat out of her neck. Snatching his phone out of her hand and stepping in front of her as she tried to walk around her, Scarlett locked eyes with Shay, put her hand up to Shay's chest, leaned her head forward and smelled Shay's t-shirt. Knowing it was Trey's signature POLO V-neck that Shay had on and smelling his cologne and scent all in it, sent Scarlett over the edge. Before Shay could react Scarlett was all over her pounding and beating, stomping and kicking, scratching and dragging her in front of Tina's house for all who was outside on this nice summer day to see. She continued to beat Shay back into the house, in the living room where she beat her some more until she was satisfied with the ass whipping she gave her. As Shay laid in Tina's house unconscious bleeding on her carpeted floor, Scarlett kicked her in her face one more time with her black and white Chuck Taylor converse before charging up the steps to find both Tina and Trey so she could do to the both of them what she had just done to Shay; kick their asses. Reaching the top of the staircase Scarlett walked past the closed bathroom door and walked straight into Tina's bedroom where the scenery and the smell of sex hit her like an open punch to the face from Muhammad Ali, George Foreman and Mike

Tyson all at the same time. Seeing Trey's clothes and the POLO boxer briefs that she had bought him along with the still chilled bottle of Rose champagne that she knew he loved, the used condom on the bed and the sound of his voice along with Tina's coming from the closed bathroom door, where they were showering together, broke Scarlett's heart all over again and had tears running down her face. Her legs felt like they was ready to give out on her at any moment. Walking out of the bedroom she stopped in the hallway directly in front of the bathroom door, with her left hand on the knob and the bottle of Rose in her right hand; which she planned to use as a weapon starting with Tina's fucking head first. Just as she twist the knob on the door, realizing it was unlocked, she felt the most excruciating pain shoot from her stomach down to her pelvis causing her to release the door handle, drop the bottle and bend over clenching her stomach. Suddenly she felt light headed with an urgency to vomit. Knowing that something was definitely wrong with her, Scarlett told herself that she had to get out of this house and fast! Still hunched over holding her stomach she descended back down Tina's steps, slowly, to the living room area where Shay had disappeared, leaving a trail of blood from the middle of the floor where she once laid to the front door where she had escaped, leaving the door wide open for anyone to come in. Scarlett walked out of Tina's house, closing the door behind her. She noticed her car keys, both hers and Trey's cell phone and his torn shirt that she had ripped off of Shay's back on the ground next to the front door. As the pain she once felt began to subside a bit, she picked up both the phones and her car keys and decided to throw his phone back down on the ground cracking the screen on impact. She got in her truck and started the ignition and drove away feeling light headed as the pain she felt in Tina's house felt like it was beginning to return.

Totally oblivious to what just took place on the opposite side of the bathroom door and what would have went down had Scarlett not felt the surge of pain that took over her body, that caused her to leave the house, Trey slapped Tina on her wet ass cheeks lightly as he stood behind her admiring the roundness of her ass when she turned her back on him giving him a show, bending forward to turn the shower nozzle, shutting the water off. "Ooooh boy that felt good. You better stop before you start something," she told him reaching from behind the curtain grabbing both of their towels off of the towel rack that sat next to the tub. Handing him his towel she opened the curtain as they both dried off, noticing for the first time the door being cracked open and not shut like she had it.

Stepping out of the shower cautiously, Tina walked towards the door telling him how she could have sworn that she shut the door completely. Wrapping the towel around her back and underneath her arms to cover her breast but leaving the bottom of her ass cheeks exposed, she opened the door completely and yelled out for Shay, "Shay! Shay I know your ass hear me calling you?!" Noticing the champagne bottle laying sideways on the floor on the other side of the door and the pink wet stain on her tan carpet, she stormed out of the bathroom grabbing the bottle off of the floor cursing under her breath as she looked in both rooms for Shay before heading downstairs.

"No, this bitch didn't!"

"What, what's wrong and why are you running around the house like a mad woman with an empty champagne bottle?"

"Because, that bitch just gonna throw the Rose bottle on the floor in front of the bathroom door and let the shit just waste out and stain my fucking carpet! I just had this fucking carpet cleaned, she gonna pay for it this fucking time! Shaaayyyy!"

Wrapping his towel around his waist, he stepped out of the bathroom, stepping over the wet stain on the carpet and entered the bedroom and began to search around for his phone as Tina called out for him from the bottom of the steps as if something was wrong. "Trey...Oh my God baby! Oh my god, please come down here! Baby look!"

"Awwww man, I know this dumb bitch ain't walk out of here with my phone," he said to himself as he headed out of the room, through the hallway and down the steps to join Tina as she stood at the bottom of the

160

stairs with her hand covering her nose and mouth as tears rolled down her cheek. "What is it babe, what you......."was all he could manage to get out as he reached the bottom of the steps and stood beside her, taking the state of the living room that was in a total disarray. "What the fuck, How the fuck, When the fuck? Don't fucking tell me....." he said to himself not realizing he was saying what he was thinking aloud, enough for her to hear as they both looked on from the broken glass table to the broken lamp that laid shattered on the floor from the trail of blood that went from the middle of the floor to the front door. Trey walked to the door trying not to step on the glass or blood, opened the door and stepped out front barefoot still dressed in just his towel. Noticing his phone on the ground, he reached down picking it up and checking out the cracked screen wondering to himself how the fuck did it get all the way out here anyway.

"Is it broken?" Tina asked standing in the door way watching him with her arms folded.

"Yeah, it's cracked pretty bad, but fuck that I can get a new one later."

"Where is the business phone though? Last time I saw it, it was on the nightstand next to my bed. Come in the house and put some clothes on and stop walking on that dirty ass ground with no shoes and socks on." Looking at her, managing a smile he walked back towards her while she continued to stand in the doorway with her arms folded with his face inches from hers and said, "What are you my mother or my ummmmm?"

"Ummmm shit, don't play with me Trey" she told him grabbing his towel and pulling him inside of the house with her. "Help me clean this shit up in here and then we can call them hoes to find out what the fuck happened, because they are going to pay for my shit! Then we can get back to business and the money. Ain't that's how you say it baby?" she asked him as they both started to laugh at her trying to talk like him. "Yeah that's it babe, we definitely need to get to the money. I got a date with a client around 5 pm, but I will call her in a minute to let her know that I am still gonna be there. But fuck all of that right now, come and sit down on these steps so I can taste what's under that towel!" Walking up a few steps, Tina took off her towel and laid it down underneath of her as she sat on it and laid back on the steps behind her. She proceeded to put her legs up and spread them apart as far as she could, continued to smile while looking him directly in his eyes and said, "Bon Appetite!!"

Chapter 11

Tone entered the hotel suite allowing Scarlett to open the door for him to come in and then shutting it back behind him and securing the locks once he was inside. Dressed in nothing but a purple lace LaPerla boy shorts with the matching purple lace bra looking as if her garments were painted on and she just jumped out of the pages of a LaPerla catalogue or 'Straight Stuntin' magazine. After locking up she turned around to face him catching him looking down at her ass and walked into him with open arms. While they stood there in a tight embrace, Tone's hands found her ass cheeks as he palmed them and then smacked and rubbed them while whispering in her ear. "Damn, you feel good in my arms girl. And you know I love the way you pin your hair up like that, it is soooo sexy to me!" She smiled at him thinking to herself he was just saying that cause he wanted to get some of her pussy, 'and giving him some is what I plan on doing after

162

having the type of day that I had; shit, if it's good for the goose then it's definitely good for the gander!' Stepping out of his embrace she walked to the bed holding his hand as he followed. Feeling his eyes on her ass again, she put a little extra switch in her hips allowing her ass to jiggle a little more than usual giving him a show. "Sit down, I need to talk to you about something." she told him crawling up on the bed and then under the covers leaving the upper half of her body out as she leaned against the head board facing him. "What's up Scarlett, what is bothering you?" he asked her, kicking his shoes off and taking a seat on the bed in front of her giving her his undivided attention. "I'm pregnant......."

"So are you going to come and move in with me and live like the king that you are or are you just gonna let me and all of this beauty pass you by?" Consuela asked waving her hands around in the air motioning the atmosphere around them, before allowing it to rest on his chest. Trey laid back on the presidential king size bed in Consuela's master bedroom dressed in nothing but a pair of Hermes boxer briefs she had purchased him earlier that day when she took him on a fifty thousand dollar shopping spree. Palming her ass cheeks as she sat atop him in her yellow, silk and lace Hermes panties while loving the way the material looked and felt on her soft, smooth skin. Trey just sat there smiling and thinking to himself how he could get rich quickly and benefit from this crazy ass chick, Consuela, that was willing to share everything she had with someone she barely knew.

◊◊◊

After making love with Tina on her steps and helping her clean the mess Scarlett and Shay made, he eventually left her house and hooked up with Consuela having her to meet him in front of the grocery store, cause he was very careful about letting her know where he or anyone that could lead to him resided. While waiting for her to pull up, he called Scarlett's phone back to back only to get her voicemail. After the twentieth time he gave up and figured that she must have been ignoring him because she was mad. That is when he decided that he would call Shay instead. "Hey boo?!" Shay answered. "Don't boo me bitch, what the fuck happened at Tina's with you and Scarlett? And where is my $200 that mysteriously disappeared from my pants pocket when you did?"

"I'm sorry Trey baby," she told him as she began to cry into the phone. "But I was so upset over the way you and Tina treated me as if I wasn't shit, that I just took the money without thinking clearly. So then when I was leaving, I figured I would tell Scarlett that you fucked me and Tina and let her catch the two of you in the shower together, then I would have gotten even with you both for the way I was treated! Trey, I'm so sorry." Trey couldn't believe the words that were coming out of this dumb bitch's mouth.

"So what happened once you let her in, and how did all the blood get on the floor and Tina's shit get broken up?" he questioned her.

"Trey, she beat my ass and all I can really remember was her smelling your t-shirt that I had put on to cover myself up with and she must have smelled your scent or something cause then she just went crazy. I remember waking up with my nose, mouth and right eye bleeding badly on Tina's floor, then I just got up and drove myself home bleeding all over my car?" Trey almost felt sorry for Shay cause he knew that Scarlett only got physical when she was extremely pissed off, and knowing Shay must have pushed her buttons to the limit then she deserved the ass whipping that she got. Besides she had stolen from him which was another reason why she deserved exactly what she had got. Just as the thought ran across his mind, Consuela was calling him on the other line to let him know that she had arrived.

"Alright Shay, look I will deal with you on this matter later, I got some other business to attend to so clean yourself up and I will talk to you later when I'm done."

"Ok, Trey baby and I wanna make..." was all she could manage to say as Trey clicked her off and spoke with Consuela.

"I'm pulling up as we speak, mi poppy amor!" she told him. Looking straight ahead out of the Mercedes windshield Trey saw when the white Maybach Landaulet pulled up in front of the grocery store. Knowing it was her he managed to grab everything out of his car starting with his blue 'magic' pills, wallet, condoms and both phones. Exiting the vehicle he locked the locks, walked across the parking lot and entered the elegant car as the driver opened the rear door for him, closing it back once he was inside. Before he could settle comfortably in his seat, Consuela jumped on his lap and showered him with kisses. From the time he entered the vehicle with her, throughout the whole day they were shopping nonstop going from store to store and buying everything he had dreamed about having from items he couldn't afford to expensive clothing he couldn't pronounce as well as expensive jewelry, he got laced.

◊◊◊

Laying there underneath her while admiring her beauty, he tried everything to keep Scarlett off of his mind, but no matter what he did or how hard he tried she kept dancing across his brain. "I would love to move in with you, but before I do there are a few things that we are gonna have to discuss and get a clear and concise understanding on." Laying her breast against his chest she leaned in and gave him a peck on the lips. "Anything for you papi, we can talk. I just want to spoil you and make you my man, treat you like a king and show you how it feels to live like a boss with a boss bitch on your arm." Trey laughed at the way Consuela spoke, he found it sexy but humorous at the same time. "What, why you laugh at me?"
"No reason baby, I just love the way you talk that's all. It is soo sexy to me." Grabbing the remote off of the bed Consuela pressed a button and Anita Baker's greatest hits CD began softly playing throughout the surround sound in the room. "I love this album, it is one of my favorites!" he told her.

"Mine too Trey. So what do we need to do to move you in our home tonight, cause I enjoy your company and I think I love you!" Trey couldn't believe his ears or his luck. On one end he was willing to move in with Consuela and enjoy the fruits of her labor but on the other hand he knew that he would have to be committed to her cuckoo ass, and being committed to her was something that he wasn't able to do because his mind and heart belonged to someone else or better yet belonged to others. He knew in order to make things work to his benefit in dealing with this type of woman he had to come up with a plan but first he needed to get with

Tina so they could put their minds together on how they could profit from Consuela.

"Consuela baby, give me a few days to make my mind up on what I want to do and I will let you know. I will stay the night with you tonight and then leave tomorrow afternoon. Is that okay with you?" Trey asked her as she sat up looking down at him smiling from ear to ear.

"Okay papi, we need to celebrate!" Trey just laid there shaking his head thinking to himself, 'damn this is a nutty ass broad'. Grabbing his new IPhone that she had purchased him earlier that laid beside him, he decided to call Tone while Consuela left the bedroom only to return with a small mirror, a sandwich bag of cocaine and a pack of top rolling paper. Trey continued to watch her while listening in on the phone, waiting for Tone to pick up, only to get his voicemail. After calling twice, and still not getting no answer he decided to text him letting him know that it was important for him to call back as soon as possible. Deciding to call Keisha to see if she had heard from him while still keeping his eyes glued to Consuela, Keisha eventually picked up on the third ring.

"Oh my God, I was just thinking about you and then my phone rang. I miss you!" Keisha told him.

"I miss you too Keisha, but I was trying to reach your father, have you talked to that nigga?"

"Oh, so you just called me to look for him... and I thought you was feeling me like I am feeling you?!"

Not wanting to piss Keisha off, he knew he had to fake it with her so his plan that he had in store for her and her deceitful ass parents would play out how he planned it. Lifting up off of the bed, he decided to excuse himself and have his conversation with Keisha in private. "I'll be back," he told Consuela digging in his pants pockets grabbing his business phone while she just sat there on the bed Indian style dumping cocaine on the mirror. "Ok, hurry up back papi, you want something to drink?" "Yeah, Patron and sprite Consuela, give me a minute or two." he told her putting the phone back to his ear as he stepped in the bathroom closing the mirrored door behind him. "Listen Keisha, I am feeling your sexy little ass, you and them sweet ass lips."

"Oh so you did like how I use these sexy lips? What about this sweet, tight pussy?"

"Awww man Keisha, that pussy is the best." He told her. Sitting down on the steps of the hot tub he checked the missed calls on the business phone and smiled while continuing to converse with her, thinking how it was true that she did have some good pussy, head and ass! "So tell me Trey, how about you come over and get up with me tonight so we can finish where we left off?!" she suggested. Ready to end the call with her, he let her know that tonight wasn't a good night but tomorrow would be better. He then told her to have Tone to get in contact with him if she talked to him before he did. After hanging up with Keisha, he then called Tone's wife. "Hello," said Seleste answering the call trying to talk over the loud music that was playing in her background. "Hold on a second, I can barely hear you." Listening in on the call, Trey noticed that the noisy background on Seleste's end got quiet as she came back and spoke into the phone. "Hello, Trey?"

"Yeah babe, is this Seleste?" he asked not immediately recognizing her voice. "This is she, excuse me for all the loud noise in the background. I had to step out to take the call so I can hear you, but what's up boo?"

"Damn, where are you and why didn't I get an invite?" he flirted.

"Ok, you can come join me if you like. I'm at the 5 mile house by my lonesome having a few drinks."

"Alright that's cool babe, I might just take you up on that offer. But I was really calling to see if you heard from your husband. I been trying to reach him but he hasn't answered the phone."

"No, I haven't spoken to him since earlier, we got into a little argument about him not spending enough time with me and always running and playing in them streets. Then on top of that I overheard him on the phone trying to be sneaky telling some bitch he was gonna meet up with her. I know it was a bitch because I could overhear her voice coming through the phone when I walked down on his ass and he tried to turn the volume down on the phone. I'm not stupid." she told him then added, "But anyway how are you doing boo? How about you come down and have a few drinks with me cause I could definitely use some company." Trey thought about what she had just said to him and wondered if Tone was somewhere with Scarlett frolicking like two love struck fucking birds. "Yeah, that's cool babe. Give me about an hour and I will meet you there." Trey told her raising up from the steps of the hot tub.

Ending the call with Seleste, Trey took a leak in the gold plated toilet, washed his hands and stepped back in the room to join a waiting Consuela as she rose her

169

face from the mirror after taking a snort of a line of the white powder through a rolled up hundred dollar bill. Walking toward the mini bar that sat in the corner of the room, Trey took a glass and filled it halfway with the Patron Tequila and filled the rest of the glass with some chilled Sprite soda, just how he liked. By the time he reached the bed, Consuela was looking at him smiling while smoking a rolled up joint of the fruity smelling marijuana. Admitting to himself that the smell did smell good, but there was no way he was going to take a hit being as though he hated the way it made him feel. "Come here papi, come stand around here by the bed, I wanna taste that dick." Walking around to the side of the massive bed where she sat, Trey guzzled down the drink in his glass while allowing her to push his briefs down his legs until they reached the floor. Sitting the remainder of the still lit joint in the ashtray and pushing it down towards the bottom of the bed where the rest of her party favors were. She laid on her stomach while he stood before her and buried his penis in her mouth. Within seconds he was grabbing her hair and slowly pumping his erectness in and out of her mouth as she slurped, licked and deep throated him with perfection.

"Consuela baby, I have to make a run cause something has come up." he told her releasing her hair, he then stopped pumping in and out of her mouth and tried to concentrate on not cumming in her mouth although he know at the rate she was going if she continued he would cum down her throat any minute. Taking him out of her mouth she grabbed the neck of his dick and licked the pre-cum that was oozing out of his mushroom head. "Why you gotta go, and are you going to come back to sleep here with me?" she asked him looking up at him with the head of his dick inches away from her lips as if she was talking into a microphone. "Yes I'm coming back, but a friend of mines is in trouble and needs my assistance. So I'm gonna need you to drop me off to my car or get me a ride to it." Giving his mushroom head one last kiss, she raised up on the bed sitting on her knees and wrapped her arms around his neck and gave him a peck on the lips.

"Baby, do what you need to do. You can just borrow one of my cars for as long as you need it. But just make sure you call me and let me know if you're going to make it back to me as soon as you can because I need to be with you tonight, me and her." she told him slipping her right middle finger in her panties and then bringing it back out glistening. She rubbed it across his lips then stuck it in his mouth allowing him to taste her juices.

After washing up and changing into something that she had purchased for him earlier that day she handed him the keys to her black on black Bentley coupe, told him if he needed any cash that there was a nice amount stashed inside of the glove compartment, that she kept there in case of an emergency. Grabbing one of the many robes she owned out of her bedroom walk-in closet; 'she may as well be wearing nothing', he thought to himself as she placed the purple see through robe on tying the string around her waist as if to cover herself while still leaving everything exposed. She walked him to the garage and hugged him once more with a long passionate tongue wrestling kiss, and told him to drive careful and reminded him if he couldn't make it back to call and let her know as soon as possible. "But call me papi as soon as you make it to your destination so I can know that you made it safely."

Impressed with the way the Bentley took to the road and the way people in other cars stared at him when he pulled up to a light, Trey told himself there was no way he could let Consuela get away from him, especially the way she frivolously spent money on him. 'And who in the hell let's someone they barely know borrow their *Bentley*.' Dropping the top and exposing the black leather interior, Trey turned the music up, leaned his seat back and drove smoothly down the highway making his way to see the lovely Ms. Seleste.

◊◊◊

"Oh shit Scarlett, I'm about to cum!!!" Tone said as he held onto her waist pumping in and out of her in the dimly lit hotel room king size bed. "I'm cummminnnng!!" she cried out in ecstasy as they both climaxed at the same time. Head spinning from the combination of pain, frustration, revenge, pleasure and too much alcohol had Scarlett laying on her stomach sweating with tears streaming down her face. As she watched along at her man's friend, Tone, laying naked beside her after they just committed the ultimate act of betrayal, sex, for the second time since he had arrived earlier that morning. She began to feel the guilt overcome her, after the anger swept over her and she suddenly felt the need to be rid of him and to be alone to clear her head and figure out what her next move was going to be.

◊◊◊

After leaving University hospital's emergency room, Scarlett finally found out that this newfound sickness came from her being 8 weeks pregnant. She knew that calling Tone would be a bad idea at this point, but she needed the companionship of another man as well as a strong drink. All those feelings rushing through her made her continue to dial his number on her cell while checking into the nearest hotel. "I need a dose of satisfaction, like immediately!" she told him. He could hear it in her voice that something was bothering her and wanting to see her again anyway after their last encounter was definitely on his to do list, so he dropped what he was doing and ran to her aid. Once the phone call ended and Scarlett was able to strip down out of the mini jean shorts and one of Trey's POLO wife beaters she wore, she kicked off her Prada flip flops and placed her phone's ringer on silent. From the small bar in the room she poured herself a glass of Red Berry CIROC to the brim of the glass, leaving no room for a chaser. Every so often she would check her phone to see if Tone had called her to let her know that he had arrived and to her disappointment the only missed calls she would have would be from Trey and Tina, two people she did not have the energy to speak with at this time. She did have a missed call from Deb, whom she really needed to call back but under her condition she didn't have the energy to talk about work either. By the time Tone arrived, she was pouring her second round and feeling extra good from the first one. The look in his eyes when she settled back in the bed after she told him that she was pregnant was priceless and she couldn't hold back from laughing in his face once she explained that contrary to what he believed, she was pregnant by his homie and not him, or so she thought. With a big sigh of relief he then poured himself a drink, wiping the beads of sweat that had suddenly appeared on his forehead and sat back on the bed giving her his undivided attention as she began telling him how her day went. From the time she had seen and fucked Trey, to her whipping Shay's ass in Tina's house, down to fact that she had actually went over there to forgive him since she knew that was where he would be down to the moment that she found out that she was pregnant. She told him how he kept calling her back to back and leaving text after text telling her to call him. During the time that past, as they talked, when Trey would call she would show him her phone screen with his name and number and he would do the same, showing her when Seleste would call or when Trey would be calling him and they would both laugh making their significant others the butt of their jokes as they continued to ignore them. As if a magnetic force was pulling them together, his eyes found her breasts, while her eyes found his lips and before you knew it they were all over each other, kissing, touching and stripping off each other's clothes until they were fucking like wild animals. They stopped to take a CIROC break and was back at it again, steadily climaxing at the same time for the second time. "Damn that was good, Scarlett baby," Tone told her as he turned on his side to face her, leaning up on his elbow while resting his head on his hand. With the other hand he began rubbing her ass, then slipped his middle finger inside of her, gliding it in and out of her pussy, feeling the wetness from both her cum and his from him cumming inside of her. "How do you feel, are you ok?"

"No, I'm not ok Tone, and I wish you wouldn't do that!" she snapped in between sobs as she laid there sniffling with tears still streaming down her eyes. "I just wanna be left alone. Can you please leave?!" Stunned over her response, he removed his hands from between her legs and tried to take another approach and began rubbing her back while giving her small kisses on her shoulder telling her not to cry and that he was there for her. Still she didn't want to be bothered,

174

she arose from the bed and before entering the shower she told him to leave again, but this time with anger behind her every word. "Can you please get the fuck out of my hotel room and fucking leave me be! Please Tone, just go... I need to be alone." Tone sat up on the bed thinking to himself that 'bitches are truly fucking crazy' and just as the thought crossed his mind his phone began to ring. Seeing that it was Trey he went ahead and answered this time knowing that Scarlett was in the shower. "What's up Trey? Me and one of my good female friends was just talking about you." he said laying back on the bed resting his head on the pillow with his legs crossed with one hand behind his head and the other holding the phone to his ear. Scarlett emerged from the bathroom once she heard Tone mention Trey's name and listened on as he continued to have a conversation with him. Still nude, she walked on the side of the bed where he laid and put her hands on her hips and stared daggers into his eyes wondering what the hell his slick ass was up to. "As a matter of fact, here she is right here. She wants to speak with you." Tone said passing Scarlett the phone. "What the fuck type of shit are you on?" she whispered under her breath while snatching the phone out of his hands. She thought to herself, "Oh yea mother fucker, fuck you and Trey. Let's see how you like it when I tell your boy that we are fucking and I may be pregnant with your baby! Hello" she answered.

"Scarlett, what the fuck are you doing with Tone and where the hell are you at and why the fuck have you been ignoring my calls?!" Trey screamed, fully knowing the answers to each question before he asked them.

"Don't worry about where I'm at, as a matter of fact since you wanna know where I'm at....." before she could finish the sentence Tone jumped up from the bed trying to grab her arm and snatch the phone from her hand before she did something stupid and told Trey the truth about their dealings. Before Tone could grab her, Scarlett kicked him in the groin area and running towards the bathroom. Once inside the bathroom, she locked the door behind her as she listened to Tone behind the door crying out in pain telling her to give him his phone and not do nothing stupid by telling Trey anything that went down with the two of them. Sinking to the floor, she put the phone back to her ear while Trey was steady talking asking her what the hell is going on, "Talk to me Scarlett, I said what the fuck is going on with ya'll two and where the fuck are you at?"

"I'm in a hotel bathroom that's where I am, from just letting your friend Tone fuck me good for the second time today! Does that answer your question? Oh and yes it was good and NO this isn't the first time we fuck either and OH one more thing, I am pregnant and I really don't know who the fuck the father is!" Scarlett screamed in the phone hoping that he heard and digested everything she said.

"Bitch, I'm gonna kill you and that bitch ass nigga!" was all Trey said as he ended the call. Not realizing that he had hung up Scarlett continued to scream and yell obscenities in the phone as she stood back up opening the bathroom door to a fully dressed angry looking Tone.

"Fuck you, mother fucker! You wanna fuck all of these different bitches and cheat on me, you bitch. I'm gonna destroy you and that hoe Tina!!! Hello?!... Hello!" While standing there face to face with Tone, she handed him his phone as he ignored the gesture.

Dropping the phone at his feet, she looked him in the eyes and stood her ground as he raised his hand and slapped the cowboy shit out of her face, hard, bringing down more tears than the ones she was already shedding. Her face began swelling from the vicious slap, making the other side do the same as her neck spun and she hit her face on the door frame while falling to her knees. With rage in his eyes, Tone stared down at Scarlett and began to feel bad at the fact that the secret between them had been put on blast. He knew deep inside that what they had done was bound to come out because he truly believed in Karma and what is done in the dark, will come to the light and as he saw it the light was Scarlett's tongue. He sat back down on the bed and put his hands on his head as Scarlett rose from the floor. With all her energy, she dove on him and began swinging and kicking him wildly catching him off guard. Since he didn't want to put his hands on her, he grabbed her around her waist as she continued to kick and yell while screaming obscenities and tossed her to the opposite side of the bed, causing her to tumble off of the bed, hitting her forehead on the corner of the nightstand beside the bed leaving a huge swelling as her body hit the floor. Tone took that moment to grab his phone and exit out of the room before things got worse than what they already were. Walking out of the hotel, Tone entered his car and shook his head over what had just took place between him and Scarlett. While sitting there in silence he knew he would have to face Trey sooner or later and getting into a physical altercation was a no win situation for him seeing as though he had seen Trey in a number of scuffles while he never lost.

'Shit I can't kill my man over no pussy and I hope this nigga don't wanna take it there. I gotta clean this shit up.' he continued to think to himself as he came up with a plan to just deny everything that Scarlett had said. Still sitting there in deep thought Tone's phone began to ring breaking his train of thought. Looking down on the caller I.D. he realized it was Trey and decided he may as well pick up. "Look Trey before you....."

"So that was the good friend you was conversing with about me huh?" Trey asked cutting him off in mid-sentence.

"I was just joking with yo you, but all that shit she said about her and I fucking isn't true though yo. Man that woman is drunk and she invited me to her hotel room to talk about all the shit that ya'll have been going through. Man you my boy and I didn't fuck her yo and I wouldn't do that shit to you homey." Trey just sat back and laughed to himself cause deep down inside he knew that Tone had no idea that he knew the absolute truth about their secret affair or better yet their secret encounters they have kept secret up until this moment.

"Oh yeah, she on some bullshit huh? I know you wouldn't do no shit like that to me yo....I believe you." he lied, knowing that he had a plan in the works that was going to blow Tone's mind when it came into fruition. "You still there with her? Let me speak to her."

"Naw she still at the room, she flipped the fuck out on me and I had to get the fuck out of there!" Tone said, laughing aloud trying to lighten the conversation.

"Oh alright, so where are you on your way to now?" Trey asked ready to end the call so he could go back in the room and get further acquainted with Seleste.

178

"Man, I'm about to go and holla at my bitch over east Baltimore and go hit that pussy real good before I go back home to wifey."

"Oh yea, what's up with ya'll two?" Trey asked already aware of the situation between Seleste and Tone since she had briefed him earlier. "How is Seleste doing anyway? Her and Keisha, what's up with them two?"

"Man same ol shit, she probably home waiting on me to get there so she can complain about me not spending any time with her and I don't have time for that shit yo cause I'm feeding her with this money that I'm out here chasing. She got the baddest crib and the sickest whip, so she needs to just lay back, be happy and not complain. As for Keisha, that my baby girl so she cool man. Her little ass probably running around with her little boyfriend or one of them phat ass girlfriends of hers."

"Oh, ok homey... I'm about to try to get back in contact with Scarlett and tend to some other shit I got going on on my end, so I will call you later to see what you are up to."

"Alright Trey, be easy pimp!"

"You too homey!" Tone heard Trey say before hanging up.

Satisfied with the way the conversation with Trey went, Tone laughed aloud thinking he had just gotten over on his friend not knowing that Trey had a few tricks up his sleeve as well and was about to perform them on his one woman audience member or two depending on if he could get the second one nice and drunk like the first one so the three of them could have a nice magic show together. Tone pulled out of the parking lot and instead of going over East Baltimore with his other woman like he had told Trey, he decided to make his way home to patch things up with his wife, hoping that she wouldn't be still tripping about him not spending no time with her like she was earlier that day before he walked out on her to go and meet up with Scarlett.

CHAPTER 12

Tina hated seeing clients after midnight especially if it was an outcall and she had to go to them, even if they did pay extra. But the type of money that this client was willing to spend, had her going against what she usually didn't and had her rushing to get one of her regulars to cum extra fast so that she could be out the door. "Slow down Tee, you are stroking me too fast baby. I don't want to cum yet, just give me a few more minutes with you jerking me slowly, lick your lips and look me in the eyes." Tina had to laugh to herself for Logan's suggestions. Although he was one of her easy going clients that did not require much and she enjoyed servicing, she knew that time was of the essence and sitting on her knees stroking baby oil up and down his 10 inch dick while looking up into his eyes, licking her lips under the circumstances was starting to annoy her.

"Logan baby, you know how I enjoy pleasing you and making you happy, I just really have to be somewhere that is important in 20 minutes." she said as she stopped stroking his dick, releasing it making it flop back quickly hitting the bottom of his stomach. "Ok, Ok Tina. I hate to be a spoiler, but you just make me feel so good and you are the only one that does it for me."

"I know baby, but I really do have to get going. I assure you that I will make it up to you the next time. Ok?" she told him raising up off of the bed not waiting for his response. Turning the lights on she then blow out the candles, stopped the music and turned the TV off that displayed a naked Latina woman bouncing up and down on her Latin lover enjoying what looked like to be a 20 inch dick.

"So, can I come back after you're done doing what you have to do?" he asked standing next to her bed looking like a sad puppy. Looking up at him as she danced her ass in the one size too small fitted red body skirt, she couldn't help but smile as her eyes took his 6 foot 2 inch cocoa brown chiseled rock hard muscular statuesque frame that had her pussy getting moist and her thoughts clouded ready to give in on the temptation and let him have his way with her.

"Logan, please get dressed sweetie, I really have to get out of this house and you standing there like that is not helping." she told him snapping out of the reverie. Not wasting her time to look for a shirt she grabbed her black short sleeved blazer along with her 5 inch black open toed Christian Louboutin booties from out of the closet. By the time she grabbed her Black Louboutin clutch, checking to make sure she had her lip gloss, both house and car keys, driver's license, bank card and last but not least her pink pearl handled .380 for protection, just in case her next client couldn't control himself and things got out of hand. When she realized Logan was fully dressed and handing her $275 for her work, or lack thereof. She pretty much had to push him down the steps and out the door to get him to leave. Once he was gone she locked her door leaned her head and body against the door and let out a big sigh and to no one in particular she mumbled, "Finally, I'm glad his sexy ass is out of here! Let me hurry my horny ass up!" Looking out of the peephole to make sure he was gone, she relaxed a little when she seen him pull off in his car. She stuffed the cash Logan just gave her in her clutch and stepped out of her house, locking the bottom lock behind her, jumped in her Range Rover and made her way to the hour long drive to York, PA where her client was waiting for her with a hard on and seventeen hundred bucks in cash. During the hour long trip, she sat back listening to Melanie Fiona deep in thought wondering what would life be like with Trey as her man and she as his woman starting anew in a brand new city away from all distractions. Turning the music down she grabbed her phone and decided to give him a call. When he didn't answer she decided to leave him a voicemail letting him know that she was on her way to a client's house and she was thinking about him constantly. She gave him the address to where she was going in case something went wrong and told him she loved him and ended the call. Settling back in her seat, she turned her music back up and began to feel queasy as if she suddenly felt the urge to vomit. Immediately her womanly instincts kicked in and she thought about the last time she came on her period. Realizing that she was a whole month late, another pain shot through her pelvis simultaneously causing her to swerve on the road into another lane, almost causing an accident.

Relieved that her exit was finally here, she exited off of 83 N and made a couple of turns and found herself sitting in a 711 parking lot with her truck still running but geared in park while she flung the door open, leaning half of her body out throwing up. Once she was done she reached on the backseat and grabbed her out call bag. Sitting it on her lap, she reached in it and pulled a few baby wipes out along with some mouthwash and began wiping her face before and after gargling the nasty mint flavor that had her feeling as if she wanted to vomit again. Once she spat it out she continued to wipe her mouth with the wipes thinking aloud, 'uggghhhhh, that shit was nasty, what the fuck is wrong with me. Trey boo I think you may have gotten me knocked the fuck up baby!' Closing her truck door she reached in her clutch, grabbed her lip gloss and looking in the rearview mirror Tina applied a few coats, giving her lips that extra wet look. She picked up her phone and called the client while backing up and exiting the 711 parking lot. Once she had him on the phone, she informed him that she should be pulling up at his hotel in less than three minutes. Before ending the call he gave her his room number and promised her a good time when she did arrive.

◊◊◊

Pulling up to the Hilton hotel in the Bentley coupe that Consuela had loaned him, Trey felt like a superstar when the valet walked up to his driver side door and opened it up for him, then to the passenger side doing the same for Seleste as she stepped out trying to fix the too short miniskirt that barely covered her voluptuous ass. She Stumbled and barely was able to keep her balance, on account of the one too many shots of the 1800 Tequila Gold she had. Grabbing her arm and accepting the valet ticket, Trey hurriedly walked through the lobby constantly looking around making sure they weren't spotted by anyone as they approached the front desk and he began conversing to the female attendant that begin checking them into the suite that was booked an hour ago. Using Seleste credit card to pay for the one night stay at the hotel, too busy focusing on Trey with kissing and touching and gyrating on him, Seleste never once looked at the attendant or the price of the suite she just signed her signature any kind of way and dropped the pen to the floor. Trey accepted the room keys along with her driver's license, credit card and the receipt. Thanking the blonde haired attendant for what seemed like the millionth time, Trey winked at her making her blush and then pulled on Seleste's arm as they entered the elevator; where he felt comfortable now knowing they were on their way up to the suite on the top floor of the hotel. Never paying any attention to the old couple that was on the elevator with them, nor the fact that the elevator had opened and closed to let them off; Trey and Seleste seemed like a couple of newlyweds that gave a whole new meaning to the saying 'public displays of affection'. They passionately kissed with him touching and squeezing her ass and breast while she fumbled with his belt buckle digging her hands in his pants while rubbing and clawing at his chest.

Finally reaching their floor, they exited the elevator still fondling each other as they made their way down the hall and to their room for the night. Once inside they continued with their charades, still kissing and trying to rip the clothes off of one another while bumping against everything from the wall to the closet, door, table, and then to the bed where Seleste laid back and begin to give him a show. Trey grabbed the TV remote and clicked a porn station on the 42 inch flat screen TV. that hung from the wall, dropped the remote on the table and made his way to the bar pouring both of them a double shot of Jack Daniels mixed with coke soda. He walked back to the bed handing Seleste the one he made for her, as she stood on her knees naked from head to toe accepting the glass from him. Before she took a sip he handed her a red pill of ecstasy shaped like a heart telling her to swallow it. "Here, swallow this sexy and chase it with your drink. This shit here gonna have your pussy dripping!" Without saying a word or asking any questions, Seleste threw the pill back down her throat and looking into his eyes begin taking sips of the jack and coke. "Boy, you gonna have me fucked up." She told him as she got off of the bed, staggering her way to the living room. "Take them clothes off and give me that surprise that you said you had for me, I know she is in here somewhere. Here kitty, kitty." Trey took that as his time to put his plans into motion, knowing Seleste was drunk and feeling her liquor. He grabbed her hand and guided her back to the bedroom, sat her down on the bed and told her he had forgotten something in the car. He assured her that he would be bringing up the surprise after he went down to the car and reassured her that she would be joining them soon enough so they could have the time of their lives tonight. "Ok, sexy man... Hurry up back cause this super juicy wet pussy needs a good licking and some overtime dicking!" she seductively told him while lying back on the bed with her knees up and legs apart. Trey shook his head from side to side in total disbelief at how lovely and wet Seleste's pink pussy looked. Amazed at how her flawless brown skin complexion glowed from head to toe and with her 5ft7 inch tall, 36D, 25, 44inch frame laying there in the position she was in, touching herself, had him mesmerized and licking his lips. His dick was growing harder and harder as he stared on thinking how he was about to fuck the shit out of her and suck the life out of that pussy when he came back. Stepping out of the suite Trey glanced down at his phone while making his way to the elevator. Slowly walking down the hallway with his face buried in his phone, he noticed the different noises coming from each room he passed from loud talking to loud music, moaning and laughter as if everyone in the building was up enjoying themselves and one another. Reaching the elevator and finding the number in his phone that he was looking for, he pressed the number 14 floor and dialed the number in his cell phone as the elevator descended down. Stepping out of the elevator with his phone to his ear listening as it rung, he smiled to himself when a female picked up on the third ring. "Hey sexy-face, I was just looking at the clock wondering when you was gonna call and if you had the plan still in motion!"

"Yeah babe, you can come on now. I'm on the seventeenth floor, room 1711." he told her, sitting down on the bench outside of the room he was about to enter. "How long will take you to get here sexy?"

"No longer than 15 minutes babe, I was waiting on you so I'm pretty much ready. So on that note, I'm walking out of the house now sweetie." she told him.

"Ok, sexy I will see you in a few then." Ending the call, Trey decided to make one more call before entering the room. "Hey papi, I was just thinking about you, I miss you. Are you ok?" Consuela asked with excitement in her tone.

"Yeah, I'm ok baby. I might be here a little longer than I anticipated. I'm thinking I won't be back for another 3 hours or so."

"Ok Trey, but I'm so fucked up I may be out when you get back. There is a spare key to the house in the glove compartment behind the cash and the code to deactivate the alarm is 1206. So when are you done taking care of your business, come on home to me and wake me up if I'm asleep with your dick pounding me like I like."

"Ok, Consuela let me go and finish my business so I can hurry back up to you." Trey told her ready to end the call so he could get down to the task at hand. "You promise to hurry up papi, ok?"

"Ok, papi promises and I will see you then." he told her before hanging up and ending the call.

Rising from the bench he walked over to the door he was about to enter. He lifted up the welcome mat, grabbing the room key that was beneath it and used it to unlock and enter the room. Soon as he entered the room he was greeted by the sounds of Drake blasting from the IPOD speakers that set atop the room's dresser, along with two half naked women dressed in matching leotards that differed in color, fishnet stockings and heels. He could tell they were both drunk as they both held half empty bottles of champagne and vodka in the air, grinding and dancing on one another as if they were in the middle of the club.

"Heyyyyyyyyy boo!!!" Keisha screamed running towards him, jumping into his arms while wrapping her legs around his waist. He held her in the air as she began kissing him and wrapping her arms around his neck. Her friend Destiny walked over and grabbing the bottle from out of her hand joined in on the kiss. Breaking the 3 way kiss, Keisha grabbed the back of Trey and Destiny's head bringing their faces together, forcing them to kiss. She jumped out of his arms and grabbed his hands and pulled him over to the love sofa, while Destiny followed. Trey sat in the middle while both women sat on opposite sides of him. "I'm so fucking high and drunk boo, I can suck your dick and eat her pussy at the same time!!" Keisha said aloud as the music stopped playing.

"Yes, bitch I'm with you on that." Destiny added. "Oh my Gawwwwdd. I'm sooooo fucking high, that molly got me horny too... Shit!!! Let's take this shit to the bed. Trey you sexy as fuck baby, lemme see that dick!!!" Trey grabbed the vodka bottle out of Destiny's hand and rose from the couch as Keisha had begun to reach for his belt buckle.

"Let's take this shit upstairs to my room baby. I told you I got a sexy ass chick from Philly that I brought with me that wants to party with us." he said looking from one to the other. Keisha rose from the love sofa, grabbed Destiny's hand as the three of them exited the room and made their way to the elevator. The two women were so intoxicated from the x pills and liquor that they began crawling to the elevator on their hands and knees like nasty felines, making all kinds of animals noises from meowing like cats to barking like small dogs, while laughing uncontrollably until they were inside the closed doors of the spacious elevator. 'Yeah these bitches are really fucked up', Trey thought to himself. Trey pushed the button to the seventeenth floor and leaned his body against the elevator wall as he began to feel the effects of his pill and the jack and coke he had with Seleste. He watched on as Destiny and Keisha crouched in the corner of the elevator on their knees, kissing and feeling on each other's asses. When the elevator door opened Trey exited first, letting them know they had reached their floor. They continued to crawl on their hands and knees through the hall behind Trey as he walked ahead of them. Once he was in front of the door to the suite he told them to sit and wait on the bench while he made sure the mood was right in the room before they entered. "Ok baby, we will be good girls and promise not to eat each other up while you are gone!" Keisha said smacking Destiny on her exposed ass cheeks as they continued to crawl and laugh as if someone had just told a joke.

When Trey entered the suite, Seleste had all of the lights off with the music blasting to the point you couldn't hear yourself speak or think. Noticing her silhouette on the bed, he walked over to her thinking to himself, 'this bitch is in the same position that I left her in'. As he got closer to her body, he crawled between her legs ready to taste her when he realized that she was already pleasuring herself with a silver bullet, letting it vibrate uncontrollably on her clitoris. Totally oblivious to the fact that Trey have even entered the room, Trey rose from the bed and walked over to the door motioning to Keisha and Destiny that it was time to come inside of the room, watching on at the two of them as they both staggered in. Once inside the two women found their way to the bed and without introductions or even being able to see each other in the pitch black room, the mother had no idea that she was in the presence of her daughter Keisha and her daughter's best friend, Destiny. The three women were all over one another kissing, licking and nibbling on each other's bodies like they were dangerously in lust. Trey's phone began to ring, illuminating in the darkness in his jeans pocket. He pulled it out and saw that it was a text message from Deb letting him know she had just gotten off of the elevator and was outside of the room door. Looking out of the peephole to see if she was outside of the right room, Trey opened the door and let her inside when she appeared. Shutting the door behind her, he gave her a hug as she whispered in his ear about how dark it was in the room and how the loud music didn't seem that loud on the outside of the room.

"Damn you look sexy as shit, lets hurry up and get this over with baby and thanks for even helping me with this." With her one free hand she pulled his ear back down to her lips and said,

"Don't worry about it baby, I told you that I would do anything for you, but you are right, I just wanna hurry up and get this over with." She kissed him on his lips and with the light from his phone he held her hand and guided her through the room and into the living room. Walking past the bed with the three lust filled bodies who were engrossed in making out with one another, without a care in the world or a clue who they were being intimate with. Deb set the digital camera on a stand in the middle of the living room floor so she could capture the whole bedroom scene. She hit the record button along with another button as a small sniper like light lit up and shined, causing the picture displayed on the four inch screen that was attached to the camera to be sharp and crystal clean as if she was filming the scene in broad daylight under a magnifying glass. The light was bright, but not bright enough for the bodies in the room to know who was who unless one of them came in the living room and looked at the 4 inch screen or if they all came into the living room together and figured it out. While Deb was now in the room focusing on snapping pictures with her camera, Trey decided to pull his dick out and let each woman get a taste of his dick while Deb snapped away. After capturing about 7 great photos, Deb walked up to Trey and pulled him in the living room with her while the other three women continued to get it on. Deb pushed Trey down on the sofa and got on her knees and began sucking his dick like she couldn't control the feelings that overcame her. She sucked him for a good ten minutes before jumping to her feet and whispering in his ear, "I wanna watch you fuck these three hoes while I sit back and play with this camcorder." Trey had to smile cause fucking those three bitches was exactly what he intended to do. "You sure you don't wanna join?" he asked her raising up from the couch.

"I'm ok boo, those bitches can't do nothing for me but piss me off. Now hurry up and get your nut so we can get out of here! As soon as you cum boo, we out of here!" she told him, smacking him on his ass as he got undressed right there in front of her. Condoms in Hand, he walked to the bedroom and joined in on the all-female threesome making it a foursome. For the next hour, Trey took his time sexing each woman while they continued to sex each other. When he finally came, he made sure to cum down both Seleste and Keisha's throats, then put their faces together and made them kiss, transferring his semen from one mouth to the other. As soon as Deb seen this she stopped the recording, closed the screen on the camcorder along with the stand and with the light from her phone she made her way through the bedroom and out of the door. In a rush to not be noticed by any of the women, Trey slipped out of the suite right behind her, struggling to pull his pants up while quickly walking down the hall trying to make it to the elevator. Once inside, Trey thanked Deb for being a part of his scheme as she smiled looking at him with admiration in her eyes. "You are very welcome Trey, and this will be our little secret. Shit baby, I'm just glad I'm on your good side cause having you as an enemy...Lord knows, your ass is crazzzzzy!!!" Deb told him smiling from ear to ear but meaning every word she said. "So, are you gonna let me take you home with me and wash you up or do you have something else or should I say somebody else to tend to this morning?" Trey fixed his clothes in the elevator mirror watching Deb the whole ride down as she inched closer to him and planted a kiss on his cheek. He grinned to himself cause he knew his face smelled of pussy and knew that she smelled it as well when she kissed him. But almost giving in to her temptation and letting Deb cater to him, he knew he had to snap out of it and stick to his code of 'business over pleasure.' He politely turned her offer down, keeping in mind that he owed her not only his time, but also an orgasm or three. He promised to see her before the day was over and assured her that it would be worth the wait. As the elevator reached the lobby, they exited the elevator and made their way to the valet.

"Ok, Trey boy. And you better not stand me up cause I really like you and want to spend some more time getting to know you." When they stepped out of the hotel they handed valet their cards and waited until he returned with their cars, one after the other bringing Trey's first.

"Yeah, I like you too Deb. You're a cool ass sexy ass chick and like I said, we will definitely get together later babe."

Trey smiled when he seen the expression on her face when she seen valet pulled up in the foreign car, hop out and hand him the keys. "Damn boo, that is a nice ass ride!" she told him holding her arms out for him to hug and embrace her before they departed. When they hugged she whispered in his ear, "Trey my pussy is so wet and moist for you right now, please come home with me!"

"Like I said Deb, let me go and handle my business and I will call you as soon as I am done. I assure you I will, cause I can't wait to feel your insides and taste that pussy." he told her brushing his lips against her neck and squeezing her ass before releasing her from their tight embrace. Just as he let her go valet was walking up to her to hand her the keys to her 760 Li BMW. "Ok boo and don't forget!" They both jumped in their vehicles, pulled off and went in opposite directions. Trey decided to give Consuela a call letting her know that he would be on his way to her, while still thinking about all that had took place in the last few hours. He was still high as a kite feeling like he was flying from the effects of the ecstasy and liquor he had in his system. After calling her phone twice and not getting an answer he decided to continue to make his way to her house and give Tone a call.

"Yoooo, what's up pimp?" Tone answered, picking up on the first ring.

"Damn homey, what you had the phone in your hand cause I didn't even hear it ring?"

"Yeah man, I was sitting here texting fucking Seleste for the twentieth time, cause she not answering her phone or her text messages and this is not like her. I was even calling and texting my damn daughter to see if she heard from her but I can't seem to get in contact with either one of them. I don't know what the fuck is going on, but that shit got me pissed. But anyway enough about my shit, what's up with you pimp?" Tone asked curious to know why Trey was calling him 5:30 am.

"Awe man, I wished you was with me last night through this morning nigga!!! Man I had the time of my life fucking these three freak ass bitches, man you would have loved it cause them bitches was nasty as fuck and doing all kinds of shit. I mean they were

193

sucking each other pussies, to letting me fuck them in their asses and pussies to letting me nut all down their throats. I'm talking these bitches got to kissing and spitting my nut back and forth in one another's mouths and everything yo! Damn I wish you coulda been there." Trey told him enjoying the sweet revenge he had got on this fake ass backstabbing ass want-to-be friend turned foe of his. "Mannnnnn, gawd damn yo! Why the fuck you ain't call me?" Tone asked, just as excited as Trey was, unaware that the joke was really on him as they both laughed from opposite ends of the phone.

"Because you told me you was going over some female house and I didn't wanna disturb you, but I swear everything in me was telling me to call you and invite you! That shit was sweet shorty. I got it on DVD and everything!"

"Hell no, you lying now man. Yo you gotta let me see that bitch!" I got you my nigga, I'm gonna make sure you get that bitch first thing later on today!"

"Trey, you betta not be kidding me homey, shit, I need some kind of entertainment after the night I had with sitting in this fucking house all night stressing over my sneaky ass wife. She probably was out fucking one of them cornball ass west Baltimore dudes trying to get back at me." Trey decided that he had grown tired of hearing Tone's voice and was ready to end the call. He continued to make his way to Consuela while being extra careful to stay in control of the car and not do anything that would have him getting pulled over by the state troopers that usually sat on the side of the highway waiting to pull someone over during the wee hours of the morning. "Naw she probably was fucking with a real stand up west Baltimore guy, somebody that ain't like your crazy ass!" Tone just laughed not even catching on to what Trey was really trying to tell him; the truth, and nothing but it.

"Yeah alright, I would put my foot in both of their asses. She not crazy enough to go out and fuck around on me anyway. That's my bitch, I got that pussy on lock!" Trey continued to smile to himself and decided at that moment to end the call. He gave him his word that he would be in touch and get that DVD to him sometime later on, ended the call and continued on to his destination with a devious smile spread across his face. Just as he sat the phone in his lap, it began to ring, alerting him that he had a message from Deb letting him know that 'her pussy was gushing and she would be waiting for him horny and impatiently with open arms and legs!!' Trey ignored her message as he turned into the winding road that led to Consuela's estate. He went through the gate punching in the code that she had given him earlier, pulled up to the garage, then with a press of a button on the steering wheel the garage door rose allowing him to enter it. He then pressed the same button to close it once he was all the way inside, put the top up on the car, turned off the ignition and got out making sure he locked the Bentley doors behind him. Trey punched the same code on the security dial pad that was on the wall next to the door, turning the alarm off. After entering the massive house he shut and locked the garage door pressing the same buttons on the dial pad to reactivate the alarm. Remembering where the elevator was that lead to her bathroom he decided to take it up just to avoid from climbing the many steps that led to her top floor. Getting off of the elevator, Trey thought to himself, 'I can get used to this riding elevators in my house shit'. He walked through the bathroom and entered her bedroom noticing that she wasn't even there. Sitting down on the bed he pulled out his phone and decided to give her another call again. "Hey sexy sexy, where are you?" she questioned.

"In your bedroom about to take a shower. I have been calling your pretty ass, where are you?"

"Papi, mi amor. I'm in the study room, I'm so pleased that you made it back to me like you promised. Ok, I'm on my way up now so go ahead and get in the shower and I will be up to wash you real good papi. Gimme a second!" she told him before ending the call. Trey could tell she was high off of probably everything she put her hands on and also was glad he was now beginning to get his second wind from the effects that the ecstasy had on him. He stripped out of his clothes, leaving them in a heap on the floor, walked to the shower and stepped in, closing the glass doors behind him. Lifting the lever to adjust the water temperature to his liking, steam filled the room while Trey stood there deep in thought, impressed with the way the water begin spraying and massaging his body from all angles.

CHAPTER 13

Tina stirred underneath the blanket trying to pull herself together feeling like she got hit with a ton of bricks and run over by a MACK truck at the same time. She struggled to open her eyes in the dimly lit room, feeling as if someone was sitting on her eyelids. She managed to open them halfway, focusing in on the blinking clock that she knew was wrong, telling herself that there was no way it was 12:00. Noticing her cell phone illuminating she wondered if it was a missed call or text as she reached from underneath of the blanket and grabbed it, accidentally knocking her clutch to the floor. Ignoring her clutch, she brought the phone beneath the blanket with her and noticed she had missed calls from Trey, Shay and Scarlett; as well as a few unknown numbers that she didn't recognize and a few text messages. She glanced down at the clock on her phone realizing it was only 8 a.m. and thought to herself 'there is no way my ass is getting up this damn early!' She closed her eyes back and tried to recall all the events that happened last night but everything just seemed to be a blur. As she laid there she thought about the last thing she did as the thought of entering the hotel room with her last sick ass client started coming back to her.

"C'mon in Tina, why you are as beautiful as you sound over the phone!" The short bald headed overweight white man said, opening the door for her to come inside. When Tina entered the room she had to stop herself from laughing at the short man that stood in front of her, dressed in a blue and black bra and woman's panty set, corset and garter belt with the strings hanging down his thighs with matching black pantyhose pulled just above his knees like a schoolgirl. 'OMG', she mumbled under her breath as he backed up closing the door and faced her with the biggest devilish smile spread across his face. Everything in her told her to just leave, but thinking about the money had her ignoring her better judgment, that and the hour long drive under her conditions didn't help either. "Thank you, Grant. You are definitely the sweetest!" she said, sitting down in a chair at a table that sat in the corner of the room. "So, you want to get a massage tonight baby, if so I'm ready!" Grant walked into the bathroom and came back clutching a black and white leather zebra fanny pack in one hand and a stack of

197

hundred dollar bills in the other. He sat down on the chair opposite of Tina and handed her the bills, watching her reaction as she counted out $2,000. Tina thanked him as he began pouring the two of them a glass of Remy Martin LOUIS XIII filled to the brim. 'Why the fuck does this weirdo keep staring at me with this stupid ass smile on his face', she thought to herself as she flashed him a smile back stuffing the bills in her clutch behind her .380.

"I changed my mind, I don't want a massage Tina. I'm not a cop or anything so I don't want you to get that impression, but what I want from you is a conversation. I want you to be topless over a nice glass of Cognac," he paused for a moment while taking a sip from his glass then added, " then I want to introduce you to Mr. Bunny and cream on your pretty legs." Tina continued to smile while reaching for her glass of the expensive cognac and decided to swallow the smooth Cognac down in three gulps. She told herself that she would have to be tipsy to get through the morning with this guy. She rose from the chair and unbuttoned her blazer, grabbed her clutch and excused herself, making her way to the restroom. Once inside she closed the door behind her, set her clutch on the floor while she reached in it and checked the chamber of her gun, flushing the toilet to muffle the sound. Relieved that there was a bullet in the chamber she then made sure the safety was off, placed it back in her clutch and checked her breast out in the floor length mirror as she removed her blazer. Noticing the shower curtain closed peaked her curiosity. She pulled it back slightly and stepped back clutching her hands to her mouth to keep from bursting out into laughter once again from the sight of the life sized white costume bunny rabbit mask. She closed the curtain back and ran the water to make it appear that she really did use the bathroom and opened the door making her way back to the table where Grant sat with that same smile on his face. He watched her over the rim of his glass as he took another sip. Tossing her blazer behind her chair she sat down with her clutch within hands reach and grabbed her glass that was once again filled to the brim with Remy Martin. So overwhelmed with everything that was taking placed since she stepped into this hotel with this freak, without thinking she guzzled the cognac down halfway and immediately regret her actions, she began to feel strange and lose consciousness. "Are you ok Tina, you don't look too well." he told her watching as her body slumped in the chair, catching her just as she leaned forward about to fall to the floor. "Here, let me give you a hand and lay you across the bed while I go and get Mr. Bunny and show him what a good girl you are." Hearing every word that Grant was saying but unable to move or focus in on him, she felt him carry her to the bed, remove her dress and leave the room. Trying her best to use all of her strength to focus on his every move she realized it was useless, as her visions of him began to go in and out with him standing over top of her with the same rabbit mask that she just saw moments ago in the shower. Standing there she watched on, motionless, as he masturbated on her legs and seconds later everything else was a blur.

Just as she continued to lay there trying to get comfortable, it dawned on her that she was still in the hotel room with the sicko. 'O my gosh Tina, bitch do not panic!' she thought to herself as her eyes grew wide. She laid there quiet trying to listen to see where he was and if he was still in the room since her head

199

was still buried under the covers. All she could hear is the sounds of loud snoring. Lifting her head from beneath the covers, she slowly looked back to the sound where the snoring was coming from and jumped out of the bed. Falling to the floor while scrambling to her feet, she saw him sitting in the chair with his legs planted on another chair, still dressed in his lingerie with the rabbit mask still attached to his head. Tina reached down grabbing her clutch up off the floor and pulled her gun out of it, checked to make sure it was still loaded and pointed at him when she realized that it in fact was. Still snoring loudly, she quickly searched around for her skirt, noticing it was folded along with her blazer on top of it she managed to put them both on, grabbed her shoes along with the zebra fanny pack as his snoring grew increasingly louder. She tip toed back to the bed almost forgetting the phone, swooped it up placing it in her jacket pocket and exited the hotel room, placing the gun in her clutch as she hurriedly jogged down the hall making her way to the elevator. Just as she reached the elevator the doors were beginning to close as she turned her body sideways and entered it just in time. She pressed the lobby button, leaned her back against the wall, took a deep breath and closed her eyes as the elevator descended between floors making its way down. Once the elevator reached the lobby, she stepped out of it and walked through the lobby, exiting the hotel all together trying to remember where she parked her truck. After about a second it dawned on her where she parked as she perused the lot and spot it. Fumbling with the things that she carried in her arms, she managed to stick her hands in her clutch while thanking God when she felt her keys and pressed the driver's side door button to unlock the locks. She opened the door, hopped in sideways and threw everything that was in her hand and under her arms on the passenger side seat. She reached in the glove compartment, grabbed her GPS and set it in the dash, put the key in the ignition placing her car in drive and drove out of the lot as fast as she could while punching the home icon on the GPS touch screen. Not one time making any detours or turns, Tina got on the highway feeling dirty as if she had been taken advantage of. Nothing on her body felt touched, sore or misused so that was a good thing but with that being said, she couldn't understand the purpose for mickeying her drink. Just as the thought of him standing over top of her with that creepy ass mask on masturbating all over her leg crossed her mind, her leg began to itch as tears began to stream down her face.

Taking quick glances down at her thighs she noticed the dry semen that flaked from the top of her left thigh down to her ankles as if he kept releasing on her until his body couldn't produce any more semen. "Sick fuck!" she yelled aloud punching the steering wheel as anger began to take over her sadness. She told herself that she would go home and scrub herself clean and then take a trip to her doctor's office to get a physical. As she continued to drive down the highway, she couldn't help but rub her stomach thinking about a part of Trey being inside of her. Tina reached down to grab her phone to give him a call when she noticed the zebra patterned fanny pack that she had took from Grant and wondered what was inside of it. After dialing Trey's number, then placing him on speaker phone, she unzipped the bag as Trey's phone just rung. Struggling to unzip the bag she sat it on her lap, guided the steering wheel with her knees and upper thigh, then with using both hands she opened the bag as Trey answered the line. "Tina baby, what's up?"

"Oh my God boo, I need you where are you?" she asked as her mouth fell open and a smile formed across the lips at the sight of the contents in the bag.

"No wonder this bitch was so heavy and hard to fucking open!"

"Tina, you're losing me babe. What are you talking about or rather who are you talking to?"

"I'm sorry boo but where are you, I need to see you like yesterday!"

"I'm still in bed with Consuela, I haven't too long......"

"Well you need to get ya ass up and leave that bitch and be making your way to my house right now! I should be there in about 40 minutes and if you so happen to get there before I do, don't leave! I need you boo!" Tina told him. She began to feel as if she was hungry and at the same time she needed to throw up. Trey told her he would be on his way now and ended the call. Tina could not believe all of the hundred dollar bills that was neatly stuffed in the fanny pack looking as if they were crisp fresh out of a bank. She guessed that it had to be well over $50k in it while she wiped the tear that ran down her cheek and smiled at the thought of getting ahold of that much extra cash on a humble, that she knew her and Trey could definitely use. Now she just needed to make it home, shower and carry her ass to the doctors to make sure Grant didn't infect or inject her with anything while she was unconscious.

◊◊◊

Keisha whipped the covers off of her body and placed her hands on her head while she sat on the side of the massive king sized bed with her feet touching the floor. She looked back and realized that there was a body still in the covers balled up in the fetal position lightly snoring. Whipping the covers back she smiled when Destiny looked up at her frowning as if she was disturbed and pulled the covers back over her head. Just then she heard the sound of the shower water running coming from the other room and pulled the covers back off of Destiny's head.

"Nooooooo Keish, I'm still fucked up boo. I don't wanna move, I swear I could lay here all week!" Destiny whined.

"Bitch come on and get up and let's take our asses to our own room. Shit my head is spinning too but I need my damn phone. I already know Seleste and Tone been blowing me up all night long, especially since they beefing right now. You know I'm always the arbitrator of their bullshit!" she said rising from the bed. "And where the fuck is Trey ass at, he better not be in the shower with that bitch from last night! Shit, bitch we was so fucked up, I don't even know what this bitch looked like."

"Girl I don't either…Trey?!" Keisha added calling out his name hoping he would hear her so she didn't have to go into the bathroom. Destiny climbed out of the bed still nude, picked up her leotard and danced her ass in it, pulling it up halfway just above her stomach leaving her perky breast out as she walked to the back of the room heading to the bathroom. "Ooooooh bitch, I gotta pee and that probably is him in the shower washing that good ass dick off," she said as they both giggled simultaneously, "I wasn't that fucked up bitch,

I remembered that!" Keisha just looked on as she watched Destiny disappear and then hollered back there to her saying, "Shiiiiiit bitch, leave my man alone that is my good ass dick!!" Destiny entered the bathroom, grabbed the toilet paper from beneath the sink and begin to lace the seat before she sat down with her hands on her head and elbows on her knees and began peeing as if she had been holding it for days. Thinking it was Trey in the shower, she sat up and pulled the curtain back and was surprised and slightly embarrassed to see it was a woman whom she didn't know or recognize. 'Damn, this must be the bitch from last night. She is a pretty older chick with a phatty!' she thought putting her hand to her mouth.

"Girl I am so sorry, I thought you was Trey's ass," stated Destiny as Seleste smiled and pulled the shower curtain back.

"No girl, it's just little ole me," she said yelling over the sound of the water, "his ass must have left out sometime this morning!" Just then Keisha had put on her leotard grabbing both her and Destiny's shoes and began to walk through the room heading in the direction of the bathroom as Destiny was coming out of the bathroom closing the door behind her, smiling with her hand to her mouth. "Girl, what the hell is wrong with you? And why you got that stupid ass grin on your face?" Keisha asked handing Destiny her shoes. Accepting her shoes, Destiny grabbed Keisha's arm and pulled her back with her to the bedroom. "Girl that is not no damn Trey in there, it's the chick from last night!" she told her pulling up the top half of her leotard putting her arms in and covering her breasts.

"So Trey isn't in there? Is that what you telling me?" Keisha questioned looking confused.

"No bitch, the bitch we was fucking last night silly is. Let's get the fuck out of here cause I don't even want to be bothered by another pussy this morning."

"Me either, so Trey sneaky ass left us in here with that bitch. Girl, I'm gonna cuss his ass the fuck out. I should bust in that damn bathroom and beat that bitch ass for the hell of it. Come on, let's get the fuck out of this room before that bitch get out of the shower asking dumb ass questions!" Keisha said now pulling Destiny's arm heading for the door to leave.

"Bitch, hold up. I forgot my damn fishnets over there on the floor!"

"Girl, fuck them damn fishnets!" she added still pulling her out of the hotel room, laughing as they both speed walked down the hallway trying to make it to the elevator looking as if they had just committed a crime and didn't want to be caught. Once back inside of their hotel room, they both stripped naked out of their leotards, grabbed their phones and climbed back under the covers. Keisha decided to call down to the lobby and book their room for another day. After she did that she called Trey's phone three times in a row, leaving him a voice message letting him know that it would be wise for him to call her when he checked his messages, "You left me and my bitch in the room with that fuckin hoe, you lucky I didn't get a chance to see the bitch before I left out. Her scared ass was hiding in the bathroom, so she lucky her ass didn't come out or I would've taken my frustrations out on her and we would've beat that bitch. But call me when you get this message boo." she told him ending the call. Just then she checked her text messages and missed calls and wondered why she only had missed calls and texts from Tone, her father, and none from her mom. She decided to call Seleste, but when she didn't get an answer she decided to text her phone letting her know that she was ok and to call her back as soon as she could. She then decided to call her dad, while his phone rung she snuggled up under Destiny and spooned with her as she laid with her breasts against her back and up. "I saw you calling and texting me at 5 am, what's up?"

"My bad babygirl, I was trying to see if you had heard from your mother cause I couldn't get in contact with her and she didn't come home last night."

"No, I haven't talked to her since earlier yesterday, but I do know she was pissed at you and said she was meeting up with a friend of hers for drinks and she was more than likely gonna stay with whoever it was if she ended up drinking too much."

"Ok cool. Are you alright?" Tone asked her.

"Yeah, I'm ok daddy. Bout to get some more rest. Me and my girlfriend Destiny had got a hotel room last night cause we was way too gone to drive home, so were both in here laid up and hung over!" "Alright babygirl, go ahead and get u some more rest, but if you talk to that mother of yours before I do, tell her ass I said to call me!"

"Alright daddy, I will." she said, listening to his goodbye before she ended the call. She turned the volume up on her phone in case it rang while she was asleep, turned over and placed it on the opposite side of the bed as far as her arm would extend and turned back over and snuggled up under Destiny and fell into a deep sleep.

◊◊◊

Seleste paced the hotel room floor naked trying to figure out why she was alone in the room and where the hell had Trey gone, as the ex pill she took last night began to kick back in. Feeling high and hornier than before, she grabbed her phone from off of the night stand and instantly caught an attitude when she noticed all of the missed calls from her husband. Searching through her text messages she wondered why Trey hadn't called or texted to let her know anything. 'Trey boo, you better not be fucking with me,' she said to herself dialing his number while laying down on the bed. As his phone rang she reached over and grabbed the television remote from the bottom of the bed, clicked it on and began flicking the channels as his voicemail picked up. Hanging up she tried calling him back but accidentally pressed the send button answering the call for Tone. "Seleste!" she heard him say when she put the phone to her ear. "I hope you are not calling me to fight Tone, cause I swear I will hang up if so." she told him. Settling back on the pillows she focused her attention on the black porn movie that was playing on the TV while waiting for him to speak.

"Seleste, don't fuck with me. Where are you and why the hell didn't you come home last night?"

"Tone I was drinking and having fun with my girls and was too drunk and high to drive so I got a hotel room and stayed there." she answered in the most nonchalant voice she could muster. Feeling relaxed from the pill she decided to get up from the bed and make herself another drink while listening to her husband rant. "So this is the bullshit you are on with me Seleste? You actually want me to believe that bullshit, right?"

"Look nigga, your lying ass do it all the fucking time. Now you are the one that is home looking like a bitch calling my fucking phone back to back all damn night!" she calmly stated then added, "Baby if you're worried about where I was and am up to, you can come and meet me at the hotel where I am staying and come spank me."

"Oh yea, your ass is high. Where the hell are you Seleste cause I'm on my way to come and get you." "There's no need baby, I will just see you when I get home."

"Seleste I am going to ask your ass again, where the fuck are you at?" After telling him where she was, by looking on the back of the key card, she had to go out into the hallway and check the wall beside the door to give him the room number. Tossing her phone on the bed without a care in the world, not even caring whether he was still on the line or not, she laid back on the bed taking sips of her Hennessey and coke soda and watched on at the ebony porn chick get fucked from behind by a skinny black BBC on the screen. While she laid there sipping her drink, she thought about Tone coming to the hotel and decided that it wasn't a good idea to bring him into an environment where she just had sex with his friend at, along with two strange woman whom she didn't have a clue about who they were or where they came from, and that's even down to the ecstasy and drinking. 'No I do not think that will be a good idea Seleste, bitch get it together. You do not need his simple minded ass coming here tripping and tearing shit up!' she said under her breath. Picking up her phone she dialed his number back, placed the call on speaker and let it rest on her breast. "What is it now Seleste?" he asked opening his front door ready to walk out of it. Looking

208

down, he noticed a black box with a black ribbon on it, picked it up and carried it in the house listening on as she spoke on the other end of the phone.

"Never mind Tone, don't worry about coming to get me. I can manage on my own. I will be home, but for now I just want to be alone for a bit and think."

"Soooooo, how and when will you get home and where is your car?" he asked setting the box on the kitchen table. Noticing the black card and making his way out of the kitchen and out of the front door. Locking the locks to his house, Tone figured there was no need to fight with her because when he thought about it everything they were going through was all his fault. As he got into his car, tossing the card on the passenger seat, he decided to just bite the bullet and apologize to his wife to make things right with her with a bouquet of roses, a bottle of champagne and some quality time. "Alright Seleste. Baby just come on home, I don't wanna fight with you anymore and I promise when you get home we can do something special and get away from all the drama that we have been dealing with the last few days."

"You promise, Tone?" she asked, taken aback by his sudden different approach.

"I promise baby, just come on home and let me make it right. I love you Seleste."

"I love you too baby, and I don't want to fight anymore. But when I come home can you promise me that you will eat me real good and make passionate love to your wife?"

Tone smiled to himself, promising her that he would do everything she wanted and more then ended the call on that note while pulling out of the parking space in an attempt to get what he needed from the store and making it back home before she did.

Happy with the way the conversation ended with her husband, Seleste decided against bringing herself to an orgasm with her bullet and making Tone further pay for his wrongful actions with the way he had been treating her. Turning off the television, Seleste rose from the bed, opened up the window curtains allowing the sunlight to brighten the suite up and searched for her white and purple leopard print Entice thongs that Tone had gotten her for Valentine's Day. Never one to leave out pantiless she knew that she had worn them because they matched the white skirt and purple sequined halter she wore. Giving up her search she placed her clothes on and said hell with the panties, called the hotel front desk and had them to have a cab waiting outside for her. She grabbed her shoes, placing them under her arm, grabbed her bullet and phone placing them both in her purse. Making sure she had everything and giving the suite a once over, she thought to herself how the trifling two bitches she slept with had to have been high to leave their stockings balled up in the corner on the floor. Then they had left the room without even showering. 'Nasty whores,' she thought to herself as she exited the suite making her way to the elevator. By the time she got off of the elevator and made it to the lobby her cab was sitting in front of the main entrance waiting for her. Once inside the cab, she gave the Indian driver the address to the 5 MILE house where she had left her and paid him $20 up front for the ride and sat back listening to him speak in his ear piece to someone in a language she didn't understand. Pulling into the parking lot Seleste pointed

210

him to her car, placed her Giuseppe Zanotti heels on and got out of the cab feeling his eyes burn a hole in her ass as she walked to her car. Using her key to unlock the front door of her AUDI A8L she got behind the wheel closing the door behind her, sat her purse on the passenger side floor and stuck her key in the ignition switch while putting the car in drive, exiting the parking lot. Pulling up to a red light, Seleste's phone began to ring in her purse. Reaching down and grabbing the phone, she looked at the caller I.D. and seen that it was her daughter, Keisha calling. "Hey baby" she said answering the phone. "Hey mommy, how are you and where did you stay last night cause I heard you didn't make it home." she stated letting her know that she had talked to her dad.

"Girl my ass is still tore up, just leaving a hotel and making my way home to your bipolar ass father. I see he done called you looking for me cause I wasn't taking any of his calls. Anyway, where are you cause you ain't been home either and it sounds like you driving?"

"I'm dropping my homegirl Destiny off and then making my way home myself. Are you and daddy ok now cause he was pretty upset with you for not coming home last night?"

"Yeah we fine now, shit that's my damn house and he knows if he keep acting up somebody else gonna be climbing in this good pussy!"

"Mommmmmmmm, watch your mouth round these virgin ears!" Keisha began laughing. Seleste overheard Keisha telling her friend Destiny good bye and that she would get up with her later, she then heard the door open and close as Keisha got back on the phone. "Oh my gosh mommy, your ass is crazy. And then you wonder where I get my craziness from, both you and daddy bipolar." Seleste laughed at her daughter knowing that she was telling the truth. They both agreed that they would be home in twenty minutes and would wait for the other to pull up, whoever got home first. They said their goodbyes and ended the call with both of them still intoxicated from the drugs and liquor that was lurking in their systems'.

Tone walked through the front door of his house, champagne in hand along with a dozen of white and pink roses, chocolate covered strawberries, whip cream and the black card from the box that he hadn't put down yet. Kicking the door closed with the back of his foot, he headed straight for the kitchen setting everything down on the island that sat in the middle of the floor. He then sat in one of the barstools in front of the island and opened up the black card and began reading. *"Just a small token of my appreciation. This one is for you "homey"... Enjoy!!"*
Trey

Tone read the card again and wondered what the hell Trey was talking about and then it dawned on him that the box must have contained the DVD that Trey told him about this morning. He wondered what else was in the box and why the fancy wrapping. Tone sat the card down on the island, rose from the bar stool and grabbed the champagne bucket from out of the bo tom cabinet drawer. Filling the bucket with ice, he then sat the champagne in the middle of the bucket, then sat the flowers next to it in the middle of the island. Then grabbing a glass tray from one of the cupboards he spread the strawberries around on it forming a heart, sitting the chocolate and whipped cream next to the tray and hurriedly grabbed the black box off of the kitchen table. With an attempt to check out the DVD and the contents in the box before Seleste walked in, he walked out the kitchen and into the living room, sat down on the couch, opened the black box and noticed a pair of women's panties. "Trey, you are a freak nigga," he said aloud smiling to himself. As quickly as his smile spread across his lips, it vanished and turned upside down when he noticed his name written in cursive in diamonds on the front of the thongs, the same white and purple leopard print thongs he had gotten Seleste for Valentine's Day. Snatching the thongs out of the box he held them in the air with both hands, checking the label in the inside noticing they were the thousand dollar Entice thongs he brought her and threw them down on the couch. Snatching the DVD out of the box that had a black and white smiley face sticker on it, he inserted it in the DVD player, grabbed the remote control off of the table and powered on the 52 inch television that hung on the wall and pressed play on the DVD player. Tone stood there watching as the DVD began to play, he took a few steps back, dropping the remote to the floor and almost fainted as anger, shock and total disbelief took over his whole being from the scene that was playing out before him on the screen. "What the fuck type of shit is this!!!" he screamed. Watching his daughter eating her mother's pussy while Trey was fucking her in the ass. "Damn baby, this dick feels so good inside me!! Awwwwww shit, hit it baby while I suck this bitch pussy!!!" Just then Tone noticed Destiny come in the picture as Trey pulled his dick out of Seleste and placed it in Destiny's mouth. After 10 minutes of being caught up in front of the television watching his best friend fucking his daughter, wife and his daughter's girlfriend, he never heard Seleste and

Keisha enter the house as they stood behind him seeing what was being displayed on the TV screen.

"Oooooohhhhhhh my Gaaaawd!!!" Seleste screamed out. Tone looked back noticing them both for the first time, looking from one to the other, full of rage as tears began to fill his eyes and roll down the faces of his daughter and wife's as well. Pulling his gun from out of his dip, never once taking his eyes off of them both while tears began running down his cheeks uncontrollably, he asked just one question before pointing and pulling the trigger, "Whyyyyy?"
BOOM

CHAPTER 14

Scarlett set in her office in front of her computer going over Trey's bank account Summary, having a bittersweet moment while rubbing her basketball size protruding belly. On one hand she missed him so much and was happy as well as convinced she was having his baby. She was also happy to see that he was exceptionally well financially, but knew he was still up to no good fucking with Tina and their massaging business, but at the same time loving the fact that he had actually kept his word when she refused to see him and continued to front her the money to pay her bills. Reflecting on the morning that Trey came and picked her up from the hotel where she stayed for a week after finding out she was pregnant and dealing with the incident with Tone. She stayed there for a week to try to get her head together from all of the nonsense she had been dealing with since the beginning. When she fucked up and let her guards down and fucked Al in the house where she and Trey called home, that is where everything changed. Since Tina had caught her and Al and decided that she would blackmail Scarlett

214

with that fact, Scarlett felt as if she was in a no win situation and from that point on her world seemed to crumble day by day. She knew that Tina's blood sucking ass took pleasure in blackmailing her, mostly because she wanted everything to do with Trey including being his woman and she knew that as long as Scarlett was around it wasn't going to happen. At the same time Scarlett sat there disgusted with Trey for all of the things that he had done in relation to her wrongdoings. Not only was Trey selling his body

Scarlett

for money and cheating on her with every set of open legs with a pussy, she had recently heard through the vine about him sleeping with both Seleste and her daughter, Keisha after having them drugged and videotaped on camera, sleeping with one another and sending the complete DVD to Tone. Although she couldn't stand Tone's ass or the ground he walked upon for putting his hands on her that day in the hotel room, nor for the shit he did after viewing the DVD. She still didn't think Trey should have went that far, especially since that was supposed to be his best friend. She understood the method behind his madness in a sense, and she knew that he was using sex as a weapon to get back at Tone for going behind his back and sleeping with his woman, 'ok, I get that. But he should've handled it in a different way just like this pussy had belonged to him and still does, shit, that dick belongs to me and he shouldn't have been giving them bitches the satisfaction of getting a piece of mines!' she thought to herself.

Over the months Scarlett had been applying all of her energy into her work, going in early when she wasn't overcome with morning sickness and leaving late to keep her mind off of Trey and other negative energy. She visited her mom and family every so often even though she wasn't fond of them because of their lack of interest in her growing up. She had even made amends with Maya after apology after apology from her for doing what she had done to her. Maya forgave her and began visiting her more, even staying weeks at a time with her helping her with her pregnancy and being an ear for her when she needed to vent or when she needed a shoulder to lean on. Scarlett even allowed Maya to fill-in after Deb just up and decided to put her two weeks' notice in and quit. Although she didn't think it was a wise idea to have Maya working in the same office with her, she switched things up by sending her to another one of the locations and sent one of the receptionists from the other location to replace Deb. Maya took the job of being a part time assistant for Scarlett when she visited until a permanent replacement was found, while continuing to work at the popular strip club in her town called SugaWalls as a bartender on a full time basis. As she continued to look at Trey's account summary, she smiled in the inside when she had noticed all of the baby items he had purchased from various department stores and decided at that exact moment she wanted, needed and intended to get her man back. As if instantly wanting to begin the process, she logged off the computer and rose from her desk in her makeshift office that was actually her walk-in closet and headed to the living room to grab her cell phone to give Trey a call. Dressed in nothing but a plain white V-neck POLO t-shirt that had belonged to Trey, one of the many things of his that she did not pack purposely when she had put him out, she noticed herself in the wall mirror. Lifting the already too short shirt that barely covered her ass, she pulled it up above her breast and turned sideways to admire and examine her body while rubbing on her belly. "Damn Scar! Eeeeeel bitch, put some clothes on. Don't nobody wanna see your goodies, with your pregnant naked ass!" Maya said to her as she made her way to the bathroom for her morning routine and added, "Sike girl you look soooo cute pregnant. Oh my gawd girl and then you got a booty with it" Scarlett continued to smile checking her ass out in the mirror thinking that she actually was getting a phat booty.

"If only this big ole thing I got back here don't deflate after I have lil Trey or I'mma have to get me some of them ass shots to make my ass sit up round and perfect. Come here Maya let me feel your ass and see how soft it is." Maya walked back to Scarlett, turning her back to her so she could get a feel of her ass in the black thongs she had been wearing to lounge around the house in. Getting a good feel of her ass, Scarlett gave it a light smack as Maya jumped holding her cheek where Scarlett had smacked it.

"Owwwwww, girl that felt good. I might have to get you to do that again." she said in between laughter making her way to the bathroom. Entering the living room Scarlett picked her phone up and decided to give Trey a call. "Hello" a female voice answered, "Ummmmmm, can I speak with Trey." Scarlett asked taking the phone from her ear and looking at the screen to make sure she dialed the right number.

"He's asleep right now may I ask who is calling or leave him a message. At first the voice didn't sound familiar but as the female continued to talk she then realized that it was her ex assistant who was answering her man's phone. "No wonder this bitch quit", Scarlett began to think, "she's been creeping and fucking with my man behind my back the whole time." What other reason would she be answering his phone, talking about he's asleep and I know she seen my name pop up on his caller ID.' "Deb?"

"Yes it's me, the one and only." she replied sarcastically. Scarlett went from being in a good mood to becoming irate. 'The nerve of this sneaky bitch trying to play me!'

"I know you know who the fuck I am, because I know my name popped up on that caller ID but I am gonna tell your man stealing ass one more time bitch to put my man on the phone and I'm not trying to hear the fuck that he is sleep!" Scarlett screamed into her ear. She could hear Deb in the background laughing and telling Trey to wake up and get his psychotic ex bitch in check, "cause she is on the phone and being disrespectful. Here get up and talk to her before I cuss her ass the fuck out!!!"

"Hello" Trey took the phone sounding as if he was in a deep sleep and just waking up.

"Deb Trey? Really? So you are sleeping with bitches who are my former employees now?"

"Look Scarlett, stop cussing and yelling in my ear. What can I do for you sweetie?"

"Trey just answer my fucking question, are you fucking Deb? And where are you? I hope you not laid up with that bitch at her house!" Just then, Maya came back in the living room sitting beside Scarlett on the couch. "Oh my Gawd girl, I know he not fucking your old assistant now? Girl fuck him, his ass ain't shit."

"Chill Maya! Answer my fucking question Trey!" she said as tears formed in her eyes.

"Look, I'm on my way to your house, I will talk to you when I see you."

"Not before you answer my question, Trey!"

"Scarlett!"

"Yes Trey?"

219

"I said I am on my way and will talk with you when I get there." he told her matter of factly.

"Alright boy bye, I fucking hate you!" Scarlett hung up the phone and tossed it on the love seat that sat a few feet in front of the couch she was sitting on. Even though her and Trey was not a couple anymore and free to date whomever they wanted, she still felt as though he belonged to her and whoever he dealt with needed to know that she would always come first. "Girl, I know you are not letting that shit bother you? You already know how he is. You need to think about you and that baby and not focus your energy on him or that bitch Debbie or Deb or whatever the fuck her name is. What the fuck is that bitch name anyways?" Scarlett looked at Maya and then burst out laughing.

"It's Deborah, girl your ass is so damn crazy."

"Deborah?" Maya said as if she was surprised to learn her name. "Well is the bitch black? What black person you know with a name like Deborah!?! No wonder they call her ass Deb, that bitch's mother was probably smoking crack and getting fucked by a white man that had her speaking in tongues and shit! Talking about some fucking Deborah!" Scarlett couldn't stop laughing as Maya continued to make fun of Deb's government name, to the point that she had tears rolling down her cheeks.

"Bitch that was mean, and I didn't know you was a racist and a heathen!" she said in between laughter. "Girl, I'm not no damn racist, I love me some white dick! Black dick...Green dick...shit, I like dead presidents with white faces on them. Shitttttt girl I like all people, but not no got damn black bitch with a name like Deborah!" Scarlett got serious and let a tear

220

roll from her face from the sadness that was beginning to take over her. "I don't know Maya, I want my man back even though we done both put each other through hell and I want my child to grow up with both parents in his or her life, under the same fucking roof." Scarlett wiped the tears away from her face at the same time tears began to run down Maya's face. "Now see bitch, you got my sentimental ass in here crying and shit! Please Scarlett baby, I understand you are missing Trey and you wanna raise your child in a home with a daddy, but Trey is a dog and it don't seem like he gonna change. So you need to have that baby and find you a Mr. Right that will take care of you and your baby." Maya told her. The whole time Maya sat there she thought about how much she wanted to fuck Trey again and dreamed on a many of nights about sucking his dick one more time while she sat there pretending to have Scarlett's back.

"But, I really think he can change Maya."

"Change what Scar, his boxers?!"

"Why do you speak so negative of him?" Scarlett asked picking up the hatred that Maya was trying to disguise as concern. "I'm not speaking negative of him babe, but I think there are just some people that are capable of changing and some that aren't ever going to change. Trey is the latter. Just my thoughts sweetie. Besides I'm your girl and I'm gonna always have your back."

"Well that is not what it sounds like SWEETIE, so if you don't mind I would like to be alone when he arrives." Scarlett rose from the couch and walked to her bedroom slamming the door shut behind her. "Ooooookk, I will leave you two love birds to attempt to rekindle." she said to herself. Noticing Scarlett's

221

phone on the love seat, Maya rose from the couch and made her way to the phone and began looking through it. As she scanned through the phone, she went straight to her pictures albums and began to look at and lust over the nude pics she had of Trey. She licked her lips and began perspiring while becoming more and more turned on at the site of him being nude as she reflected on the times when they were intimate or when she would watch his dick print jump around when he walked around the house with sweatpants on. Searching through Scarlett's phone further, she came across a phone number and saved it in her own phone. Tossing the phone back on the chair, she rose from the couch and went into the room Scarlett used as her walk-in closet/office. Once inside she went through her suitcase and pulled out one of her tight white Victoria Secret jogging suits that fit her like second skin and put on her matching grey and white Nike sneakers and headed back to the living room. She grabbed her phone and purse, told Scarlett that she was heading out and she would call her to let her know if she was coming back for the night. "Ok Maya, just lock my door behind you please!" she yelled through the closed bedroom door. Maya headed downstairs and out of the house. Once inside her car she dialed the number she had just stored from Scarlett's phone as a sexy male voice answered, "Yeah, who is this?"

"Hey boo, how are you? This is Scarlett' friend, Maya."

"Oh hey, what's up Maya? How did you get my number and how can I help you?" Al asked trying to figure out this chick's angle. "Well, let's just say I had to sneak and jump through hoops to get your number! she said seductively laughing while adding, "I was here visiting Scarlett and since she so love drunk over her boyfriend I was bored and lonely and was trying to hang out with a real boss type nigga and see if you wanted to show a girl a nice time." Al didn't even have to think about what she had said cause he wanted a piece of Maya for years while him and Scarlett were together and even when they broke up but he was leery about stepping to her because he feared she would go back and run her mouth like most bitches. "Damn girl, you couldn't have called at a better time cause right now I am on my way to Hooligan's to have a few drinks and your sexy ass would be the perfect company. How about you meet me there in a half an hour?"

"Not a problem boo, I was actually sitting in my car letting it run hoping you would say to come and meet up with you. Alright Al, I will call you when I am parking."

"Cool Maya baby, see you then." he told her ending the call. Maya placed the car in drive, buckled her seat belt and pulled off headed to the sports bar to meet up with Al. She planned to get fucked up, drunk and let Al fuck her in every way imaginable. Scarlett walked away from the window seal after seeing Maya pull off in the rented Chevy Impala, stepped out of her bedroom and made her way to the living room and grabbed her phone off of the sofa. She dialed Trey's number again to check to see if he was on his way. Once he answered and confirmed he would be there in about 20 minutes they ended the call with each other as she made her way downstairs to unlock the door for him. She was excited and smiling from the anticipation of seeing him. Making her way back to her bedroom she turned her TV on, laid back in the bed on her many pillows and began watching the Bad Chicks Club awaiting his arrival.

◊◊◊

Trey laid there in Deb's bed half asleep after his mini workout routine which consisted of Pull-ups and pushups and a steamy hot shower he had taken immediately afterwards. He heard when his phone had rung and Deb answered it. Wanting to say something to her about answering his phone without his permission crossed his mind, but he just let it slide for the moment promising himself when he got up and was fully alert he would. When she passed him the phone letting him know that it was Scarlett on the line, everything in him wanted to slap the shit out of her for being so disrespectful to his ex and possible child mother. After ending the call with her he checked Deb's simple ass, letting her know not to ever do that shit again. She tried to put up a fight with words saying how Scarlett deserved to be disrespected and how she couldn't believe he was taking up for her when she didn't give a fuck about him, adding, "It's a possibility that she is pregnant with your home boys baby. Fuck off Trey, she disrespected you and you wanna still take up for that bitch after the fact and I have been nothing but good to your ass!" Trey reached over while lying next to her and put his index finger in her mouth before she can say another word. Catching her totally off guard he placed his other index finger to his lips telling her to shush and be quiet. Slowly sliding his finger out of her mouth letting it run across her tongue and bottom lip, he then pulled his dick out from his boxer briefs and simply told her, "Wake him up!" Doing as she was told Deb rolled her eyes at him, bent her head down in his lap and wrapped her lips around his semi erectness and slowly sucked him in and out of her mouth the way she knew he loved. Trey laid there enjoying the satisfaction, as he quietly began to release his load in her mouth and down her throat while she swallowed his massive load down to the last drop. She continued to lick his dick and testicles clean like a cat. Trey removed himself from her mouth, pulled his boxer briefs up and arose from the bed putting his clothes on. "So, where are you going Trey," she asked. "Lemme guess, you are about to go and run to Scarlett's aid or is it the other one, Tina?" Ignoring her, Trey got dressed and sprayed on some cologne, grabbed his keys from off of her dresser and walked out of her house without ever saying a word. He laughed at himself at the way he just carried her. 'Stupid ass chick' he thought to himself as he got in his black on black Bentley coupe that Consuela had gifted him and drove in silence to Scarlett's house. At this point in Trey's life, he felt on top of the world and although things were going his way financially, he still felt like something was missing out of his life. His relationship with Deb was becoming more annoying every day, mostly because of her demanding more and more of his time which was something he wasn't trying to give, and also because of the other women in his life. At least that is what she thought. She figured her sex with him, allowing him to do whatever he wanted to and with her, from the threesomes with other women including her friends, as well as other random chicks, allowing him to bring his clientele to her house and fucking them while she would be in the other room listening. To the moans and cries of him catering to other women, while she would cater to him by washing his back and dick when he was done with them, would be enough to keep his mind focused on her and only her. Never one time did she think that he just wasn't willing to commit to her no matter what she did and she was pretty much locked in the friend zone; nothing more and nothing less, no matter how much she put it on him sexually and complained when he wasn't around her. Trey knew that the time had come for him to delete Deb out of his life, but every time he was ready to he would convince himself that after he slept with her one last time and every time that one last time she would pull a trick out of her sleeve, making him think with the head in his pants instead of the one underneath his fitted cap causing him to have a change of heart and keeping her around a little longer. Knowing that Scarlett would be pissed whether they were together or not if she found out about him dealing with Deb, was one of the main reasons that he kept it a secret from her for the past 6 months. Not to mention Tina who had been skeptical of his dealings with Deb but never interfered, telling him once that 'he had better not slip up and give his heart to another woman other than her and any woman he dealt with it had better be strictly business and business only or she would make him pay in the worst way.

"If you ever hurt my heart and share your heart and emotions with one of these bitches out here, or even give my dick away to a bitch that we are not benefiting from financially, I'm gonna fuck you and that bitch's shit all the way up, make your life a living hell and you will never see me or this baby of ours that is growing inside me, at least not in this lifetime. Do you understand me Trey, baby?" she threatened him one night while laying on top of him with her head laying on his chest after they had just finished making love for the prior 2 hours. "Yeah, whatever Tina. Your ass is not stupid." was his only reply but deep in his heart he believed every word that had just come out of her mouth as they both remained silent falling into a deep sleep.

From that day on, living with her under her roof he kept his dealings with other women outside of clients, a secret or he would lie and act as if they were clients when she would get suspicious and began asking too many questions. Even keeping it a secret that he had his own little penthouse downtown that he had been staying at when he got away with Consuela whom had purchased it for him in his name as a gift to go along with the Bentley coupe she had given him. He knew he had it made with having a woman like Tina on his side and loving everything about her from her pretty yellow pedicured toes to the top of her number one inch smooth blonde head and he showed her daily by being her protector, provider, lover and friend. When he found out she was pregnant and he was going to be the father, everything in him was excited and happy but it was still a piece of him that was hurting, because he knew at some point he would have to share this same information with Scarlett whom a part of him still loved and yearned for despite all the shit they been through.

He figured he would tell her when the time was right, because a part of him felt like what they had together wasn't over until he was ready for it to be over. But in the meantime he figured he would apply his focus and energy into getting to the money and loving and being there for the one he was with since he couldn't be there for the one he truly was in love with. He had wanted so badly to combine both Scarlett and Tina together and make them as one, because of their differences and what they both represented for which was the main reasons why he loved them both and why it was so hard for him to focus on just one. But then it was also that night life that he was also in love with that he wasn't ready to give up on, so to him he felt like he was in love with three women living life a hundred miles per hour with no plans on stopping. A good friend of his sat him down one day and told him something that he would never forget, "Trey my friend, you gotta slow down a little bit because you have too many balls in the air and when they come crashing down they all will fall at once and nothing good will come out of that."

"I hear you my friend, but as sure as my name is Trey, I have everything under control so I will be good."

From that day on, Trey always thought about what was told to him and never forgot, more so taking those words as a warning to stay 10 steps ahead of the game and not to slip. Now on this cool night with the air still and his top down, sunk deep in the plush black leather seats. Trey pulled up in front of Scarlett's house as the thought of him being in control crossed his mind. He had to laugh as he put the top of the Bentley back up, placed the car in park, turned the ignition off and grabbed his phone dialing her number while exiting his vehicle. "The door is unlocked Trey, come on in." she answered. He told her he would see her in a sec, ended the call and made his way to her front door. As he approached Scarlett's door he received a call from Tina.

"Hey Tina baby, what's up?" he answered stopping to take her call before entering Scarlett's.

"Baby, I am laying here lonely, bored and hungry. I need you, where are you?" Hesitating before answering the question with the truth, which he knew she picked up on, he still went on and told her the truth knowing how pissed she would be.

"Baby, I'm just arriving at Scarlett's house, about to see her for a minute."

"For what Trey!?"

"I don't know, she called me over saying she needed to talk to me about something." he told her.

"So you go and run to her aid while I'm laying here pregnant with your child, missing you. Then on top of that instead of you bringing your ass home to check on me all I get is a phone call last night. So where did you stay? But before you answer that question Trey, answer me this, Is Scarlett pregnant and about to have your baby?"

Becoming irate at the way the conversation was going, Trey sighed and turned to face Scarlett as she stood in the doorway arms folded with his black silk Versace robe opened, revealing her protruding stomach and nude body.

"Look, I will be there when she and I are finished talking, ok?"

"No, it's not ok Trey, so what you're telling me is that you are choosing her over your family, what you have at home with me?" Tina was trying everything in her power not to scream and raise her voice, but she knew Trey was up to no good and trying to play her on the back burner for Scarlett. "But then again I'll let you go boo, I will see you whenever. Just know that you are fucking up Trey, go ahead with your conversation, and so you know I'm not feeling this shit at all!"

Hanging up in his, Trey looked down at this phone, smiled and placed it in his pocket as Scarlett pulled him in her arms, giving him a hug that showed how much she missed him. "Boy, come on in this house, its cold out here." Scarlett said. Taking his hand, she pulled him inside locking her locks as they made their way to her bedroom. Once inside her bedroom Scarlett sat her back against the headboard as Trey sat at the bottom of the bed facing her with that famous smile of his planted on his face. Giving him the once over, she had to admit that he was looking good in his black Gucci polo shirt, black Gucci belt, jeans and shoes. 'Damn he smelling so fucking good. I miss you Trey so fucking much! Awwwwww I miss that smile' she began thinking as she looked him in the eye with one eyebrow raised. "So tell me Trey, how are you doing and was that your girlfriend on the phone?" she asked.

"Scarlett, you know who that was on the phone and yes that was my chick and I am doing good, how about yourself?"

"Miserable!"

"Enlighten me Scarlett, why are you so miserable? Last time I checked you were happy and things were looking up for you and going your way."

"Move closer to me Trey, I'm not gonna hit you!" she told him fist raised in the air wagging her index finger suggesting him to come closer. Moving inches apart from her, he reached out and began rubbing her stomach. "Do you love her?" she asked him catching him totally off guard with her question.

"Of course I do Scarlett, just like I love you!"

"Trey I'm pregnant with your baby, does that mean anything to you? Matter of fact, you don't even need to answer that question."

"No, it's cool Scarlett, yes it means something to me, but you know how I feel about that. I'm still having doubts that your baby is mine, honestly." he told her. Just as the words rolled off of his tongue a tear rolled down her eye.

"Trey baby, if you have doubts then why are you out buying baby clothes and shit like that?"

"Baby clothes??" Trey was puzzled and caught by surprise that she knew about his baby shopping that he was doing with Tina.

"Yes cause she's pregnant Scarlett and that is what she and I do from time to time. Where did you see us at?" Having no idea that she didn't see nor know that whoever he was talking about was pregnant, his words hit her like a knife to the heart, and feeling like her whole being was shattered like broken glass. "So you got Deb running around pregnant with your fucking baby, are you kidding me?"

"No, just Tina. I thought you knew that already. You think I'm that crazy to get Deb pregnant?!" Trey got serious trying to figure out where Scarlett was going with her questions. She reached out and slapped him making his head turn and face turn red. Swinging her legs off of the bed she rose to her feet and charged at him, swinging at his face and head. Catching her hands, Trey wrapped his arms around her waist as she gave in and cried in his arms. She wrapped her arms around his waist and continued to sob as the tears continuously rolled down her face onto his sleeve. "Why Trey, Why did you have to do me like this? Do I mean anything to you? I fucking love you with my whole heart and soul!" Trey was at a loss of words as he continued to hold her feeling all of her pain and what she was going through.

"Do you love me Trey?"

"Yes Scarlett, I do. But I can't change what I've done in the past nor the shit that we have been through." he told her while still in her embrace.

"Come back home Trey, please I need you. We need you?!" Before he could respond his phone began to ring, after ignoring it for the third time he dug in his pocket, looked at the screen and seen it was Tina again. Just as he noticed it, so did Scarlett. She released him, climbed back in her bed and watched him as tears continued to flow down her face and into her pillow, while lying in the fetal position holding her stomach.

"Yeah Tina, what's up?"

"So you decided to not come home and basically choose that bitch over me, huh?" she calmly questioned him.

"Look Tina, I said I will be home after her and I talk baby. So chill, what is your problem?"

"You are so right Trey, don't even worry about it. I will let you know face to face when I get there!" Tina said ending the call in his ear without saying another word. Trey stood there not knowing what to do, because everything in him knew that Tina was seriously about to knock on Scarlett's door. He knew he couldn't let both of these pregnant emotional women whom were supposedly pregnant behind him get into an altercation against one another so at that point he decided to leave Scarlett's house, get control of Tina and make his decision on whom he wanted to spend his life with, if he chose to be with anyone. Sitting down on the bed next to her he removed a strand of hair away from her face and wiped the tears that were streaming down her face. "Listen to me Scarlett, I do miss you and would love for us to try and rekindle what we once had, but I just really need to sit down and get my life in order and get my thoughts together on the upcoming decisions I need to make." Lifting her chin, he wiped the tears from her eyes and further told her, "I am serious Scarlett, if you love me like you say you do then I need you to give me some time. Do you hear me?" Sitting up in the bed, Scarlett wrapped her arms around his neck.

"Yes, Trey I hear you baby. Just don't make me wait too long, cause you know I hate waiting." As their lips met, Trey felt the connection that they once shared. He knew he had to get going so he could deal with Tina's crazy ass. Hugging her tightly, he broke the kiss along with the hug and rose from the bed. Helping her to her feet he opened up her robe and looked at her nude pregnant body and began feeling that familiar tingle in the head of his dick. "Damn, your body is sexy as shit even while you are pregnant!"

"Oh yeah, well you know what they say about that pregnant pussy. Besides, maybe if you hurry up and make your way back home with me or stay the night with me I will think about giving you some." Loving the way that sounded Trey smiled at the thought and was considering on taking her up on her offer, but just not tonight. "How about we make this happen tomorrow?" he asked her.

"What, you spending the night with me or coming back home?" she had to smile at her own question as everything in her lit up with hope for the latter.

"How about if I spend some time with you tomorrow and you show me what that pregnant pussy like?"

233

"How about I tie your ass up and hold you hostage so you won't go anywhere or ever leave me?" she questioned him with a serious look on her face. Trey continued to laugh as he told her to walk him to the door, giving her a hug. Releasing each other he unlocked the door and as he began to walk out she yelled out to him, "Trey, you don't have to call. I'm pretty sure you still have your key, use it!"

"Alright Scarlett baby, now carry your ass in the house. You standing there all exposed and shit, you're gonna make me fuck somebody up!" Scarlett blushed as she stepped in the house, closing and securing her locks. Trey noticed Tina's Range Rover pull up behind his Bentley while he was walking around to his driver's side to get in and leave. Pissed off that she had the audacity to pop up at Scarlett's house but not at all surprised, Trey walked up to her tinted driver side window ready to hear her excuse as to why she showed up and to give her a taste of how he felt about her pulling this stupid ass stunt. "Man, roll the window down silly!" Trey grabbed the door handle pulling on it realizing it was still locked. He stepped closer to the window as it rolled down giving him the surprise of his life from what happened next, but by then it was too late.

CHAPTER 15

Keisha watched as Trey exited Scarlett's house through her binoculars from two blocks away. 'This bitch is standing in the damn door in a fucking robe, naked, without a fucking care in the world about who may see her pregnant ass. "Mmmmhmmmmmm, she pretty and that's a cute robe, Versace, bitch I see you."

"Ohhhhh bitch, let me see" Destiny said snatching the binoculars.

"Girl pull off, she just shut the door and he walking to his car now. Damn this nigga pushing a Bentley!" Cutting her high beams on Keisha placed the car in drive and pulled away from the curb. Pulling up behind Trey's car as he was about to get in, they watched as he walked up to the driver's side window assuming it was Tina telling her to roll down the window while checking the door handle to see if it was unlocked. "Awwwww, he must think you're his bitch!" joked Destiny. "I kind of miss his ugly ass, girl I had a crush on his ass for years. But fuck all of that shit, I'mma make his ass pay for that shit he did, especially with Tone ass being locked up and Seleste in the fucking looney bin with the rest of the crazy mother fuckers! Bitch, let's go!" With the car in park, Keisha rolled the driver's side window down while leaving her seat laid back slightly knowing Trey would stick his head in the window. As soon as he placed his hands on the window seal and stuck his head in halfway, he noticed Keisha sitting behind the wheel instead. Taken aback by the sight of her, he was caught off guard when she sprayed him with a can of pepper spray mace catching him not only in the eyes but in the mouth also, while his mouth hung open in shock. "Bitch!!!" Trey yelled out while falling to his knees choking. Seizing the moment, both Keisha and Destiny jumped out the truck, gun drawn while Destiny had a Louisville slugger metal baseball bat. "Get your punk ass up and get the fuck in the backseat before I shoot your ass!" Keisha screamed. Trying to focus and see as much as he could, Trey did notice the silver gun Keisha was now pressing to his temple. "You heard me nigga, get the fuck up!!" Continuing to choke Trey did the best he could to stand up and prevent her from shooting him. Destiny swung the bat hitting him in his left arm, "She said get up. NOW NIGGA!"

Doing as he was told Trey found his way in the back seat of the truck with Keisha kicking him in his ass and climbing in the back of the truck with him, never once taking the gun away from his head. Destiny jumped in the driver's seat, placed the car back in drive while Trey continued to complain about his eyes burning and face feeling numb. "So what about his car, Keish?"

"Fuck your eyes and your fucking pain, bitch you lucky I don't shoot your ass right here!" Keisha screamed, "Fuck his car, we will get that shit later, for now let's take him to his bitch so we can deal with these mother fuckers together!" Destiny pulled off from in front of Scarlett's house and began driving back to Tina house where they had left her blindfolded and duct taped to a chair in the middle of her living room floor. While Keisha kept the gun pointed on him, she had a flash back of the dreadful day that sent her father to jail and her mom to the insane asylum, all because of the man that sat before her.

"Why?" Tone said pointing the gun at Seleste head then pulling the trigger. Seleste never had a chance to duck or dodge the bullet as it grazed the right side of her temple, just inches away from entering her brain. With both hands clutching her tear filled face, Seleste fell to her knees as Tone rushed to where she kneeled, knocking her to the floor full of rage, choking her with one hand and beating her in the head with the butt of the gun with the other hand. "Daddy, what the fuck are you doing? Get the fuck off of her!!" Keisha yelled trying to fight her father off of Seleste, while Seleste tried fighting and kicking from beneath him for dear life. "This is all your fault bitch!!" Tone screamed. Tone's eyes seemed to go black as he continued to beat Seleste over the head with the gun while choking the life out of her at the same time. Keisha continued to swing on him as she crashed a vase against his head. Trey rose from above Seleste and hit Keisha with a two piece punch to her face as she fell to the floor crying, holding her face. "You little bitch, you are a fucking whore, just like your fucking mother!!!" While Tone began tearing up everything in the house that he could get his hands on, like breaking tables and glass flower pots, he ripped TV's off the walls and stomped on the screens of them in a rage like Keisha had never witnessed before. Not knowing what else he was capable of, she crawled to her purse to retrieve her phone and called 911 while he moved on to a new part of the house up, yelling and screaming obscenities in a language she couldn't make out or understand! Talking to the dispatcher she tried her best to let her know what was going on, but dropped the phone to the floor in mid-sentence when she looked up and noticed Seleste laying still as if she was dead. Still dazed from the two punches she took to the face, she crawled to where her mother was lying motionless on the floor bleeding profusely from her head and face, felt for her pulse and put her hands under her bleeding nose realizing that she was indeed still alive. Wiping the blood from her bleeding nose, Keisha picked her phone back up and before dropping the phone back to the floor, she gave the dispatcher her address telling her to send a medic because her mother had been shot and beaten and looked as if she were growing unconscious. When the police and ambulance arrived, Tone was still full of rage taking his anger out on the officers as well as the mess he had made in the house. It took four officers to restrain him. As they even had to hit him with a taser guns just to be able to arrest him and allow the medics to work on Keisha and Seleste and be able to rush them out of the house and to the hospital quickly. When they arrived at the hospital, Keisha convinced the doctors that she didn't need no medical treatment but to please save her mother, who was slipping in and out of consciousness, due to the severe head trauma and beating Tone had put on her. Seleste stayed in a coma for a month while her daughter stayed by her side day and night praying she would wake up normal like she was before this trauma. Tone admitted to the beating of both his wife and daughter and sat in jail with a "NO BAIL" awaiting his trial date. Keisha had visited him when she could and sometimes he would accept her visit but most of the time he refused, saying that he wanted nothing to do with her or the rest of his family, not even his wife that was in the hospital fighting for her life. Only calling Keisha collect when he wanted her to handle business for him, regarding his lawyer and making sure that his commissary account stayed full of money, which she always did.

When Seleste finally came out of the coma, she was extremely delusional and would talk to herself, randomly bursting out into laughing fits while she was alone and even trying to fight on the medical staff, while telling everyone she was from another planet and she was being held hostage by aliens. Everyday Keisha prayed that her life was actually a bad nightmare that she would soon be awakened from and everything would go back to how it was before the events. She sought revenge on Trey, dedicating her days to finding out everything she could about him,

238

from the stakeout like stalking sessions where she would just sit outside of both Scarlett and Tina's houses. Keisha planned to take Trey down for the all of the abrupt life changes that he had managed to take her and her family through in such a short time.

Now sitting in the backseat beside him with a gun pointed to his head, she realized that she didn't necessarily want to kill him but she did need him to pay for the pain and the betrayal. But before she would make him pay she felt like she needed to hear his excuse on why he did what he did, not that it really mattered. Pulling up outside of Tina's house, both Keisha and Destiny jumped out of the truck looking normal like they could have been one of Tina's friends, to anyone who noticed them. Opening the back door where Trey was still hunched over fighting the pain and the burning of not only his eyes but also his face. Keisha smacked him in his forehead with the front of the Glock 23, then pushing it into his neck calming him down when he was about to jump at her in reflex, she hurried him to the doorway as Destiny stood waiting. Once inside locking the door behind them, Keisha pushed Trey down on the love sofa as Tina watched on, duct taped to one of the dining room chairs that sat in the middle of the living room floor with tear filled eyes. In her head, Tina sat there praying that the two crazy bitches would not hurt her, Trey or their unborn child.

"Bitch duct tape this mother fucker up and if he flinch wrong I'm gonna put a fucking hole in his head...Him and his bitch!" Keisha said blowing a kiss at Tina.

"Keisha, what the fuck is this about?!" asked Trey as if he had no idea and then added, "If it is money that you want, bitch you can get it!" screamed Trey.

Destiny swung the bat hitting him in his arm when he looked as if he wanted to rise. Falling back to the couch, Destiny dropped the bat and began duct taping his hands behind his back and his ankles together so he couldn't get away as Keisha looked on, never taking the gun away from his head. Only being able to see out of one of his eyes but unable to move, Trey cursed aloud for letting these two bitches get the best of him and endangering his woman and unborn child. Keisha went into the kitchen and came back with a quart of milk, kissed Tina on the duct tape that covered her lips, walked past her and set atop Trey's lap. With one hand she wrapped them around his neck pushing his head back and unscrewing the milk with other as she began pouring milk all over his face and eyes to reverse the effects of the pepper spray. "Open your fucking eyes Trey! I'm trying to help your stupid ass out because I want you to see what you have gotten yourself into." Doing as he was told, Trey opened his eyes allowing her to pour the milk in them, enjoying the cool sensation it gave by cooling off the burning feeling of the pepper spray. Tossing the empty milk carton to the floor, Keisha raised his shirt and flipped it over top of his head. "Destiny hand me a towel boo, and what do you think we should do with him while we let his fat ass girlfriend watch?"

"Hold that thought Keish, cause I have plenty of ideas for this mother fucker." Destiny told her looking around the kitchen then coming back with a towel handing it to her.

"We can get his dick rock hard and then cut that mother fucker off and feed it to his bald headed ass girlfriend over here." Accepting the towel from her, Keisha continued to sit on his lap and dab the liquid dry from his face to his chest. "Nawwwww, that's why her ass is pregnant now, he keeps feeding her that good dick, so that would be a treat for her. Wouldn't it bitch!?" Keisha rose from his lap and walked over to where Tina sat and ripped the tape from her mouth and said, "I said feeding you his dick would be a treat for your hungry nasty ass, wouldn't it bitch!" Tina just sat there feeling defeated and deep down blaming Trey for this madness that they were currently enduring. She felt as if she needed some questions answered in order to measure the extremities that these bitches would go through with seeking revenge on Trey at this costs with inflicting pain the mental and physical. "Look what is it that the two of you want?" questioned Tina, "If it is money, jewelry or electronics you can have whatever you want in here, there is a safe upstairs in the closet…Take everything in it and you don't have to worry about the police being involved, I promise that!" Waiting for a response, Tina just sat there fuming mad on the inside and for that instant she thought, 'if only I wasn't pregnant!' She knew she could take both of the women and beat their asses senseless but the thought of her losing her baby brought her back to reality and she knew she needed to play her position and keep cool with these crazy chicks if she wanted to come out on top. She knew being hostile and belligerent wasn't going to do it. Keisha pulled Destiny into the kitchen with her and as soon as they were out of ear shot she handed her the gun and told her to get the code for the safe that Tina spoke of and place everything in a bag, as well as grab anything else that she saw profitable, while she dealt with Trey and his bitch alone. Doing just that, Destiny walked out of the kitchen and made Tina give her the code to the safe. Once she retrieved it she winked at Trey before walking up the stairs toward the bedroom to do as she was told. Keisha came out of the kitchen

241

with a butcher knife in hand smiling as if she was up to no good, overhearing Trey tell Tina 'not to worry cause he was going to get them out of the situation unharmed. "Is that so Trey?!" Keisha retorted catching him off guard. Climbing back atop his lap, she placed the butcher knife against his neck and began applying pressure until she saw a tiny spec of blood trickle down the blade.

"Bitch, I swear on everything if you lay a finger on or harm Tina, I am going to rip your fucking heart out with my bare hands! That shit I did to you and your mother was out of anger Keisha!"

"What the fuck is going on Trey?" questioned Tina struggling to free herself from the tape.

"Bitch, shut the fuck up," screamed Keisha. "But why Trey? My fucking mother is wacked the fuck out in a crazy home, while Tone is in the county jail facing Life plus, because of what you did to us! Does that mean anything to you Trey? I should cut your fucking head off, SO ANSWER ME NOW TREY!! Why the fuck did you do it!" Trey felt the knife beginning to cut through his flesh as more blood began running down his throat and chest. Seeing the anger in her eyes, while still sensing her weakness, Trey knew he had to get control of the situation and at that moment he wondered what the fuck Destiny was doing. Trey began laughing in Keisha's face and told her,

"Man look, before you kill me at least suck my dick and let me die with a smile on my face, bitch!" Cocking her head to the right, Keisha squinted her eyes in disgust, as well as lust, wondering how someone could ooze sexiness even with his life on the line and the possibility of death. Making her temperature rise and blood boil at the same time, Keisha removed the knife from his throat gripped his face and kissed his lips, pushing her tongue in his mouth. Breaking the kiss she began to cut his pants off of him and added, "I plan to, then I am going to fuck you one last time in front of your bitch. So say good bye to her ass cause once you blow, you got to go and then her ass is next... Ok, bitch!" she said as she glanced back at Tina while she continued to cut his pants until he was bare from the waist down. She kept a firm hold of the knife as she proceeded to get on her knees in front of him and began to suck his flaccid dick. Trey looked at Tina who was just sitting there in shock not believing what was taking place before her eyes. Tina smiled at him and pulled her hands to the side to reveal that she had freed her hands and was planning to make a move. Trey shook his head as to give her a nonverbal no. Starting to feel that familiar tingle in his dick, Trey was starting to swell up in her mouth as he looked up and noticed Destiny peeking from the wall of the staircase. Putting her index finger up to her lips to tell Tina and Trey to keep quiet, Destiny came from behind the wall and fired the gun in the air making Keisha jump off of Trey's dick and fall back landing on her back, scared shitless trying to scramble to her feet to see where the shot came from and what was hit.

"Stay the fuck on the ground you snake ass bitch! Yeah, that's right bitch I'm TEAM TREY! Did you really think I wasn't gonna find out about that fake shit you been doing behind my back, huh bitch??!" Destiny said as she kicked Keisha in her chest and watched as Keisha scooted back trying to get away from her. "Bitch, you tried to fuck my man in my bed and sucked his dick after you pillow talked him to death about me! You did some sheisty shit stealing the money from my account when I was taking care of you! You a trifling ass hoe!" While Destiny and Keisha was caught up in one another's madness, Tina untaped her legs from the chair and ran to Trey, helping him pull and unravel the tape from his wrist while he turned to his side. Once she untaped his hands, he reached down to free his ankles and turned to Tina and whispered for her to go upstairs while he deal with these two women. As Tina got up to do what Trey said, she turned to run up the stairs and grabbed her stomach and stumbled to the floor with Trey behind her catching her before she hit the ground. Trey helped to carry her up the stairs as her body and breathing became heavier. By the time they got into her bedroom Tina's water had broken just as they heard two gunshots go off downstairs, followed by two loud thumps as if it were raining 200 lb. weights.

"Oh my gosh, what the fuck Trey! I'm not going to have my baby in here with these two crazy bitches downstairs trying to kill one another!" Trey told her to sit still and stay there while he ran downstairs to see what was going on. Digging in her closet, Trey grabbed his .45 automatic and crept back down the stairs to survey the damage. When he got halfway down the stairs he peeked around the wall to see Keisha lying motionless looking dead against the door bleeding from a bullet wound in her neck and through her forehead, while Destiny was on the floor laying on her back fighting for her life with the same butcher knife that Keisha had earlier plunged deeply through her neck. The point of the blade came out of the back of her neck while blood sprayed profusely all over the living room. Trey ran back upstairs just in time to hear Tina calling out for him. Grabbing the house phone, Trey tossed the phone to Tina and told her to call the police and ambulance while he got his self together. Tina did as told and in five minutes the cops were outside of the house banging on the door. Trey ran in the other bedroom and stashed the gun in the safe that was untouched by Destiny. Realizing that he was still bleeding from the neck, he grabbed a towel out of the closet and pressed it against the open cut. Ready to let the cops in he glanced down and laughed to himself when he realized he was still nude from the waist down. He quickly walked back in the bedroom where Tina was looking at him smiling and clutching her stomach, "Naked ass, hurry up and put something on so you can let them in before I have your baby right here on this fucking futon." Grabbing a pair of his gray Yves Saint Laurent sweatpants out of the closet he put his legs in them without taking his shoes off and pulled them up to his waist, tossed the shirt he had on to the floor, grabbing the matching sweatshirt to the pants he'd just put on and walked out the room making his way to open the door. "Trey, hurry up please boooo!" Looking down at Destiny as he walked past her he cursed himself for not having her back like she had his. It was because of Destiny that he learned of Keisha's plan of revenge and how she planned to make him pay for what he had done to her family.

◊◊◊

"Hello, is this Trey?" the unfamiliar female voice asked on the opposite end of Trey's phone.

"Yeah, this be me, what's up?" Trey asked. Sitting on Tina's bed massaging her swollen feet and ankles while she laid back admiring the way he curved his lips as he talked.

"Hi, Trey this is Destiny. I don't know if you remember me or not but I was the chick at the hotel with Keisha that night when you pulled that dope ass stunt on that ugly ass bitch and her crazy ass mother." she said laughing into the phone. Trey began laughing with her sensing the dislike she had for Keisha but also wondered why was she calling him. "I know you are probably wondering why I am calling you, but you are a cool ass cutie and I just wanted to put you on point about that bitch Keisha and what she plans to try to pull on you because of what you did to her and her mother as well as exposing her slut ass."

"Oh yeah, so how do I know that you're not in cahoots with that bitch or handling some shit for Tone trying to win my trust and then snake the shit out of me. I mean, I haven't been hiding out or nothing and no one has expressed beef with me but I'm definitely smart enough to know that all is fair in war, right?"

"Yeah, I feel you. I definitely feel you boo, and I know you don't have no reason to trust me but I

assure you that I am loyal and that bitch Keisha has crossed the line with me and did some cruddy shit to me behind my back, but she thinks that I don't know so when she came to me discussing how she found out where both of your babies mothers lived and what she planned to do, I felt the need to call you and put you on point with that scheming ass hoe!" Destiny assured him so he would be clear on where she was coming from and the type of real woman she actually was on the contrary.

"Look, I was in the middle of something with a special lady of mine. How about we meet up in a few to further discuss this shit face to face?! And if it is money you are seeking we can handle that as well." Trey told her very ready to end the call and get back to the task at hand.

"No boo I'm good, you can keep your money," she said laughing in between her words, "just get a bitch nails did and give me another round with that thing between your legs that you got these bitches losing their minds over while I'm sober this time and in the right frame of mind, is that a deal?"

"Yeah, that's cool D. I will text you the address and location where to meet me as soon as I am done with what I'm doing, alright?"

"Alright, Trey boo. See you soon sweetie."

After hanging up with Destiny and making sure Tina was satisfied with his work, he eventually texted "D" the location where they would meet to seal the deal. Once he was in the company of Destiny again, he had to admit that she had looked better than he remembered. He kept his end of the deal up and paid for her manicure and pedicure as she asked, while they spoke about everything from what Tina had in store for him and when she planned on doing it, the reason why he fucked the three of them on camera in the first place, as well as the whole Keisha and Celeste incestuous relationship. Destiny realized that she loved his style and swag and he was definitely feeling hers, they eventually made it back to Destiny's house where they planned to seal the deal. They continued to converse for damn near the whole night getting to know one another while sipping on Patron silver and a sparkling Moscato until they found themselves laying on opposite sides of each other, sweating and out of breath in Destiny's bed, as a result of the animalistic sex they had engaged in until the sun came up. It felt heaven sent to the both of them, but little did either know.

◊◊◊

Now walking past Destiny, seeing her lifeless body sprawled across Tina's living room floor laying in a pool of blood, a warm chill ran through his body and he felt a tinge of sympathy for her because to him she was a really cool and down to earth bitch who didn't deserve to die. Before Trey opened the door, he glanced down at Keisha and the only thoughts that crossed his mind when it came to her was that she was a good HOE turned sour. Opening the door for the officers and medics, they all rushed in and immediately began interrogating him. A couple of officers rushed up the steps with the medics and rushed to Tina's aid to help tend to her and their unborn baby. Removing Tina and Trey from the scene the medics rushed them to the nearest hospital in the back of the same ambulance since they refused to be separated from one another. They watched on as news crews from several local channels began to broadcast LIVE the crime scene of their home, calling it a 'kidnapping and attempted robbery gone wrong between feuding girlfriends who brutally took the lives of each other execution style'. Trey sat in the hospital beside Tina's hospital bed holding her hand through each and every contraction, while watching the news on the television as the coroners carried the bodies of Keisha and Destiny out of the house in black oversized bags. That night after the police questioned Tina and Trey about the motives for the tragic deaths of both Keisha and Destiny who took the lives of one, they marked them in their case file as 'victimized witnesses' and crossed them out as being conspiring suspects.

◇◇◇

Tone stood in the dayroom of BCDC (Baltimore City Detention Center) the day after his daughter had been murdered watching the story on the news of the tragic death of her and her girlfriend. Having just came from an attorney visit where he was already informed of the murders and the fact that it was all over the local news, he rushed back to the unit where he slept to catch the heart breaking news for himself just to make it all true in his mind. After watching the breaking news, Tone stepped out of the dayroom feeling like someone had snatched his soul straight out of his body. A couple guys he knew spoke to him and tried to talk to him wondering what was on his mind after he returned from the attorney visit, but he just kept walking past them ignoring their questions while making his way to his cell with his head down as if they didn't exist. Stepping into his cell, Tone sat on his bunk placing his head in his hands as the harsh reality set in that he would never see the streets again and he would die in the hands of justice as a grieving old man with no family. At the thought of his court trial quickly approaching in a few days Tone decided at that very moment that he wasn't going to give the judge or jury the satisfaction of finding him guilty of any crime, especially not one that consisted of him causing the brain damage of his wife, and painting the picture of him being a merciless overprotective woman beater who got a kick out of beating his wife and daughter in addition to officers of the law. Rising from his bunk, Tone took a razor blade and cut his bed sheet down the middle and tied both pieces together securely and meticulously. Grabbing another double edge razor, he placed both of them in his mouth and quickly exited his cell. While no one was paying any attention he tied the sheet to the pole of the top tier. Tone quickly climbed over the pole, tied the sheet around his neck, pulling on it a few times to ensure it wouldn't break before finishing its job and without hesitation he jumped over and swallowed both razor blades a split second before the sheet tightened, cutting off his wind supply and snapping his neck. Tone's soul levitated from his body at 12:00 p.m.

◊◊◊

Tina looking Amazing

Tina gave birth to a healthy baby girl at 12:00 p.m., whom she and Trey named Demeanor J. Essence. Both excited to have become parents of their first child and proud of the precious gem they brought into existence, they just sat there and reflected. Trey danced the room with Demeanor in his arms while Tina looked on with tears of joy in her eyes forgetting about the crazy events that had occurred just the day before. "Trey, give me my baby before you drop her and I have to kick your ass and then Italy's!" she said to him. Hearing Italy's name roll out of Tina's mouth, Trey instantly felt bad because he hadn't heard from his mother in a couple of months and she had no idea that she was a grandmother. Checking his pants pocket he realized he didn't have his phone on him or anything else for that matter. Handing Tina their baby girl, he told her that he needed to run to the house to get a few things they would need because it was no way he was going to bring his family back to that place, because after all that had occurred he no longer considered it home. "So, where do you plan on moving us to Trey?" she asked looking at him quizzically. He walked over to her and kissed both her and Demeanor on the cheek and with the most serious face she had ever seen on him he told her, "We are going to move in with Scarlett." Seeing her face turn instantly red he covered Tina's mouth before she could say anything and told her that he was just kidding. They both began laughing at the thought of all of them living under the same roof together. Moving his hand from her mouth she looked at him, smiling telling him not to fucking play with her like that, "You play too damn much Trey! Now again babe, where are we gonna move to because I'm not shacking up in no damn hotel or none of your skank ass bitches houses with my newborn baby!"

"Girl, I got this! Gimme the keys to the house so I can do what I have to do so I can hurry back to my two lovely ladies."

Tina pointed to the drawer that was in the corner of the room, beneath the television, telling Trey once again to hurry back and not to keep them waiting. Trey promised he would be back as soon as he could, exited the room and made his way to the hospital lobby. Once outside he got in the back of the first cab he saw and made his way back to Tina's house. Deep in thought Trey didn't realize that he was ignoring the cabbie who was trying to make small talk. Trey thought about how good it felt to be a father with his first child and thought about the lifestyle that he was living with being involved with the different women and getting paid to service them around the clock. Then he thought of Scarlett and what she meant to him. The fact that she was also pregnant and ready to give birth to his child within the next month, he knew he had to keep her close to make some decisions on what he wanted to do with both her and Tina to keep the peace amongst the three of them for the sake of the children. Trey knew he had to do something to bring in some more money and going back to a regular nine to five was out of the question. Making a mental note to count all the money he and Tina had made together over the past year, he knew he would have to continue to fuck with Consuela at least until he came off with a few million from her to be able to kick his feet up, make a few investments and take care of his kids, himself and whatever woman he chose to spend his life with. When the cab driver pulled up to the address Trey had given him they both noticed the yellow tape that was crisscrossed over the door. "That will be seventeen dollars sir" the cabbie said to him glancing back through the rearview mirror. Trey explained to him that he just needed to run in the house to get the money; but having been played too many times to count, he cautiously gave Trey the once over looking at him closely before unlocking the back doors to let him out. Picking up on the vibes, Trey assured him that he had enough problems and didn't need to have a cab driver hunting him down for $17.

"If you give me a minute sir, I will run in and run back out. That's my word!" Trey stepped out of the cab and began removing the yellow tape from the door's entryway, looking back to see if the cab driver was still watching him. Using his key he stepped into Tina's house and immediately felt the presence of a black cloud hovering over the living room. Rushing upstairs to where his shredded pants were he reached in them and grabbed a $50 bill and walked back out to the cab and handed the money to the driver who was now out of the car leaning against the hood smoking a cigarette while telling him to keep the change. "Thank you my friend! Thank you." the cab driver said to him looking at the bill making sure it was authentic. "Yeah, yeah mother fucker, get the fuck out of here!" Trey told him. Walking back in the house Trey opened the window shades to let some light in, walked back to his pants where he found his phone and began searching for the keys to his Bentley coupe. After looking everywhere for them, he sat down in Tina's bedroom on her futon and began going through all of his missed calls and text messages. Seeing that he had calls from Deb, Consuela, Scarlett and a few other numbers he didn't recognize he decided to call Italy to give her the good news.

"Hey Trey baby, bout damn time you called me. I was beginning to think you didn't miss your mother!" Italy answered. Trey laughed at his mom's sarcasm but he knew part of what she told him was how she truly felt.

"Mom, I'm great! I have some wonderful news for you."

"Aww boy, what is it now Trey?! Cause we all know how your surprises be?!" she told him.

"Well, congrats cause you are now a glam-mom!"

Italy sat on her lounge chair, drink in hand staring out at the clear blue water, smiling from ear to ear happy to hear the news that Trey had just shared with her. "Oh my Trey, that is so wonderful baby. So where is Scarlett and my grandbaby anyway?"

"No mom, not Scarlett, although she is still pregnant and ready to have the baby soon, but Tina mom. Tina just gave birth today to a beautiful baby girl and we named her Demeanor Tei'Osha Essence. I'm so excited mom and she looks just like you!"

"I'm excited too baby, but Tina? Trey are you sure?"

"Yes mom I'm sure she is mine!" he told her interrupting before she even asked the question.

With Scarlett being her favorite she didn't give Tina a chance, nor any other woman that came into Trey's life, she just thought Scarlett was the perfect woman for him cause although they didn't grow up the same way, she valued and admired her womanly ways and she knew Scarlett truly loved her son. Trey continued to converse with his mom promising he would be visiting her really soon and would text her some pictures of Demeanor as soon as he got back around Tina. She gave Trey the updates on what was going on with her and Ronnie and how they both were working and enjoying life in Puerto Rico, not missing anything about the states. When Italy asked him about Tone he told her nonchalantly, "He's probably running around screwing somebody's wife while running from their husband, either that or he is in jail." Not wanting to tell her the truth that he no longer dealt with or cared about the air his fake ass old friend breathed he quickly dismissed the thought and changed the subject.

"So yeah mom, I will be sure to visit you really soon and kiss Demeanor for you!"

"Ok, Trey baby. I love you and you make sure you stay out of trouble. Trey before I hang up, remember there is nothing worse than a woman scorned baby, she will do any and everything in her power to bring you down and make your life a living hell, even if it consists of hurting herself in the process!"

After hanging up with Italy, Trey always had to take a few minutes to digest their conversation, they would either motivate him making him feel like the happiest man alive or piss him off by making him mad at the world, drained not in the mood for nothing or dealing with nobody. Still sitting there on the futon, the thought of the things Keisha tried to do to him crossed his mind again, as his phone began ringing in his hand.

Glancing down at the screen he couldn't put his finger on the strange number that looked familiar. "Trey speaking?!" he answered, curious to know who the caller was, but eventually brushed it off as just another client. As the line went dead and whoever the caller was hung up in his ear.

CHAPTER 16

Maya pulled up in front of Scarlett's house behind Trey's Bentley thinking to herself, 'damn somebody around here got some damn money!' Placed the car in park and turned off the ignition. Instead of getting out she sat back in the driver's seat thinking to herself how she hated Al for getting too drunk to perform sexually, cursing people out in the hotel lobby and falling asleep on her after he pushed her around the hotel room calling her disrespectful names like bitches, sluts and back stabbing whores. Stripping him completely naked while he laid on his stomach asleep snoring, Maya dumped everything out of his pockets, leaving his keys, cell phone and wallet. She left the hotel room with all of his cash along with his clothes. Once outside the hotel she handed over his clothes to a homeless man that was rummaging through the dumpster in the alley and got in her car, texting Scarlett letting her know she was on her way to her house.

Now digging in her purse she grabbed the wad of money that she took from Al and smiled to herself when she counted out thirty seven hundred dollars. Placing the money back in her purse she stepped out of the rental Impala and kicked what looked like a set of keys further into the street. Closing and locking the car doors behind her, Maya walked over to where she kicked the keys and picked them up noticing that they were the keys to the Bentley that set in front of her car, parked. Pressing the unlock button on the keys, she walked over to the Bentley hearing the doors unlock and seeing the brake lights flash. Maya opened the car door and got in, sitting behind the driver's wheel as if it were her own and closing the door behind her. Impressed with what she saw, she looked around the car and immediately spotted Trey's driver license. She then opened the glove compartment and felt her pussy get moist at the sight of the 12 $10k Stacks. She reached inside, grabbing the registration and the title of the car and saw that the car was in Trey's name along with a Consuela Vasquez. At that moment she decided to call Trey on his cell phone while starting the car and pulling off with devilish intentions. "Hello" answered Trey.

"Where are you Trey?" Maya questioned. Pulling into the parking lot of the Giants supermarket Maya parked the car, turned off the ignition and listened in on the phone at the sound of Trey closing a car door while waiting for him to answer her. "Who is this and what difference does it make where I am?" he asked answering her question with a question.

"Look, this is Maya boy and I have something that belongs to you and if you tell me where you are I can deliver it to you!"

"Maya, Maya, Maya. I thought you would have quit playing games by now but I see that you are still on the same dumb shit. So what is it that you have of mines?"

"A pretty hot shiny black Bentley coupe, your driver's license, $100k cash and some wet ass pussy with your name on it!" she told him with a devilish grin on her face. At that moment, Trey sat down on Tina's living room sofa after just stuffing as much of her things as he could fit in her trunk along with everything they kept hidden in the safe. Knowing full well he must have dropped his car keys when things first kicked off with him, Keisha and Destiny; and wishing like hell that ANYBODY instead of Maya, from Scarlett to a stranger would have found those keys, he knew that getting his car back was going to come with a price especially seeing the way he treated her the last time that they were in one another's company. Not really in the mood or mind frame to deal with her, he figured he would just play along with her little game, get his shit back and then send her crazy ass about her way as if she never existed.

"So Maya, I assume after I tell you where I am you are going to bring me what belongs to me and I'm gonna have to drop you back off to where ever you may need to go?"

"Yes Trey, what the hell do you think? You are going to send me off smiling and clicking my heels like you do all the rest of your bozo ass bitches?! I don't fucking think so! Now stop playing mind games boo and let me know where I need to bring this car! Oh and I do have to tinkle and would hate to go on these soft leather seats!" Trey gave Maya Tina's address on that note and poured himself a glass of Patron silver with two ice cubes and sipped on his drink while waiting for her to arrive. Once she finally arrived, Trey was feeling good from the two glasses of alcohol he drank waiting for her while talking to Tina, letting her know to call him as soon as the hospital was ready to release her and Demeanor, in the meantime he would be setting their place up. Opening the door for her, Trey knew it wasn't a good idea to have her in Tina's home after the events that had taken place and looking as thick as she was, sashaying past him in the skin tight sweat suit that she wore.

"Alright Maya, let's cut the crap bitch! Where are my car keys and what the fuck is these bags and shit?"

"Calm down! Damn! Can a bitch use the bathroom and freshen up a little bit?" she questioned turning around catching his eyes looking at her figure up and down, she smiled and continued knowing she would fuck him before he sent her about her way.

"How about being a gentleman and showing me to the ladies room? Oh and after that pour me a glass of whatever that is you're sipping on." Placing her bags down Maya glanced in the kitchen hoping the upstairs was just as empty and he was there alone as a naughty thought crossed her mind. Walking her to the bathroom, Trey went back downstairs and began searching through her bags looking for his car keys as well as trying to see what she had purchased from the mall because whatever it was he knew she had purchased it with some of his money. After not finding the car keys he figured she must have taken them to the bathroom with her and decided he would go ahead and fuck her one last time like she wanted, drop her off wherever she needed to go and head to the penthouse to drop his and Tina's stuff off and meet her back at the hospital. Grabbing another glass out of the kitchen, Trey dropped two ice cubes in hers and two more in his glass and poured both of them a full glass of Patron. Sitting back in the white leather chair, Trey noticed the blood stains that set in the carpet and the wall and thought about the crazy events that had occurred in this same area where he planned on fucking Maya's brains out. Too disgusted with the sight before him, Trey decided to grab both of their drinks and head upstairs. By the time he got to the top of the steps, Maya emerged from the bathroom naked from head to toe. "Is this for me?" she said grabbing one of the drinks out of his hand. Taking it upon herself to walk into Tina's bedroom while Trey watched in awe at the way her ass jiggled with every step she took. Downing her drink Maya dropped to her knees as Trey stood before her looking down at her as she pulled his pants down and took him into her mouth.

Reaching down in his pocket to retrieve his ringing phone while Maya continued to suck his swollen mushroom dick head, as if her life depended upon it, he answered it mistakenly while continuing to let her do her thing. "So you are gonna be on your phone, really though?! Damn what am I am not sucking it right or something Trey?!" Maya stated holding his dick with one hand to her lips as if she was talking into a microphone. With the phone in his hand Trey glanced at the screen just to see he accidentally hit the touch screen and answered the call with Tina on the other end. Knowing she'd just heard everything Maya just said from having the phone in his left hand near her face, he knew she would pick up on Maya's voice and give him hell because of it. Hanging the call up before Maya could say anything else and make matters even worse, he placed the phone on vibrate and tossed it on the bed. "Shit!!" he said aloud cursing himself for being so reckless and fucking stupid. Standing to her feet, Maya continued to jerk his dick and leaned against the bed telling him as seductively as she could to put it in her and fuck the shit out of her! Everything in him told him not to fuck her, get what belongs to him and get her out of Tina's house and send her on her way, but thinking with the aroused head between his legs and her lips had him ignoring his instincts. Reaching in the nightstand beside the bed, he took out a condom and ripped the packet open, applied it to his dick and begin plunging deep inside of her. With every thrust, he made sure she felt every inch of him as she cried out begging him to keep it up and not stop! "Ohhhhhhhh YESSSSS!! Keep it right there Trey.... Don't stop.... Don't stooopppp!!!

Boy Damn, I love you! Ohhhhh my gawwwwwwwddddddd, I love you!!!! Aaaaggggghhhhhhh!" With no intention on stopping Trey continued to pound in and out of her, even giving her ass light smacks, letting her know he was enjoying every bit of her just as much as she was enjoying his dick. Kicking his sweatpants off, Trey made her climb all the way on the bed and resting on her hands and knees he positioned himself on his knees behind her and entered her again from behind. While Trey was deep inside of her enjoying her tight wetness he didn't notice his phone begin to vibrate again or when Maya reached between her legs and grabbed a hold of it, only to see Tina's name appear and pressed the talk button to answer it.

With Tina on the line and Trey having no idea she was listening to him having sex with another woman, Maya decided to put on a performance for the audience. Placing the phone underneath the sheet by her head Maya decided to rest her head on her arms and raise her ass higher to give Trey full access to her pussy so he could hit it harder and she could cry out in ecstasy and talk shit to him to get him to talk back so Tina could hear her man in the act. "You love hitting this pussy?! Trey, talk to me! I said do you love hitting this wet pussy Trey?" Not the one for a whole lot of talking while having sex, Trey decided to give her what she asked for and talk shit back to her. "Hell yea Maya, damn this pussy is good!!"

"You feel so good inside of me... Yesssssss! You are fucking the shit out of me Trey, all in Tina's bed aren't you baby?! Every time you sleep together in this bed I want you to think about this pussy, you hear me daddy?!"

"Hell yeah I hear you, I'm fucking the shit out of you in her bed ain't I?"

"Yes Trey you hitting it... sooooo fucking goooodddddd... Ooooohhhhh, all in her fucking bed! Aaaaaaahhhhhhhhhh.... Hold up, hold up boo. Let me lay on my back so you can taste this pussy, then I want

261

you to make love to this pussy for old times' sake!"
she told him.

Maya turned over and laid on her back with her legs
spread wide, Trey told her he was going to suck the
shit out of her pussy and then beat that pussy up like
he used to. A single tear fell from Tina's eye as she
listened to Trey having relations with another woman
in her bed and talk down on her as if she didn't mean
anything to him. Recording the whole act Tina
couldn't believe her ears and believe that the father of
her newborn child was treating her so badly while she
was waiting to be released from the hospital from just
having their child.

"I told you Trey not to hurt me. I am going to fuck your
shit all the way up when I get out of this fucking
hospital. I told you not to fuck with me or I will make
your life miserable. Stupid ass nigga!!" Tina thought
aloud, just as the nurse came back to her room letting
her know that she would be allowed to leave the
hospital with her baby in the next few hours as soon as
her release papers were prepared and signed by a
person over 18 responsible for getting her and the baby
home, as well as seeing to it that she had all her proper
medications.

Tina

Tina gave the nurse her best smile knowing deep down she was hurting to the core and couldn't wait to get even with Trey for being so careless and causing so much pain to not only her but their newborn daughter as well. When the nurse left out of the room she put the phone back to her ear in time to hear them finishing up while making small talk.

"Yeah I did miss that pussy, you almost had me ready to pull the condom off and cum all up inside of you!" "You should have, shit, you done made me cum all over your bitch bed sheets boy! Your ass better flip the mattress and change these sheets cause I know I came everywhere. You had this pussy squirting!" Maya said laughing aloud. She knew Tina was probably still on the phone listening in, so she again laughed aloud at the thought. "Trey baby, can you go and turn the shower on so I can wash up again real quick, please baby cause I just need like two minutes to get myself together." Raising up from the bed Trey stepped out of the bedroom and entered the bathroom. Maya took that time to grab his phone and blow a kiss in the mouthpiece before ending the call. Surprised to see that he didn't have a lock on his phone, she went to the last call and saw that it had last for a whole 37 minutes which meant that was how long Tina had listened to them have sex in her home and in her bed. Maya deleted the call so that Trey wouldn't realize what happened, she then went to the deleted calls folder and deleted it from there as well, erasing the call out of his phone all together just in case he so happened to be searching through that part and figured out that she had something to do with setting his dumb ass up. Rising from the bed, Maya tossed his phone back on the bed and whipped the sheet back over it, left out of the bedroom and entered the shower where Trey was waiting for her washing himself clean under the steaming hot water.

"So where do I have to take you from here?" he asked. Stepping in the shower, Maya moved Trey from underneath the water and soaked her washcloth up while letting the water run down her curvaceous body.

"To my car which is in front of Scarlett's house." At the sound of hearing Scarlett's name Trey was instantly turned off at the sight of Maya and knew he would have to call Scarlett to tell her the situation with Tina having her baby being the reason he couldn't see and spend time with her today. "Shit!" he said cursing aloud.

"What's wrong boo, are you alright?" Maya questioned.

"Yeah, lets hurry up and get out of here, I forgot I have some important shit that I need to tend to!" he replied looking her in her eyes with the most serious facial expression he could muster. "Scarlett doesn't know that we are together does she?"

"No, Trey why would you think that?"

"Because I don't have no time to be fucking around with either one of y'all like the last time, especially with her being pregnant with my fucking child. So tell me the truth Maya and on our way with me dropping you off are you going to explain to me how you got my car without her knowing?!" Rinsing the soap off of their bodies, they both dried off while Maya tried to make small talk suggesting that this would not be the last time that they see one another. Promising him that she would keep her mouth shut about their intimate rendezvous they shared and every one that they will have in the near future. Trey just agreed and assured her that he was fine with everything she was saying. After they both got dressed Trey found his phone mixed in the sheets, made sure Maya had everything she came with and departed Tina's house as she went in her purse handing him the keys to his Bentley. During the drive to her car she admitted to spending $300 of the $12k that was in his glove compartment; which he didn't mind since she could have taken all of it, along with his car and disappeared. Smiling at the thought, Trey listened as she explained to him how she found his keys in the middle of the street and got in just to be nosey when she realized that it was his. Pulling the Bentley over and parking it on a side street around the corner from where Scarlett lived Trey retrieved the money from the glove compartment and counted out one hundred and nineteen thousand seven hundred dollars and gave her the odd seven hundred dollars, telling her to go and buy herself some shoes or something.

"Alright Maya, just walk to the corner and make a right down that street and you will see your car and Scarlett's house. Again, DO NOT and I mean under any circumstances tell Scarlett that we were together!"

"I'm not BOY, calm your ass down!" she assured him. "Besides, thanks for everything boo and I wanna see you again real soon so don't be a stranger and act like you don't know my number when I call you for some more of that good ass dick!"

Leaning over, Maya kissed him on his lips, as their tongues met and danced in each other's mouths. Promising she wouldn't tell Scarlett a thing, she kissed him again on his cheek, leaving her lip gloss print, grabbed her bags and exited the car. Trey watched as her ass swayed from side to side in the tight orange skinny jeans she wore. She walked up the block as thoughts of him fucking her again crossed his mind. Pulling off, Trey glanced down at his phone wondering why Tina hadn't called him back yet. Figuring that she was pissed with over hearing him getting his dick sucked, he decided to just tell her part of the truth which was that he had to let Maya suck his dick in order to get his things back because she was adamant about wanting something in return. Turning on the car's system, Trey searched the changer and decided to listen to Miguel's song *Adorn* while he drove back to Tina's house to get her Rover and park the Bentley so he could take their belongings to the penthouse, so he could pick up Tina and his daughter in it. Trey set up and cleaned the penthouse with the help of his neighbor Elisha, a big breasted light skinned brunette chick he had met in the elevator on her way back to her own penthouse after seeing her husband off for a month long business trip. Insisting on helping him with his bags and suitcases in her deep British accent after he declined 3 times, Trey just gave up and for the past hour they had cleaned and talked about any and everything that came to mind. Reminding him of the singer Melonie Fiona in the looks department, Trey found her to be cool with a down to earth personality and finding her thick accent extremely sexy and humorous at the same time. After they were done, Trey fixed them both a glass of Moet Rose being as though it was the only thing that he had in the fridge, since he didn't spend much time at the penthouse. Trey excused himself and walked over to the balcony overlooking the Inner Harbor, closing the glass door behind him so he could talk to Tina to see if she was ready to leave the hospital.

"Hello?" Tina answered. Sensing she had an attitude about something in the way she answered, Trey had a feeling it was about what she had heard earlier with Maya.

"Babe, what's the attitude for?"

"Trey, don't fucking play with me please! What time are you coming to get me and Demeanor and what took you so long to call me back?" she asked sounding agitated.

"I was trying to get the house cleaned up and comfortable for my ladies, so I am on my way to get you girls now, ok?!" Trey smiled to himself knowing that Tina was pissed. Looking through the glass at Elisha as she sat on the chocolate alligator love seat

267

smiling, she waved at him when she noticed he was looking. Trey began to get side tracked as he waved back and wondered what her body looked like under the white tank top and pink silk Fendi pajama pants she wore.

"Ummmmm yes Trey" Tina began to further say breaking him out of the trance like state he was in focusing on Elisha, "I think it would be a good idea for you to be on your way to get me. NOW!" "Alright woman I should be there in about a half an hour alright?!"

"Whatever Trey!" Cursing under his breath when she hung up on him, he dismissed the thought of calling her back and was about to step inside when his phone began to ring in his hand. Thinking it was Tina calling back Trey answered the phone without looking at the name that appeared on the screen, "Babe, I'm leaving out now!"

"Babe? So where are you on your way to and when was the last time you saw Maya, Trey?" Questioned Scarlett.

"Scarlett?" Trey asked caught totally off guard by it being her on the other end of his phone, not to mention the question that she had just asked. Trey kicked himself in the ass for not screening his calls before he answered.

"Don't play with me Trey. Why the fuck is your phone and driver's license in her pocketbook and DO NOT LIE TO ME! I know you had to have been with her because I looked through her phone and seen your other number all through her recent call log!"

"Soooooo ask her Scarlett, what the fuck!" he told her knowing he had been caught up. "Look babe, I don't have time for this shit right now, Tina just had my daughter and I am on my way to the hospital to pick them up, so I will give you a call when I am done." Trey explained.

"So, you can make time for Tina and ya'll baby, fuck my friend AGAIN, after you promised you wouldn't hurt me anymore and just say fuck me and our baby, huh Trey!" screamed Scarlett.

"Babe, I promise I will call you and explain things further later once I pick Tina and my daughter up."

"No Trey! Fuck you, fuck Tina and that fucking baby!!!" she furiously stated. "Don't worry about doing shit for me, I'm about to go back in this fucking house and ask this bitch if she was with you. If she tell me that she was with you in any way Trey, your ass is going to be sorry! Say goodbye to me and this baby that I am carrying, you fucking asshole!" Trey just shook his head at his luck at the moment. Both of his children mothers were angry with him and he knew that he had fucked up with the two he cared for the most, he had been cussed out and caught the fuck up. With a wave of nonchalance, Trey placed his phone in the pockets of his Derogatori sweats and stepped back inside of the penthouse with Elisha, locking the glass balcony door behind him. "This champagne is good Trey, you have got to come by my place sometime and let me introduce you to my boring life over a bottle of my favorite champagne, Vive Cliquot Rose." Placing his matching yellow Derogatori sweatshirt on from off of the back of the crocodile couch, he walked to where Elisha was sitting and reached down to grabbed her hand and helped her up from where she sat. "I would love to take you up on that offer at a later date, but as of now I must get going to pick up my girlfriend and newborn baby." Walking her to the door, Elisha slid her pretty pedicured toes into her Louis Vuitton slippers as they exchanged phone numbers and hugged saying their goodbyes as she walked out of the penthouse. Trey took a couple of seconds to watch her pajama pants slide between her ass cheeks as she walked down the hallway making her way to her penthouse on the opposite side of the building. Closing the door behind him, Trey went back inside and grabbed the keys to the Rover, $10k cash, his wallet and exited the penthouse. Thinking about Elisha's her hard nipples that strained to break through the tank top she wore, and the soft jiggly ass he had a chance to bump, when he was holding the door for her to enter the penthouse when she backed up on him trying to carry one of the many big bags of clothes that belong to Tina. "Mmmmmhmmmm, I gotta hit that one day", he said aloud to himself. Locking the door, he walked to the elevator and rode down to the ground floor thinking that he would park there in the garage when he came back. As that thought crossed his mind he couldn't help but think how he knew he fucked up when he decided to fuck Maya again and she probably had spilled the beans and told Scarlett everything. Hoping that she didn't, he just pushed the thought into the back of his mind and figured he would get out of the dog house with both Scarlett and Tina eventually. Stepping out of the elevator, he bumped square into Consuela who was about to enter as he exited.

"Trey baby!" she said wrapping her arms around him.

"Consuela baby, where are you on your way to?" he asked. Hoping she didn't state the obvious, she told him what he already knew.

"To see you papi, I was about to come to your penthouse to see if you were home and you surprise me mi amor! I see you are leaving though, so where are you on your way to?" Grabbing her hand, Trey walked her back outside to her Maybach Landaulet, explained to her that he had to run to the hospital where his girlfriend was waiting on him to pick her and their child up and as soon he had them settled he would call her and make some time for her. "Ok, Trey papi. You hurry up because I have a surprise for you and I just miss you papi!"

"I miss you too baby. Now hurry up and make your way home and wait for my call because I have some things to speak with you about." he told her as the driver opened the door for her once she stepped inside. Consuela rolled the window down and reached out grabbing his sweater pulling his face down to hers.

"Papi, call me as soon as you are done and I do mean AS SOON AS you are done! Do you hear me?" Leaning inside the back passenger window, Trey kissed her in the mouth passionately, reached inside and began fondling and squeezing on her breasts. Breaking the kiss he promised he would call her after he was done with what he had to do. Releasing his shirt, she took her hand and wiped her smeared lipstick from his lips and told him again not to forget. Backing away from the car, he watched the window roll up and seen as she signaled the driver to pull off. Trey breathed in and out deeply, happy that Tina wasn't there to see Consuela cause he knew that would've been an even uglier scene than the one he was already in store for. He had to appreciate Consuela, for not only all the financial things she did for him, but also for the fact that she was so understanding to his situation. He knew he had to definitely make sure he called her once he had Tina and Demeanor settled. Climbing behind the wheel of Tina's Rover, Trey buckled his seat belt and turned on the ignition before pulling off in the direction of the hospital where his two special ladies awaited. He knew Tina was going to be furious when she saw him and all he could muster was an 'Oh well' to himself as he turned the radio up and began singing along with the song by Drake, "Take a shot for me", while thinking about all the women in his life.

Maya emerged from the bathroom to a Scarlett who was standing in the doorway with her arms folded looking as if she wanted to strangle her. "What's up Scar?! Bitch, you scared me shitless!" Maya said picking up on the tension between the two of them. "What's wrong baby?"

"What's wrong Maya? What's wrong is that we need to talk, so you can come in the study and have a seat with me." Turning her back on her while she spoke, Scarlett led Maya to the living room where she sat down on her couch Indian style holding the lower abdomen of her belly. Maya sat down directly in front of her, looking as if she knew nothing, when she knew exactly what the preceding conversation was about. "Maya, what the fuck are you doing, honestly?" she asked her finishing up with what she had to say before Maya could respond. "Sooooo, you went through my phone and got Al's number, hooked up with him and stole over $3k from his pocket, along with his clothing while he was drunk and passed out in a hotel?" she stopped for just a breath. "Then you meet up with Trey, fuck him and run off with his driver's license and phone! You need to talk to me Maya and tell me something! You are supposed to be my best fucking friend!"

With tears in her eyes, Maya rose from the couch, grabbed her purse and sat back down across from Scarlett. Dumping all of the contents of the purse out on the glass coffee table, Maya lied about the allegation that she went through Scarlett's phone to get Al's number; saying that he had contacted her and insinuated that they have a private affair that Scarlett couldn't and wouldn't find out about. Simultaneously grabbing the money, Maya offered half of it to her as she began to continue with her lies, telling Scarlett how Al had totally disrespected her calling her bitches and hoes just to name a few. "And after he realized that I had no intentions on betraying my friend and fucking him, his bitch ass was so drunk he wanted me to walk him up to his room to make sure he was good! After the 100th bitch he called me, while trying to rough me the fuck up, I was over it and taught his ass a fuckin lesson and TOOK HIS SHIT!" Maya stood up grabbing the two thousand dollars, which equaled half of the money and walked around the table to where Scarlett sat and handed her the cash. Scarlett grabbed the money from her hand with one eyebrow raised trying as hard as she could not to jump up and hit Maya across the head with something and said, "And Trey?"

"Scarlett, I'm not going to lie to you," she told her sitting next to her. "I did sleep with Trey earlier today. I met up with him earlier to take him his car because I found his keys in the street when I came here earlier. We starting drinking and before I knew it, one thing led to another and we fucked!" "Where Maya, and how did you know that it was his car? Also when you found that out the first thing to do was come and tell me!"

"I fucked him in the bitch Tina house. I'm sorry Scarlett, I just wasn't thinking with the right body part.

I saw him checking me out, the liquor kicked in and I wanted him. I'm so sorry Scar, I really am." Maya admitted.

"So why do you still have his phone and his L's? Let me guess, so you would have a reason to make the same "mistake" again and sit it my face like shit is all fucking good?!" Scarlett asked her while laughing psychotically at the thought.

"Scarlett, for what it's worth Trey isn't shit and he ain't never going to be shit! He don't give a fuck about me, you or the next bitch for that matter! He actually fucked me in that girl's bed without a second thought, that should tell you something right there!"

"Maya, just answer the fucking question, if Trey isn't shit like you say, why would you allow him to fuck you in another bitches bed while she is God knows where and you know full well all these things; what does that make you?!" Sitting there with the dumbest look on her face, Maya just smiled and told Scarlett how she never thought about it like that and rose from the couch stuffing the things from the table back into her purse. Grabbing the gun from between the cushion where she was sitting, Scarlett shook her head with disgust and released it thinking Maya had no clue on how she wanted to shoot her in the fucking head, emptying all eight shots out of Trey's .45 automatic she just held in her hand. "Maya, get your suitcase and the rest of the shit you came with, minus Trey's phone and license and get out of my home please." Grabbing the remote from the glass table, Scarlett clicked the TV on and began laughing at Jerry chasing Tom with an axe on her favorite cartoon show. Maya walked into Scarlett's walk-in closet that she used as her office and came out wheeling her suitcase. She stopped by the table placing Trey's phone, license and $700 cash on it. "Scarlett, this is the $700 that Trey gave me to keep quiet about what happened between him and I today. I'm going to go, but if you ever need me boo I'll be here." Still laughing at the cartoon and never giving Maya any more of her attention, she looked up with the most serious face as if she weren't just laughing and said, "Are you still here?" Maya turned and left Scarlett's house without saying another word leaving her to continue to focus her attention on the cartoon that displayed on her 3D 57'' flat screen TV. Scarlett placed the 3D glassed on her face and continued to laugh at the cat and mouse as they now seemed to be running through her living room, while thoughts of making Trey's life a living hell crossed her mind. Removing the glassed from her face and tossing them on the couch, Scarlett clicked the television off, rose from the couch and went to her front door locking both locks. Back in the bedroom she laid in her bed in the dark trying to come up with the ultimate plan to destroy Trey's existence for hurting her once again.

CHAPTER 17

It had been a month since Tina had been living under Trey's roof in the penthouse with their precious newborn baby girl, Demeanor. Watching how he catered to her every need and interactions with their daughter made Tina happy and often cry real tears of joy. She wanted so desperately for them to be and stay a happy family, so she began to introduce thoughts and ideas of how they could make the money they were used to making without selling their bodies. Trying to convince him to stop dealing with other women because it wasn't healthy for their relationship or baby, didn't seem to register to him because instead he would say he was going to stop and she would later

275

find out that he hadn't. And the fact that she hadn't truly gotten over him having sex with Maya in their bed while she was in the hospital, after just giving birth to their precious daughter, who he also still crept with and fucked every chance he got, had her upset and wanting to get even with him and hurt him just as bad as he had hurt her. Knowing everything there was to know about him, Tina kept a watchful eye on him and his actions while setting up her plan of escape to leave and destroy him before he did the same to her. She paid attention to his bank account summaries and knew how much he put money in or withdrew by accessing his personal codes and convincing him to let her join his bank account so she could access the account for withdrawals or deposits of her own. She kept a record of who he called, texted and emailed by having access to those accounts as well, even down to placing hidden cameras in the house and a GPS tracker on both of their cars to see where he went to and fro. Tina knew about his dealings with Elisha, who he had begun to sleep with since her husband was away on business, even fucking her on the island in their kitchen where she prepared their meals. He also had sex with her in their bedroom on both occasions when she had appointments to take Demeanor to the doctor's office. Almost catching him the most recent time when she exited the Elevator, she could see Elisha walking towards her penthouse but knew just where she was coming from. When she entered her penthouse Tina could smell the sex still lingering in the air mixed with scented candles, air freshener and Elisha's perfume while Trey showered trying to clean himself before she came back. Placing the baby in the crib, Tina logged onto the laptop and played back everything from the time Elisha first walked through the door of the penthouse they shared, when they fucked, when they were done fucking and when Elisha walked out the door which showed Tina walking in just a minute later. As she sat in the back of a parked rented limo across from Scarlett, Tina felt the urgency to question her face to face after conversing over the phone with her for the past few weeks to see just how much love she really had for Trey or lack thereof for wanting to cause him the exact amount of pain that she did when just like her she was with his child. After admitting that the love she had for him had died and how she was getting tired of explaining to Tina how she didn't wish death upon him but just wanted to see him suffer, Scarlett picked up on the worried vibe that she was getting from Tina and knew that she was trying to pick her brain to see if she was serious about coming together with her to destroy Trey, or was she contemplating to change her mind. Scarlett felt a sharp contraction run through her as she instantly buckled over in her seat clutching her stomach. "Oh my Gawd, Scarlett are you alright!" Tina asked trying to come to her aid. Just as Scarlett began to speak she felt another one and then her water broke instantly. Tina yelled to the driver to get them to the nearest hospital, immediately, as she was going into labor. By the time they arrived at the hospital there were medics standing in front of the emergency doors laughing and conversing with one another on a smoke break or out just to get some air when Tina's limo pulled up. Tina jumped out of the back and began screaming to the medics that her friend was in the back and about to have a baby. The medics instantly stopped what they were doing and rushed to the limo to assist the woman who just became their patient. After helping Scarlett out of the back of the limo into a wheel chair, they rushed her through the hospital where other nurses and doctors joined in to help, transferring her to a bed and onto the elevator to the delivery floor. Not wanting Trey to know that she and Scarlett were together, Tina convinced one of the nurses that it would be best if they contacted the father of baby so he could be there to support the soon to be mother. After giving them his number, Tina decided to wait around a little while longer to see if he was going to show up. When the medical staff rushed to her telling her they couldn't reach him, she said fuck it and decided to call herself.

"Hey babe, what's up?" he answered.

"Soooo I just got an anonymous call that your bitch Scarlett is at Sinai Hospital about to have your baby! Don't you think you should be by her side, or are you there already?" Tina asked hearing Consuela's annoying voice in his background. "But then again, you don't have to answer that. I can see you're in the presence of your taco eating, spanish speaking, coke head bitch!"

"What the fuck ever Tina, you have been on some real bullshit lately and I'm not feeling that shit!" "Is that so?" she said sarcastically.

"I'm trying to do what I have to do for us and you are over there." Trey began to speak and then dropped the phone. Tina overheard him telling Consuela that she bit him and then she heard another familiar voice in the background telling him she missed his dick and then put two and two together realizing that it was Shay. "He is having a threesome with Shay and Consuela?" she said out loud to herself. Trey got back on the phone apologizing to Tina for dropping the phone and went on to say how he would call her back once he was able to reach Scarlett or someone at the hospital to see her about her status. Hanging up in his

278

ear after he told her he loved her, Tina began feeling herself becoming irate but quickly contained herself and decided that she would use that energy for something else instead. Feeling a sudden closeness with Scarlett, she stood outside of the delivery room window and watched as Scarlett began to deliver her baby. Realizing she needed to get to her own baby she looked down and realized that she was still holding Scarlett's purse, so she walked quietly in her room, placed her purse on the chair next to the bed she was laying on and whispered in her ear that she would be back. Kissing her on the cheek, Tina watched as Scarlett shook her head to say ok. Walking past the nurses who were too engrossed in what they were doing to pay her any attention, Tina exited the hospital and hopped into the back of the limo that was patiently waiting. Tina gave the limo driver the address to her old neighbor before she moved in with Trey, Carol's house to pick up Demeanor. Thinking about Trey being involved with Shay again made her sick to her stomach when a thought popped into her head, how she would be able to get even with Trey on her own without Scarlett.

After picking up her daughter Tina returned home and logged into the hidden camera feed and saw that Trey hadn't been back in the house since she left out to meet up with Scarlett. Calling an old police officer client of hers, Paul, Tina faked a crying fit in which she poured out her heart with a story on how Trey was constantly physically and mentally abusing her and she couldn't take it anymore. "So, what do you need me to do Tee, just let me know and you know I have your back baby?!"

"Paul sweetie, I just want him arrested and out of me and my daughter's life so he can never touch me again." she cried out.

"So, where is he now Tee? Is he around you now?" A part of Tina wanted to laugh in Paul's face and tell him how stupid he was for asking that question, but she restrained herself and decided against it. "No Paul, he is prostituting himself with one of his many female clients." Paul fell straight into her plan by going on to tell her how it was a perfect scenario that Trey was in that kind of business and how they could use that to bring him into custody and that would buy her just the time she needed to get away from him. Tina just smiled, telling herself how she couldn't have agreed with him more. After being on the phone with Paul for the past hour giving him all the information needed to begin Trey's demise, from both of his cell phone numbers, the websites where he posted his advertisements at, along with the type of flashy cars he drove thanks to one of his many clients. Tina felt satisfied with her decision and happy to know that in the next few days she and Demeanor would be on their way to an unknown city without Trey to further hurt them. Tina then thought about Scarlett again and couldn't wait to share the news with her. At that exact moment she decided she would take Scarlett and her child with them, if she was game to go. Wondering what the gender of Scarlett's baby was and how the delivery went, Tina figured she would call her in the next couple of hours once she got Demeanor settled and got her thoughts together. She called the limo service and explained to them that she would no longer need their services. The dispatcher excitedly thanked her for being a valued customer. Stripping completely nude Tina stood over top of her baby girl staring down at her thinking how beautiful and precious of a gift she was. Just as she got ready to step into the bathroom to enter the shower she heard the doorbell ring and wondered who the hell that could be. Walking to the door, Tina peeped into the peephole and noticed it was Elisha standing there. "This bitch", she said out loud to no one in particular. Tina rolled her eyes and began walking off to head back to the shower when Elisha rang the doorbell for a second time. Her first instinct was to slip something on, open the door and whip Elisha's ass for thinking it was okay for her to sleep with her man in her fucking house. Suddenly Demeanor crossed Tina's mind and she wiped the previous thought out of her it. Walking back to the door, Tina opened the door not caring if Elisha saw her naked body or whoever else for that matter that could've walked past at that moment.

"What the fuck do you want besides an ass whipping bitch, because if you don't get the fuck away from my door in two seconds that is exactly what the FUCK you are going to get!" Tina barked slamming the door back shut in her face before Elisha could muster a reply. Pressing the lock button on the wall to secure the locks on the door, Tina went back upstairs to take a shower, thinking to herself that she handled that very well under the circumstances, knowing her background. After showering she stepped back inside of her bedroom wrapped in her yellow terry cloth robe, glanced at the oversized Marilyn Monroe clock on the wall and noticed it was 11:47 p.m. which meant she had been in the shower for close to an hour. Walking back to the crib where Demeanor slept she adjusted her in her crib and changed her position, laughing as her daughter fought and kicked at her in her sleep. "Oh, you wanna be a feisty lil thing like your momma, huh lil Miss Demeanor?" Tina playfully told her making her laugh before she dozed right back off as if she was never awake. "You mommy Miss Demeanor!" After playing with her daughter Tina finally sat down on her California King sized bed, disrobed and began to rub her body down from head to toe with her baby oil gel, sprayed on some Gucci Guilty perfume and laid across her bed glistening, searching through her phone. Noticing that she had two missed calls from Paul and two text messages; one being a picture from Scarlett smiling with her son in her arms with a text underneath of it saying, *'Me and my knight in shining armor.'*

"Awwwwww, Scarlett, I'm so happy for you boo" she said smiling at the picture and text message. She then went to her second message to see it was from Paul saying to call him as soon as possible. Dialing Paul's number Tina grabbed the universal remote that laid beside her and dimmed the lights of her bedroom and cut off the bathroom light while she waited for Paul to pick up. On the second ring, Paul answered sounding as if he was happy to hear back from her, "Tee baby, how are you baby?"

"I'm good sexy Pauly, laying across my bed nude from head to toe smelling like Gucci Guilty while dipped in baby oil gel sweetie." she playfully flirted in her sexy slut teacher voice.

"I was just thinking that after all of this is over with this guy Trey I would like to see you for old times' sake, since you will be leaving me for good." Paul told her then added, "Besides I haven't had a good release since the last time you stripped for me, so what do you say sexy?" Rolling her eyes, Tina figured what the hell. Paul was a very generous client whom she had a good thing with and knowing she may need him again in the future she told him how she would love to see him again and grace him with what he was apparently missing. "Sounds like a plan baby but on another note, I have briefed my team on Trey and we have already set up an appointment to meet up for a date with him at 2 a.m. this morning with one of the sexiest female officers we have in our vice squad. As soon as she gets him to perform a sexual act for some money we will nail him with no problem. They already spoke and we even have him recorded saying he will provide her with two ounces of cocaine as long as she can get him $2k. Did you know he was dealing in drugs as well?"

"No, that is definitely some news to me, but I guess good news now."

"Ok Tee, if we can meet up within the hour I can actually let you hear the conversation that they had and if you would like to see the sting go down with your own eyes for extra pleasure you can. We can set up a hotel room with hidden cameras so you can see it all if you like?" Tina smiled at the thought of Trey going down for his deceitful and disloyal ways but decided against seeing him getting cuffed through the hidden cameras, but instantly felt a certain feeling between her thighs and decided at that moment to meet up with Paul, listen to the recording and let him fuck her and then she would watch the look on Trey's face as he goes down.

"Ok, so I will see you in an hour Paul and you can bring the recording, only if you promise me a hard nonstop fuck for a good 30 minutes, showing this pussy no mercy!"

"I promise Tee baby, meet me at my house and we will take it from there." replied Paul. "You do remember where to come to right?"

"Of course I do Pauly, how could I forget?!"

"Alright Tee baby, I will see you then and remember you will be out probably until 3 a.m. depending on how soon we can nail him. Oh and one more thing, you can either sit at my house and watch the whole thing take place or you can be in the trailer with the rest of the vice squad, which ever one you like is fine with me."

"No baby, I think I would rather watch from your house as long as it is okay with you." she told him. Tina hung up with Paul and immediately texted Trey to see what he was doing on his last night free. '*Boo you are such an inconsiderate pig*!!' she text. Rising from the bed Tina walked in her closet searching for something to put on and then said forget it, deciding against wearing clothes. She walked over to her shoe rack and grabbed her six inch purple suede Salvatore Ferragamo pumps. Tossing her shoes on the bed she then read the text message she received from Trey in reply to hers saying, '*He said and so are you boo*!!' Texting him back Tina shook her head thinking, 'I can't believe he have these bitches texting and using his phone to talk shit to me. 'Well let's see who has the last laugh clown!' Tossing her phone back on her bed she then reached in her lingerie drawer grabbing her purple lace La Perla leggings and slipped them on with no panties. She then grabbed the matching purple lace La Perla bra and placed it on followed by her pumps. After applying her makeup, she got Demeanor together, putting on her clothes so that she could be dropped off at her babysitter's house. Tina put on her yellow Ralph Lauren blazer, stood in front of the mirror and got turned on looking at her own reflection. "Damn, you are a bad bitch!" she told herself. Walking back to her bed, she picked up her phone and read

Trey's text message aloud, *'Just kidding babe. I stopped by the hospital to see Scarlett and her baby and that didn't go right cause she just cussed me out and put me out of her room once she got me to sign the affidavit stating that I am the father. But I'm on my way home to see you and Demeanor but I have to leave back out because I have something to take care of around 2 a.m. Kiss my baby girl for me Tina. I <3 u :)'*

Ignoring his message, Tina dialed her old neighbor again and explained to her that something had come up and she needed her to watch Demeanor again, this time until the morning. Knowing that she would oblige, Tina was already out the door and strapping Demeanor in her baby seat in the back of her truck. Placing her personalized baby bag with everything in it from extra bibs, pacifiers, pampers, milk and extra towels and wash cloths and baby wipes on the seat beside her. She got behind the wheel and fastened her seatbelt, turned on and placed the truck in drive and made her way to drop off Demeanor and meet up with Paul to do their celebration. While driving she decided to give Scarlett a call to congratulate her and see how she was coming along. "Congratulations boo!" said Tina smiling when she heard Scarlett pick up the phone.

"Thanks Tina, so what is your crazy ass up to?" asked Scarlett.

"Well, you know I'm about to go drop Miss Demeanor off at Carol's house, and then I'm gonna go fuck one of my old clients who just so happens to be a police officer that is going to help me send Trey away to jail and I was just thinking that after I take everything from this bastard, you can come along with me and we can fly to a nice tropical spot and stay awhile!!" Scarlett laughed aloud at what Tina just said because she knew what Tina was telling her was the truth and nothing but the truth. "Of course I would love to come along with you and Miss Demeanor to stay awhile at an undisclosed tropical location." Scarlett told her. "Just as long as you split all of Trey's money with me and Diamond, we are ready to go!"

"Girrrrrl, I know you did not name that boy Diamond?!" laughed Tina.

"Bitch I damn sure did, Diamond Delux Williams!"

"Bitch I am gonna fuck you UP!" Tina screamed out bursting into laughter while saying, "I love it though....Miss Demeanor and Diamond Delux...oooooooweeeeee!" Getting sleepy, Scarlett explained to Tina that she was gonna try to get some rest while the baby slept. She then told her that the hospital planned to release her and the baby in the morning.

Scarlett

"So, I'll be here until then so you can come and pick us up by 11 a.m., but make sure you call me when everything is going down with Trey cause I assume it's going down tonight, right?"

"Yup bitch, at 2 a.m., your ass is smart. How did you know?"

"Just call it a bad bitch intuition Tina. Bye crazy ass!"

"Bye boontch!" Tina said ready to hang up.

"Boontch?" Scarlett asked wondering what the hell a Boontch was.

"That is bitch, in pretty girl language. C'mon girl, you know us pretty bitches got our own lingo!" "Oh yea I forgot, goodnight boontch!"

Tina continued to smile after she ended the call and dialed Carol's number as she pulled up outside of her house. While leaving her truck running, Tina quickly got out to help Carol with Demeanor into the house while Carol followed behind examining her outfit, toting the baby's bag. "Girl, your ass looks good and you lucky I don't swing that way cause I would have you for breakfast, dessert, lunch, dessert, breakfast and dessert again! Damn bitch, you look good. I ain't lying!" Blushing from cheek to cheek, Tina sat Demeanor down while still in her baby seat on Carol's gray and black microfiber couch.

"Thanks Carol, I'm about to go and freak the socks off of someone's yummy husband!"

"You mean like yours, Trey? And wait a damn minute Tina where are your damn panties!?" asked Carol as Tina turned to face her. Heading for the door to leave back out Tina turned to Carol and said, "Who needs them, they'll just be in the way for what I have planned!" Carol laughed at Tina telling her to drive careful. She assumed Tina was going to go meet up with Trey and that they needed some time alone without having to constantly check up on their baby.

Walking to her truck, Tina glanced back and noticed Carol watching her and before getting inside she said aloud, "Whose Trey?" Tina pushed the Range Rover doing 70 mph the whole drive to Paul house, who happened to live in a four bedroom house, alone in Owings Mills, Maryland outside of Baltimore City. Pulling outside of Paul house Tina turned her radio up louder singing the lyrics to Beyoncé song, Irreplaceable, she exited her vehicle, "You must don't know bout me, you must don't know bout me, I can have another you in a minute!" Turning the truck off she stepped out clutching her purse, locked the doors with the lock button on her keys and stood outside of his door ringing his doorbell. Paul opened his front door smiling as Tina stepped in walking past him. Turning to face him as he secured the locks on his door, Tina dropped her purse on his sofa, placed her hands on her hips pulling back the yellow blazer she wore to show off her body in the purple lacy attire she wore.

Admiring Paul's six foot one inch muscular frame as he turned to face her Tina felt her pussy get overly moist with the anticipation of feeling Paul's ten and a half inch dick, power driving in and out of her. Wearing nothing but a smile, Paul helped Tina out of her blazer, tossing it across the living room. Unsnapping her bra and tossing it to the side while shoving her lace leggings down her legs with force that turned her on even more. With one shoe at a time he kneeled down and took them off, then placed them back on once she removed her leggings from around her ankles, kicking them to the side. Now standing face to face with her he grabbed her face, shoved his tongue down her throat and began kissing her deeply. Tina jumped in his arms, wrapping her legs around his waist. Breaking the kiss Tina felt him slam her back against the wall, then felt his hard dick ramming in and out of her pussy.

"Pauly baby where's your condom boo?" Paul continued to grip her ass cheeks while plunging in and out of her then told her, "Fuck that damn condom, now stop talking and take this dick!!" For the next forty minutes Paul fucked Tina the way she needed, making her cum repeatedly and sweat profusely. With his back now against the wall, Paul flipped her around upside down with his muscular arms wrapped around her waist and began sucking her clitoris while taking his tongue delving it into her pussy, around her lips, across her asshole and then back to her clitoris. That sent her body through convulsions as her body vibrated in his arms and she came on his tongue and lips. Tina continued to suck and deepthroat his dick, feeling it jump and pulsate in her mouth as he began releasing his load down her throat. He laid her down on his couch watching her as she set up, placed his dick back in her mouth and continued to suck him making sure she got all of the nut out of him down to the last drop. Once done they both sat side by side on his couch out of breath. "You're on amazing fuck with a humongous dick for a white boy." she said laughing. She laid back on his couch and rest her legs and feet on his lap. "Tina, my mom is white and my father is black so you can blame them for creating this Mandingo white looking black man." They both laughed at what he just told her. Getting serious, Paul told her to get up and follow him to his private office upstairs so they could listen to the conversation where Trey had to set up the meeting, shower and then he would have to leave out to assist with his arrest. "Okay we can go upstairs, but only if you carry me." she told him running her foot up and down his chest. Lifting her body off of the couch, Paul carried Tina upstairs in his private office, setting her down in the bathtub. "I assume you wanna get clean first?" he asked.

"Of course I do." she told him taking her heels off and tossing them in his office. Playfully punching him in his chest, Tina pulled the curtains back in his face then opened them back up smiling at him letting him know she was kidding. Glancing at the clock on the wall Paul whistled under his breath then cursed aloud, "Shit!" Seeing how serious he became Tina asked him what was wrong while turning his shower on at a decent temperature.

"It's one fifteen and I need to be with the others making sure this bust with Trey goes down properly, ok?!" Stepping inside of the shower with her, he told her he would set up his MacBook PRO so she could watch everything go down once Trey entered the hotel room. Washing his body quickly, Paul exited the shower, dried off and got dressed in less than five minutes. He set up the live feed of the hotel room up for her on the laptop, grabbed his gun, handcuffs, keys and was out the door with his briefcase. Tina continued to shower letting the steamy hot water massage her skin. After using one of the new wash clothes that hung on his wall to wash her body, she rinsed off, turned the shower water off and stepped out using one of his towels to wrap her body in. Walking to the desk where his laptop set, she looked down and seen that Paul left an envelope with her name on it. Sitting down in the huge leather chair behind his desk, Tina opened the envelope and smiled as she counted out twenty- two hundred dollars. Placing the money back she read the message he wrote on a piece of paper, thanking her for making him feel good, '*I hope you can use the money to buy yourself something nice*

I may be gone until the morning so make sure you lock up before you leave and I will call you when I can!'

Folding the paper back up and placing it back in the envelope with the money. Tina was caught by surprise when she heard a woman's voice coming through the speakers that set on Paul's desk. Now looking at the 18 inch laptop screen in front of her, she couldn't believe the pretty scantily dressed woman on the screen in the hotel room was an officer. Turning the volume up on the speakers to hear the female on the laptop screen more clearly, Tina set back in the chair and watched on at the woman on the screen before her.

CHAPTER 18

After leaving his house to meet up with his new client Mileena, Trey began to wonder where was Tina with his baby girl. He gave up with calling her phone after her voicemail kept picking up on the first ring. Now pulling up outside of Mileena's motel room he wondered why she was staying at a super eight motel and thought about leaving because of the ill feeling he felt. Just as the thought crossed his mind his phone began to ring, as he put it to his ear and answered it.

"What's up Mileena baby, I just pulled up outside of your room."

"Is that you in the Bentley flicking your lights?"

"Yeah, that's me" he told her.

"Well, what are you waiting for baby, come on up and don't forget to bring the stuff." Snatching the duffel bag off of the passenger seat of the car, he thought about bringing his .45 handgun in case Mileena was trying to set him up but decided against it, making his way to her door. Opening the door to let him in, Trey was immediately impressed with how beautiful Mileena's dark skinned complexion was. "Hey Trey, give me a hug!" Mileena told him wrapping her arms around his neck, "You can touch my ass you know, I like it squeezed and felt on too!"

Doing just that Trey palmed and squeezed her ass then released her and set on a chair in the corner of the room. Placing the duffel bag down he told her, "Now here's the two ounces of coke you asked to buy, since you're a pretty sight for sore eyes and have a body like a goddess I'm gonna charge you $1,800 for both of them."

"Ok, so because I am a pretty hot and sexy woman you are gonna sell me your coke for just $1,800?"

"Correct?"

"So what about the massage and how much are you gonna charge me to let you fuck me and let me suck your dick?" she asked him while sitting on his lap.

"Ok, sexy this is what it's going to be. For the massage alone I'm just gonna charge you $300 since you are buying the coke from me."

Too caught up in Mileena's pretty face and voluptuous curvy body in the skin tight mini dress she wore that barely covered her booty showing a glimpse of her white panties, Trey never thought for a second that he was being set up by an undercover agent. "Ok that's fine baby let me use the bathroom while you get comfortable and when I'm done I will give you your money and we can get started." Rising off of his lap Trey smacked her on her ass, and watched as she sashayed her hips in the bathroom closing the door behind her. Trey pulled out his massaging oils, candles and towels. Spreading them out on the table he then pulled out the two ounces of cocaine, setting them on the table as well. Just as he began stripping down out of his clothes, he heard the key enter the door, that's when four officers charged into the room, in plain clothing, guns drawn with vice squad on their t-shirts telling him he was under arrest. "Put your fucking hands in the air, you are under arrest!!" Doing what he was told, Trey couldn't believe he was just set up by a pretty face with a soft voice and big ass. "Shit" he cursed under his breath. Milenna emerged from the bathroom dressed just like the other officers in her jeans, vice squad t-shirt and badge around her neck. After they cuffed him and read him his rights they made sure he understood what he was being arrested for, then escorted him outside of the room and into a squad car. After sitting there for a half an hour, finding his gun they finally drove him to the district for him to be booked. Tina just sat there in front of Paul's laptop after the sting was over and Trey was taken out in police custody thinking to herself, 'You is one stupid mother fucker, how did your dumb ass not know you were being set up Trey!' Just then she decided to log online and transfer all of their money that was in their joint account into her own personal account. "Damn that bitch Consuela transferred two million dollars in your account and you out trying to stick your dick in a bitch and sell ounces of coke for twenty two hundred dollars, your dumb ass deserve to be where you are!" Once that transaction was complete she smiled at the sight of her new two point five million dollar balance. After that she booked a flight to Maui for herself, Scarlett, Miss Demeanor and Diamond. Shutting the computer off, she left the towel in the chair, stood up and walked down the stairs to get her clothes. Tina placed her bra, leggings and blazer back on. Picked up her purse and ran back upstairs, grabbed her shoes and placed them on her feet. Dropping her purse on Paul's desk she then grabbed one of his cigars out of the drawer, lit it and took out her cell phone to call Scarlett.

"Hello", Scarlett picked up sounding sleepy. "Hey Boontch, what's up?"

"Well, it's over now and he should be on his way to the big house to be booked. Plus you know I was able to sit back and watch the whole things unfold?!" "How the fuck you finagle that boontch?"

"Well let's just say that my clients love me and no matter how long I don't see them, it's like we pick up where we left off. My client was able to set up the cameras in the motel room where it went down and I had a clear view of everything from his living room sofa! His ass is going down not only for prostitution but also for the coke he tried to sell to the undercover officer as well," she told Scarlett. "So on another note, I booked a flight for me, you and the kids to go to Maui for tomorrow evening. You don't have to worry about packing because we will go shopping once we get there for any and everything we want or need and I am going to put half of the money Trey had in his account into, for you and Diamond."

"Oh my gawd, Tina! Tell me you are serious and not joking and that bastard is going to get what is coming to him?" Scarlett asked feeling more and more excited over the thought of actually being able to take her baby and fly to another part of the world and not having Trey to worry about.

"As a mother fucking heart attack bitch! I am not playing at all. I will meet you at the hospital in the morning so I can pick ya'll up and then we can go from there and start our new lives." As she ended the call with Scarlett, Tina stubbed out the cigar and then dropped it in a cup of water that Paul had on his desk, grabbed her purse and headed out the front door locking it behind her. On the drive back to her home, Tina was feeling like a new woman already as she turned her Beyoncé album back up and snapped her fingers to the beat, thinking about what she was going to do with her life now that she was free from Trey with a million dollars in the bank. Making a mental note to pick Demeanor up before she picked up Scarlett and Diamond, she felt sure of being in control of her life as she turned the volume up on the radio a little more and leaned the seat back a little. She turned on the heat and enjoyed the twenty five minute ride to her house.

CHAPTER 19

Trey sat in the back of Consuela's Maybach sipping on a glass of Remy Martin trying to unwind after she had just bailed him out of jail, after he sat for a day and had time to get his thoughts together.

Going over his charge papers, he had been charged with a long list from Prostitution, Illegally possessing a firearm, C.D.S, Attempting to sell narcotics to an undercover officer and the list went on as he allowed the papers to fall to his feet.

"Awwww baby, you don't have to feel down." she told him. "Before you got arrested, I transferred $2 million into your bank account and that will be more than enough to get you a good lawyer and a nice vacation when all of this bullshit blows over."

"Yes you're right, Consuela baby. Thank you for bailing me out of that place as well as putting the money into my account. I know you say you have a flight to catch this afternoon and you will be gone for a month but I was just wondering if you were going to let me stay at your place while you are away?"

"Of course papi! I was going to tell you to do that anyway. You have the keys and I don't mind you bringing any guests over, just as long as they are not moved in with a key." Smiling from ear to ear, Trey smiled listening to the way Consuela spoke with her Spanish, Dominican accent. Pulling in front of his penthouse, he hugged Consuela good bye telling her to call him once she got to the airport, downed the rest of his drink and stepped out of her car waving goodbye to her as she pulled off. He rode up the elevator ready to see Tina and Demeanor and give them both the biggest hugs and kisses from being away from them so long. Stepping out of the elevator he walked up to his door and grabbed an envelope that was taped to it, placed his key in the lock and entered the penthouse. Looking around Trey was confused to see the penthouse empty as if no one ever lived there. Everything he owned was gone as if Tina had moved out and forgot to inform him. Racing upstairs, he seen everything was empty and gone from there as well. 'Everything', he thought to himself even down to his toothbrush. Going back downstairs Trey opened the envelope ripped the letter out and begin reading it aloud…

Trey,

By the time you read this letter you will be in the house wondering where all of the furniture and belongings are and what the hell is going on. Well so you will know everything in the penthouse was packed and given away along with everything in my old house, so say goodbye to all of those things because you will never see none of that shit again. As for me and Demeanor, we are doing just fine without you and should be on an island somewhere by now enjoying the breeze. As for your bank account, you don't have to worry about that, because yes I emptied it out and just so you know me and Scarlett split it right down the middle. So, so long Trey. Me, Scarlett, Demeanor and your son Diamond wish you well with whatever it is that you are going to do with the pathetic excuse of a life you are going to have. Maybe you will sit down and think about what is really important to you and stop hurting the people who loved you and who you claimed to love. Tell Elisha I said hello and that she left her ass print on the island in the kitchen where you fucked the bitch moments before I walked in the house. I bet you didn't think I knew about that huh?! Well Trey you've done did it this time sweetie, I told you a long time ago never to fuck me or I would make your life a living hell and I intend to do just that. Good luck when you go to court, I only wish you get 20 years to LIFE!

T

Trey just sat down on the step feeling like his world had just come to an end. Pulling out his phone he called his bank to check the balance of his account and almost spit up when the automated message recited, *"Your account balance is fifty three cents."*

"You have got to be kidding me, bitch I'm going to fucking kill you!" he screamed out to the top of his lungs as if anyone was around to hear him. He tried to dial Tina's phone back to back only to get her answering machine. He did the same with Scarlett and got her voicemail message as well. Feeling defeated, Trey just dropped his phone to the floor and placed his elbows on his knees with his palms to his face and for the first time in a long time he felt like he wanted to cry from losing everything and realizing there was no one to blame but himself. He reflected on the conversation he had with Italy where she explained just what measures a scorned woman would take to make a man's life a living hell. Then he thought about the pain that he had caused both Tina and Scarlett and cursed himself because he knew he needed them both in his life, because of the love that he had for them as well as his newborn children. He also realized that there was a chance that he would never see his kids again and that by hurting these women he had hurt himself in the long run. As a tear trickled down his right cheek, Trey reached down and grabbed his phone and dialed

Consuela. After she picked up, he gave her a cliff note explanation of what had happened, she agreed to pick him back up before she left town. Promising that she would send her driver after he dropped her off at the airport, Trey thanked her, ended the call and began to pace the floor deep in thought. Dialing Elisha's number he figured that he would take a load off and kick it with her until Consuela's driver arrived. Realizing her phone number was either cut off or she changed the number he thought about going down to her house and knocking on her door. Just as he opened his front door he was greeted by two officers that were simultaneously knocking on the door.

"Are you Tre'Vion Williams?" the taller of the two Caucasian officers asked. Knowing he hadn't had time to do anything else wrong he figured that the officers had to be here because of either Tina or Scarlett and at that moment his heart seemed to drop and he prayed that nothing had happened to either of them and definitely not one of his kids.

"Yeah, that is me. How can I help you officers?"

"Sir, we have a warrant for your arrest for having sexual relations with a minor." the officer explained.

"A minor? I think ya'll have me mistaken for someone else." Trey answered.

"No, sir. Elisha Larkson who happens to live next door with her father Mr. Norman Larkson"

"A minor!" Trey yelled looking from one officer to the other. "What do you mean a minor? She told me she was 23 years old and living with her husband?!"

"Try 17 buddy, now you are going to have to come with us!" Trey couldn't believe his ears as the officers arrested him and he was being hauled away to jail again for the second time in less than 48 hours. The officers cuffed him, read him his rights and escorted him out of the building. Now riding in the backseat of the police cruiser, Trey shook his head and couldn't believe how his life had flipped upside down and was going 'Every Which Way' but the right way. 'I can't believe that lil bitch fucking tricked me, Damn I fucked up!' he said to himself. After going through the formalities of being booked on statutory rape charges, Trey sat in the Central Bookings for another five hours awaiting his time with the commissioner on duty. Once he sat down with the female commissioner that reminded him of the singer Sade, he pleaded his innocence with her and explained how Elisha had lied about her age and how they had come to meet. Never once looking up from her paperwork, she continued to run copies of different sheets of papers while loudly popping the gum that she chewed. At that point, Trey gave up on trying to convince her of his innocence and knew at any second she was going to slap him with a high bail that he couldn't pay. "Sir, I am going to release you on your own recognizance," she began. "Just sign these papers and slide them back under when you are done. And next time sweetie, please be careful the next time you choose to stick your dick in another female. These young girls out here nowadays may look grown but a lot of them aren't!" Sliding her the papers back after signing them, Trey thanked her as she slid his copy back to him and told him to have a good day. Walking out of Central Booking doors, Trey couldn't believe his day and the bullshit that he was going through. Thinking to himself what could possibly go wrong next, he decided to catch a cab to the penthouse and remembered he left a ten thousand dollar stack on the top of the wall ledge that separated the kitchen from the living room. Remembering how he was carelessly tossing it and catching it in the air one day, when the last time it became stuck he said forget it, deciding to forget about it and let it stay up there for a rainy day. That day he had no idea he would be needing it so desperately. "Give me one second sir to run up and get your money, I will be in and out in a minute, I promise you!" Jumping out of the backseat of the cab, Trey walked through the lobby ignoring the stares of the attendant and security guards who had seen him being escorted out earlier that day in handcuffs. Using the elevator to ride up to his floor, again he couldn't believe that this was the same elevator he had rode down earlier in cuffs. Exiting the elevator and approaching his door he then wondered who had helped Tina to get the things moved out of the penthouse. Immediately thinking about his arrest for dealing with Elisha, he didn't want to run the risk of running into her or her father so he hurriedly stuck his key in the lock and walked back into the penthouse praying that Tina or nobody else for that matter had found the money. Climbing the wall, Trey reached his hand atop it and felt the stack of money still there while he sighed in relief that at least one thing was going his way today. Grabbing a hold of it, he smiled and blew the dust off of it and jumped down rushing to make his way back downstairs to the cab driver. Opening the door to leave out Trey jumped back, dropping his keys and the money on the ground. He was taken aback as he stared down the barrel of a gun.

"Seleste!?!"

"Going somewhere fast Trey?" Seleste questioned him. "Why, you look like you've seen a ghost, what's wrong? I would have thought you would be happy to see me." With a tear rolling down her eye she cocked the hammer on the gun while Trey stared down at her in disbelief. Noticing her index finger beginning to squeeze tightly around the trigger, Trey knew if he didn't act fast then she was going to pull the trigger and shoot him in the head ending the otherwise worst day of his life. Trey lunged forward and tried to duck while at the same time knock the gun out of her hand, but was a split second too late..."POWWWWWW!!!"

ACKNOWLEDGMENTS

You know when I sat down and wrote this book, the idea of having it published was farfetched …I couldn't see it. It took the love and support from those in my corner during the good and bad times to push me to complete and actually go forth with having it published. I always wanted to have the title "Author" beside my name, and again I thank God for having the love from not only him, but also my family and extended family (friends) in my life giving me that push to turn my dream into reality. So I thank everybody who was there for me and helped me along the way with "Every Which Way". I love you all and I would give each and every one of ya'll my last. Sometimes in life we feel alone when we have thousands of people around us, we feel discouraged when we have everything laid out properly at our feet, and we feel we can't go on because the mental strength, motivation and inspiration have exuded us. But we must not quit nor give up. We must remain strong and thank/praise God because that feeling is Him filling us with strength! That feeling is him conversing with our souls to give us that motivation we desperately need. That feeling is him giving our brain and our heart the nourishments we need to show us where we came from, where we are and where were headed; inspiration. As I've became more mature and wiser, I came to the realization that were all here in this world to serve a purpose. God placed some people here to serve a purpose greater than others, but no matter how big or small that purpose is, were all here for a reason, which makes us meaningful when we may think or feel that were meaningless. That also goes for the people around us. I used to wonder why all bad/negative things happened to me, I prayed and asked God why me?! Well one day sitting quietly alone he answered my question and made me see why all bad things were happening to me. He showed me how he placed certain situations into my life, bad and good, to shape me into a better man, the man that I am today. I told myself that I wasn't gonna write out a thousand names, just to tell my dearest family and friends what they already know. But what I will say is: Thank You!! Thank each and every one of you who helped me, not only with this book, but for being in my life whether it was for a minute, an hour, a season, a decade or a second. For my family and friends that's no longer here on God's green earth, I thank you, we will meet again! To the people who doubted me and laughed at me when I stressed to them that I would become successful, I thank you. One last thing before I go: Tawanda Trayham, my beautiful mother, tell Tia Trayham, my favorite aunt, to let everybody know we made it and we partying tonight, everything on me!!! 💻 God Bless